in the ♥ cards

in the ♥ cards

Jamie Beck

Montlake
Romance

Published by Montlake Romance, Seattle

www.apub.com

Amazon, the Amazon logo, and Montlake Romance are trademarks of Amazon.com, Inc., or its affiliates.

ISBN-13: 9781477825693
ISBN-10: 147782569X

Cover design by Laura Klynstra

Library of Congress Control Number: 2014908553

Printed in the United States of America

To my husband and children, the loves of my life.

CHAPTER ONE

Sugar Sands Beach Resort, Sanibel Island, Florida
New Year's Eve 2005

Levi

Wild kids run around the pool, splashing passersby and banging against the ends of the lounge chairs. The noisy chaos is one thing I won't miss about this place come Sunday. Some of the older folks look overwhelmed by the commotion, so I stop to help them secure seating, towels, and such. I may not hail from high society, but I'm still a Southerner with a sense of decorum.

An unruly little boy darts in front of me, nearly knocking the crate of glasses I'm carrying right out of my hands. Then I hear a familiar, heavy drawl that stops me cold.

"Better watch out, son."

I glance to my left to see my pop grinning like a shark. And here I'd been looking forward to my last day of work.

"Pop." I keep walking to the bar while I gather my wits. When I get there, I unload the glassware without giving him my full attention. "This is a surprise."

"I bet." He rests his right elbow on the bar and casually looks across the pool deck. "I was passing through the area and thought I'd come check on you."

Passing through: a euphemism for running a string of card scams and long cons from Florida to Texas.

"Yeah?" I inhale slowly and shrug, trying not to reveal how much I wish he'd disappear before my coworkers get curious. "Well, as you can see, I'm just fine."

"Fine?" He grunts and shakes his head. After glancing over his shoulder, he leans across the bar. "Making minimum wage and waiting on others? Come on, boy. I taught you better than this."

He taught me, all right. Taught me how to play poker like a pro, among other things. Yanked me out of school in favor of getting me to master the finer points of body language, pacing, and position in the back rooms of bars across the South.

I don't regret acquiring my talents, seeing as how they give me a distinct advantage in many situations. But I never want to live a drifter's life and rip off people like my pop does. He may get a thrill from those games, but I don't. And I don't enjoy causing other people grief. It's why I've been trying to make my own way.

Bottom line: I don't care much about what *other* people think of me, but I need to be able to look in the mirror without disgust.

"How long are you going to waste your God-given talent and hide behind this bar?" The disapproving look on his face doesn't surprise me. It doesn't bother me, either.

"Don't worry about me." I ignore him and let my gaze drift over the crowd.

This job's been a decent short-term gig for a guy my age. I've spent my time outdoors and collected healthy tips, especially from the middle-aged married ladies left to sit alone while their husbands play golf.

Besides, someday I'll be one of those rich men on the golf course—minus the wife, of course. But there's no need to share my plans for Vegas with Pop.

"Sorry to break up this family reunion, but I've got to get to work." Placing both hands on the bar, I look him in the eye for the first time. "Can I fix you a drink before you head out?"

"Jack and Coke, son." He chuckles and throws a twenty on the bar. "You keep the change. When you're ready for a little fun, you know how to find me. You and I could clean up in this crowd of lonely ladies." He winks and walks away, probably scoping the crowd for a new mark. At forty-eight, he's still a good-looking man. I notice a few of the women check him out as he struts toward the hotel.

It'd be easier if I could hate him for how he raised me. But I don't. He trained me not to rely on anyone for anything, and that makes me stronger than most. There are worse parents than him, even if he is an unrepentant thief.

As predicted, the outdoor bar is teeming with New Year's Eve partiers before noon. The three of us tending bar barely have time to crack a joke. I don't complain, though. Bigger crowds mean bigger tips.

Sara, a babe with a knockout figure, pockets most of the male customers' money. Fortunately, John lacks any kind of charm, so he mostly serves the impatient men and women who want drinks and nothing more. I attract the flirty female patrons to my side of the bar. I wasn't given much in this life, but I'm blessed with good looks—or so I'm told.

"I'll take a banana daiquiri, please," says a perky, wide-eyed brunette.

I've noticed her hanging around the pool all week. Up close her tawny eyes momentarily stop me in my tracks. Dazzling. Even in the bright sun, her pupils are fully dilated. Enlarged pupils are a sign of attraction or dishonesty. She's either hot for me or underage, or both. Can be drugs, too, but this little girl don't seem high.

"Miss, I need to see some ID." I tuck a lock of my hair behind my ear and glance at the line forming behind her. I don't want to lose those tips to John.

"Oh." She bats her lashes and leans into the bar, offering me a better view of her cleavage. "I didn't bring my wallet to the pool."

Her form of foreplay is yet another excellent perk of my job. I admire the way she fills out her cherry-red suit before I meet her eyes again.

"I'm not askin' for money, doll. I need proof of your age. I'd bet all my tips today you're not twenty-one."

"Am too."

Her childish remark and refusal to meet my gaze only confirm my suspicion. Part of me admires her cheeky attitude. Hell, she's damn cute. Under other circumstances she might tempt me to break a rule or two, but I won't risk getting fired today.

Unwilling to waste more time or lose paying customers, I fix her a virgin daiquiri and charge her room. She beams, apparently thinking she's fooled me into serving her alcohol, and throws a generous tip on the bar. As she struts her string-bikinied bottom away from me, I notice her sip her beverage and then stop midstride. Scowling, she turns to protest, but I'm busy with other customers. Drawing the left side of my mouth upward, I wink at her.

Accepting defeat, she skulks away, which causes me to chuckle. Nice try, little girl. Returning my attention to my other customers, I plaster a smile on my face and tend to a fetching blonde.

∽

At five o'clock, I break for dinner. Thankfully, Pop seems to have vanished as quickly as he'd arrived. Now I can enjoy an hour of sun on the beach with my burger and book before setting up for tonight's big New Year's Eve party.

I find an empty lounge chair next to Dan, a waiter here who's let me camp out in his living room for the past month. He's the ideal roommate—lives in the moment, doesn't ask a lot of questions. We've had a good time together, but I can hardly wait to hit the road. My grin must tip Dan off to my thoughts, because he smiles and shakes his head.

"I envy you, Levi," he says. "Wish I could pick up and move to Vegas."

"You're a good guy, but you can't play poker for shit." I chuckle. "Too many tells. You'd be eaten alive."

"Big talk from a small-town player." He watches me chow down on my burger. "I've seen you clean up around here. But how do you know *you* won't lose your shirt out there with all the pros?"

I hesitate, careful of what to reveal.

"'Cause when I was six, my pop was dealing me cards instead of tossing baseballs in the yard." In fact, Pop made me play some of those so-called pros. I beat them at seventeen, so I'm pretty sure I can beat them now.

"Your dad sounds cool." Dan crosses his arms.

Cool? Not really. I'd have preferred school and sports teams to the years spent living on the run. Then again, now my expertise gives me a shot at legally banking enough cash to escape the rat race for good.

"Even so, you're only twenty-three." Dan crosses his arms in front of his chest. "Lots of people have been playing longer than you."

"True, but they'll underestimate me because of my age and rough edges." I grin thinking of the sixteen grand I've already banked during the past few years while working the resort circuit along the Gulf Coast and preparing for my next step.

I'll be arriving in Vegas with enough cash to enter the better poker tournaments. I've met plenty of smart players who make steady money at the tables. If I'm careful, live cheap, and invest well, I can set myself up pretty nicely, especially if I also tend bar at some hot club and make great tips. "By the time they realize it, it'll be too late."

I consider the help Dan's given me since we met in October. He's been the closest thing I've ever had to a friend, which differs from the superficial acquaintances and one-night stands I'm most comfortable with.

"When I get settled, you can come visit. Maybe you'd be safe at the blackjack tables." I snicker.

"Sounds like a plan." Dan smiles and notices the book in my hand. "But if I come, you've got to put your books down long enough to make it fun."

I grin but don't bite back. Books saved me from being an ignorant son of a bitch I couldn't respect. And unlike people, a good story rarely disappoints. I glance at him again.

"Thanks for letting me crash at your place."

I'm mighty grateful for Dan's help. I'll be sure to leave him a generous gift for his inconvenience, though I suspect we won't actually keep in touch once I'm gone.

"No problem." Dan looks over his shoulder toward the resort. "I've got to get back to work. Later."

After he takes off, I remove my shirt to let the remaining sunlight even out my tan. I'm reading *Atlas Shrugged* and enjoying my meal when a shadow casts over me.

"You had a good laugh at my expense today," purrs a feminine voice.

I peer over the top of my sunglasses to find the saucer-eyed virgin-daiquiri girl standing at the end of my chaise. She's planted her hands on her hips and shifted her weight to her right leg. Her spirited attitude forces a grin across my face. With practiced nonchalance, I admire her long enough to make her fidget.

"Thanks for that, miss. Always appreciate a chance for humor on the job."

Her stance relaxes and her tone turns friendly. "So, how'd you know I'm not twenty-one?"

"'Cause you don't look it. Plus, you were nervous when you ordered."

She flips her silky, light-brown hair behind her shoulders and presses her glossy pink lips together in a frown. Her pert nose is sprinkled with light freckles, and her full lower lip catches my attention. She's real pretty in a natural, girl-next-door kind of way, so I don't mind extending our chat another minute.

"Here's a tip: Get a fake ID or have one of your older sorority sisters buy your drinks for you."

A victorious flash of light shines in her eyes, but I'm not sure why. I do know those eyes look like they can see through anything, or anyone.

"What are you reading?" She tips her head sideways to read the book jacket.

I hold the cover up to show her while I estimate her real age. Deciding she may be jailbait, I suspect her little victory stems from my mistaken assumption that she's already in college.

"Do you like it?" She's grasping for a reason to talk to me, because I doubt she's real interested in my thoughts about Ayn Rand's ideals.

"So far."

I don't offer more. Keeping quiet forces other people to do all the talking and all the revealing. Typically, this strategy establishes my power position, the only position that assures me protection. Her alert gaze warns me I need all the protection I can get.

Undeterred by my lack of enthusiasm, she seats herself in the sand alongside my lounge chair. Her face is now only a foot or so away from my chest. I shift to my left, uncomfortable with her proximity. She's forward, though not blatantly flirtatious. She just marched over, invaded my space, and now won't leave me alone.

Her lightly bronzed skin shimmers in the rose-colored light of a late-afternoon sky. If she were older, I might indulge in a brief fling. Unfortunately, she's an inexperienced baby, and I don't take advantage of the innocent. Plus, something about her knocks me off balance. I don't enjoy the unfamiliar feeling.

"Are you working here between semesters?" she asks. "Do you go to college nearby?"

Her questions, coupled with the fact that she's vacationing at this resort for the holiday, indicate she's probably a sheltered daddy's girl who gets whatever she wants, whenever she wants it. Despite her physical appeal, she's *not* my kind of chick. Truth be told, I'm not likely to be her kind of guy. Fortunately, I know exactly how to make her hightail it away from me.

"I don't go to college."

As expected, her eyes widen even more—if that's possible.

"Oh. Why not?"

"Why bother?" I shrug.

"For your future." Her eyebrows furrow, framing amber eyes filled with concern.

"What about my future?" I stare at her, daring her to preach to me, which is what I suspect is coming.

"Well . . ." She hesitates. "You know, for more career options."

I nearly choke on laughter at the image of me with an office job. She withdraws and narrows her eyes, confused by my response. I lean closer to her and am hit with the coconut scent of her skin. Mmm. Collecting myself, I soften my voice.

"Don't you go worrying over my future. As long as there are libraries, I'll learn whatever I need to know. Don't need to waste time and money paying some drone to tell me what to think. And anyway, a fancy job and white picket fence may be your dream, but it ain't mine. I'll take a pass on the anchors and just live my life."

There. Now she'll lose interest and run along to find her parents, or some nice rich boy just like her. Only, she doesn't.

"Anchors?" She hugs her knees to her chest while awaiting my reply.

I sigh and place my book across my lap.

"Anchors. Things that weigh you down and hold you in place—a wife, kids, a mortgage. Not interested."

Her forehead creases again as she chews on my personal philosophy. After another moment, she raises one brow in challenge. "With a good education, you could get a real job *and* still choose to be alone."

"*Real* job?" I feel the vein in my temple pulsing. "I've got a real job, thanks."

She disregards my indignity. "Based on that book, I doubt you want to tend bar forever."

Resentment burns inside me, although she's utterly unaware of her rudeness. I think she actually believes she's helping me. Damn prima donna can't even fathom a life different from her own. Despite her apparent sincerity, I snap.

"Gee, I never looked at it that way. Thanks for showing me the light." I dial back my animosity, unwilling to let her get further under my skin. "I wonder how many of you rich kids would go to college if you had to pay your own tuition. I bet very few."

Her face twitches and she casts her eyes down to her hands, which are now folded neatly in her lap. She appears both chastised and pitying, and that really chafes.

"Hey, spare me your sympathy. It's my choice. If I wanted it bad enough, I'd work to pay for college. I like my life just fine. I travel. I'm completely self-sufficient. That's more than a lot of people my age can claim. Besides, bartenders at big clubs can pull down six figures in tips. Seems more sensible than *owing* six figures and taking some entry-level cubicle position making peanuts." Her contrite posture stops me from further defending myself. "Now, unlike *you*, I'm not on vacation. Go on and run back to your sandbox, baby girl. Let me enjoy what's left of my break." I return my attention to my book.

It's unlike me to get riled up, but her condescending attitude splinters my pride. Not sure why I care what she thinks, but I want her gone before I say something I'll regret.

From the corner of my eye, I notice her bite the inside of her cheek. She rises up from her knees and brushes the sand from her legs—her toned, long legs. I keep staring at the page in front of me, but I sense her willing me to meet her eyes. Naturally, I refuse.

In response to my rebuff, she flippantly replies, "Sorry I wasted your precious time."

I don't answer or look up. When her shadow retreats, I peek and enjoy the view of her nice derriere until she disappears over toward the pool.

Too bad that little princess has no idea about the real world, and probably never will. I try to guess how she might react to that day in the future when life finally tests her. Will she rise to the challenge or will it knock the innocent light right out of those pretty eyes?

∾

Lindsey

I return to the pool to find my glamorous mother sipping a margarita and flipping through *Town & Country*. Between her looks and her attitude, it's like she's found the secret to gliding through life and bending it to her will. Of course, I inherited none of her poise or confidence. All of my attempts to mimic her flop miserably, as just demonstrated on the beach.

"Why the long face, Lindsey?" Her radar's flawless even when she doesn't give me her full attention.

"No reason . . . a little hot and bored, I guess."

I lie, unwilling to admit the truth about my failed attempt to seduce the hottie bartender. Mom wouldn't approve of him. Then again, maybe she'd understand on some level, given he resembles

Gabriel Aubry. No doubt his intense green-flecked hazel eyes, sexy smile, and dimples catch everyone's attention.

I've never seen such a beautiful man, not in real life, anyway. His Southern accent and the gravelly quality of his voice are unlike those of the boys back in Connecticut. The way he punctuates his lazy speech with intentional pauses sets me on edge, too.

Sadly, I obviously don't inspire a similar response in him.

I've wasted dozens of hours daydreaming about heated, stolen kisses—maybe a bit more. I know a vacation fling isn't a big adventure by most standards, but in my overscheduled, overmonitored life, it would've been pretty exciting. A secret rebellion. A chance to experience the kind of power my best friend Jill and my mom seem to have when it comes to guys.

But as usual, I blew it. No chance I'll leave here with any juicy scoops to share with my friends.

"The men should be back from golf soon." Mom's voice yanks me from my musings. "Why not go freshen up?"

"What time's our dinner reservation?" I ask.

"Eight," she says. "We're meeting the Campbells at seven thirty for cocktails."

"Okay, see you later."

Back at the bungalow, I lie across my bed. While staring at the white, stippled ceiling, I consider tonight's party and wish more of my friends were here with me. As if on cue, my phone rings and Jill's number pops up on the display.

"Hey, what's up?" I ask.

"Just checking in before I head out. Rick Dawson's parents will be in the city all night, so he's having a party. Too bad you'll miss it. Of course, I'd be jealous of your vacation if you weren't stuck there with Dave Campbell." Jill snickers.

The Campbell family met mine at our country club. Their son,

Dave, is my age. Dave's plain—average height and build, mousy-brown hair and eyes—but he's a nice, mellow guy. I don't mind that he's not considered cool back home. He likes hanging out with me, which is an ego boost, and he's always polite without being a kiss-ass. I know a few of Jill's male friends who'd be worse to vacation with, but I don't mention it to her.

"I guess being nicer isn't your New Year's resolution, is it?" Jill can be a bit bitchy, but she's a loyal friend and I kind of like living vicariously through her boldness. "Anyhow, there *is* a totally hot bartender here. Of course, he's a few years older."

"Really?" Jill's tone conveys heightened interest. "Have you talked to him?"

"Unfortunately." I grimace. "I stuck my foot in my mouth. Now he thinks I'm an annoying kid."

Jill dissolves into laughter on the other end of the line.

"Yeah, Linds, you've got to stop spewing your thoughts the second they occur!"

"Go ahead, laugh at me," I say halfheartedly while shuddering at the memory of the bartender's drawl thickening with sarcasm when I tried to encourage him to go to school.

"Sorry." Jill stops giggling. "So, big plans for tonight?"

"There's a party tonight around the pool." I don't share my lack of genuine enthusiasm. "It could get interesting with all the college kids around."

"More time to change the bartender's mind." Jill chuckles at her own joke.

"You're hilarious, really," I say dryly.

"You love me and you know it," she chides.

It's true, but sometimes I envy her, too. The things I like about myself—my thoughtfulness, generosity, and compassion—aren't all that valued by my peer group, so I'm not as popular as her. Maybe in college it will change.

"Sorry you aren't here, but try to have fun," Jill says. "Talk to you next year!"

"Bye." I hang up, roll over on my side, and think about the bartender again.

Even if he hadn't rejected me, it wouldn't have changed anything. In fact, I probably would've chickened out if he'd actually propositioned me. And if I had somehow managed to hook up with him, that one exploit wouldn't have magically freed me. At the end of this trip, I'll still be saddled with meeting the expectations of my parents, teachers, and friends.

I don't know exactly what I'd do differently if I could ignore them all, but I hate to let anyone down. Especially when they only want the best for me. Besides, following their advice is definitely wise. After all, my dad's a successful banker and my mom's an ex-litigator turned socialite. I could do worse. Then again, what do I know? As the hottie pointed out, I'm pretty clueless about the world outside my sheltered experience.

The effects of the sun and my embarrassing run-in this afternoon have tanked my mood. I roll over and close my eyes to escape.

Hours later, I wake up in the dark. Crap. I'm going to be late. I rush to shower and apply makeup. With little time to primp, I pull my soaking hair into a wet knot at the base of my neck and slip into a new, gold-sequined dress.

The backless minidress forces me to wear it braless. Even with the built-in liner, it's sexy. It makes me look more mature than my Lilly Pulitzer stuff. Although I'll need to figure out how to get out the door without being ordered to change, I smile at my image in the mirror. Maybe that bartender will give me another chance once he sees me in this outfit.

I'm fastening my strappy heels when my mother knocks on my door.

"Coming!" I hop on one foot, wrestling to buckle my sandal strap.

Checking myself in the mirror one last time before opening the door, I grab a wrap to hide my bare back from my dad.

~

At ten o'clock, Dave's and my parents finally give us the green light to leave the dinner table, but mine issue a one o'clock curfew. Dave and I head straight to the pool party.

"Rocking that dress, Lindsey." He smiles with a wiggle of his brows.

"Thanks." I hope the bartender shares Dave's sentiment.

Kanye West's "Gold Digger" is blaring, colorful lights are swirling, and some people are already swimming.

"So, I've got a fake ID. Let's have a few drinks," Dave announces with a huge grin. "What do you want? Something simple, like a rum and Coke?"

"Okay, but don't approach that bartender." I point at the one who can't stand me. "He'll know you aren't old enough."

Dave's puzzled expression braces me for a question, but he shrugs before setting off for the other side of the bar. Within ten minutes, he reappears with two drinks in hand.

Holding up his glass, he makes a toast. "To our last semester at Greenwich Country Day!"

"Cheers!" Gulping down a huge swig of my sweet drink, I wipe the corner of my mouth with the back of my hand. Dave smirks at me.

"So, Lindsey, why'd you suggest I avoid that particular bartender?"

Shoot. I'd hoped to sidestep this conversation.

"He carded me this afternoon when I tried to buy a daiquiri. Really embarrassing." I roll my eyes for emphasis and omit any mention of the beach tête-à-tête.

"Something tells me it wasn't really a drink you wanted." Dave winks.

Busted.

"Maybe not, but it turns out he's not too sociable."

"Guys that look like that don't need to be friendly to attract girls, do they?"

Dave's commentary shames me. Admittedly, I'm still hot for the bartender, despite his snarky attitude and dead-end choices. If he weren't so gorgeous, I probably wouldn't be all that interested in the personality he revealed this afternoon, although his book choice did surprise me.

Hopefully I'll wise up with age. Then again, why should I feel guilty about behaving the way every guy I've ever known does?

"I think that works with both genders, Dave. Hence the popular snotty girls." I grimace because most people would probably include my friend Jill in that category.

As we while away the hours getting buzzed and laughing by the pool, I occasionally steal glances at my bartender. Has he noticed me at all? Doesn't he regret giving me the brush-off earlier?

His sandy-colored hair continues to flop in his eyes, and his lazy grin only adds to his sex appeal. Not that I know anything about sex from experience, but I have a rich fantasy life. Since boys tend to view me as good-friend material rather than girlfriend material, I've racked up more imaginary boyfriends than I care to admit. I had really hoped to turn the tide during this vacation, with *that* bartender.

Despite his focus on his work, I see he still manages to flirt with all the beautiful girls. While I stare dreamily, he casts a sharp glance in my direction and catches me ogling him. An invisible bolt of electricity passes between us, or at least it feels that way to me. He cocks one brow up when he notices the drink in my hand, then shakes his head briefly before smiling at his next eager customer. Defeated, I pull my attention back to the teen scene and vow not to spy on him for the rest of the night.

After the midnight hoopla, a bunch of college kids around the pool decide to hit the beach, so Dave and I follow. Several, including

Dave, wander into the cold water fully dressed, but I don't want to ruin my new dress. Unlike one really drunk girl, I also won't strip down to my undies, especially since I'm braless.

I rake my hands through the cool sand. The shrieks of those running in and out of the water catch my attention now and then. Sitting on the outside looking in, as usual, I'm losing steam.

The breeze picks up, scattering goose bumps across my arms. Growing depressed that nothing particularly interesting or exciting happened tonight, or any night on this trip, I'm ready to go back to my room and crawl into bed. I call out to Dave, but he's not paying attention.

I guess I drank more than I realized, because I'm dizzy when I stand. I flop into one of the lounge chairs next to the cabana. I'll lie here for a bit, until everything stops rocking, then go home. Hopefully, I'll be able to sneak into the bungalow without waking my parents.

The stars sparkle like a million Swarovski crystals thrown against black velvet. I swear I see, and feel, the earth spinning on its axis. I'm studying Orion when the sound of someone striking a match nearby startles me. Sensing potential danger, my heart races. My head whirls around as I sit forward, and I stop breathing. The hot bartender is leaning against the cabana with a freshly lit cigarette.

"You scared me!" I shiver and clutch my stomach.

"Sorry," he drawls. "Didn't see you there."

"Is the bar closed already?"

"I'm taking a break." The red glow of the tip of his cigarette brightens when he inhales. "Long day."

I can't tell if he's watching me or not, but he doesn't move from his spot.

"Oh." I'm silent for a few seconds, uncomfortably aware of my slip of a dress. As my eyes adjust, his indistinct image sharpens, transforming him from a ghostly figure to a man. In a misguided desire to fill the silence, I blurt out, "Hey, I'm sorry about earlier today. I didn't mean to offend you."

"No sweat, little girl. Your opinion don't mean much to me either way." He blows smoke off to the side of his face without looking at me or saying more.

Insulted by his dig, I sit upright. "You don't need to be rude. I said I'm sorry."

He takes another drag and sighs.

"Sweetheart, let me have one break in peace." The timbre of his inflection on the word *sweetheart* coaxes a tremble from my traitorous body, which bothers me since I can't justify finding him so damn sexy on one hand and spiteful on the other. I hear his low chuckle before he continues, "Bet you missed your curfew. Maybe you should run along now."

Now I'm pissed. I approach him despite wavering a bit from the booze and the tingling sensations he inspires. For the first time, I notice the name tag pinned to his shirt.

"You know what, *Levi*? I take it back! I'm not sorry. You think you're so cool, but really you're just a sarcastic jerk. Trust me, you won't have to worry about any 'anchors,' because no one wants someone as rude as you anyway."

Only just finished, I'm breathless from my rant when he steps so close, the heat of his body warms me. His seductive glance causes me to gasp.

"That ain't true." His face is mere inches from mine. "*You* want me."

Caught off guard by his remark and proximity, my skin prickles as if I've been stung by static electricity. My mouth falls open in protest while my brain scrambles for something to say.

After blowing more smoke through the side of his mouth, he tilts his head toward me. "Go on, admit it." Staring at me with heavy-lidded eyes, he sends a delicious shiver through my entire body. He nudges even closer until we're on the verge of an embrace.

My heart pounds in my chest, awakening in an unfamiliar, yet tantalizing, way. Before I realize what's happening, his free hand touches the nape of my neck. Slowly, his fingertips trail down the length of my naked spine. At once, I lose my breath and all thought.

"Admit it," he whispers, lowering his head to mine.

His lips softly brush the corner of mine. With my eyes now closed, I smell a faint mix of smoke, salt, and alcohol. He's motionless, waiting for my answer. My head is swimming and I might fall over. All of my senses are firing at full blast. Torn between arousal and defeat, I confess.

"Yes." My eyes remain closed while I wait for the kiss I've been dying to steal for days. Then—nothing. I open my eyes. For the briefest moment, he appears to be battling himself. Then, unexpectedly, he withdraws.

"Just like I thought." He leans against the cabana again, flicking his cigarette butt into the trash can, his face obscured by the shadows.

Thank God for the darkness, because my cheeks are surely beet red. Although I'm humiliated, all the lessons my mother ever taught me about dignity kick in. Without bursting into tears or running away, I take a steadying breath.

"Feel better now that you've embarrassed me? I hope it brings you comfort in the future . . . when you're nothing but a lonely old man with poor grammar."

I storm off before he replies, leaving him standing in the shadows.

Locked in my room, I cry confused tears. How'd I let him manipulate me so easily? Lust makes us stupid, I suppose.

I sigh, exhausted from the festivities and the bitter note on which the night ended. I'm not a cruel person and I regret my snobby remarks.

He claims not to care what I think, so maybe it doesn't matter. I doubt he spent another second of his time thinking about me.

Jill always yells at me for being everyone's doormat. I swear I'm going to change. No more trying to save the bad boys from themselves. Definitely no more thinking about that bartender, either.

I'm glad we leave early tomorrow. At least I'll never have to face him again.

CHAPTER TWO

Malibu, California
May 24, 2013

Levi

Hey, Levi, whatcha doing up there?" a woman's voice calls up from the beach.

I look down from my deck and see Elena, the recent divorcée from a few doors up the block. She's not unattractive, and has a pretty tight figure for thirty-six. But as I do with everyone else in my life, I prefer to keep her at arm's length.

"Enjoying the day, darlin'." I wave.

She's fond of my dimples, so I'm careful to conceal them by replying with a closed-mouth smile.

"I'm planning a little party tonight. Care to join us?" Her hand catches her sun hat before the wind blows it off her head. "A few friends will be coming around seven. Margaritas for all!"

"Sounds real nice. I might wander in, thanks." I don't invite her to come up, which is what I suspect keeps her lingering around the base of my deck stairwell.

After an awkward moment, she waves good-bye. "All right, then, hope to see you later."

She adjusts her hat and struts away with an exaggerated sway of her hips. Without regret, I watch her depart. She's always been obvious about her attraction to me, touching me when we talk, remarking on the honey color of my hair and the way I wear a pair of blue jeans.

While I enjoy the benefits of my appearance with plenty of women, I'd never take advantage of one who hankers for more than I can give, or bed an emotionally vulnerable woman. Elena seems to be both. Plus, with her being a neighbor, it would only lead to complications. I love my little shack by the sea and don't want to be forced to consider uprooting myself because of a jealous woman.

The heat outside keeps me thirsty, so I duck back inside to grab another beer. As I toss the cap into the garbage, I hear a knock at my front door. When I answer it, I'm confronted with a cop. My body reacts to his presence—pulse skips, muscles tighten—just like when I was a kid living in fear of Pop being arrested.

"How can I help you, officer?"

"Are you Levi Hardy?"

"Yes, sir."

The cop removes his Ray-Bans. "Are you related to a James Hardy?"

Guarded, I reply, "That's my pop's name. I haven't seen him in a while. Is he in town?" If Pop somehow used one of my accounts in another one of his scams, I'm gonna wring his neck.

"No, sir. We received a call from an Officer Hopkins in the Lake Havasu Sheriff's Department. He found your name and number in your father's wallet."

Agitated, I interrupt, "What's he done now?" Facing a prison sentence is one of many risks of life with Pop I don't miss at all.

"Well, sir, I'm sorry to report he's been killed. I don't have all the details, but it appears he may have been involved in some illegal activity. Since you're next of kin, they'd like you to come identify the body and answer some questions."

I fall silent, dumbfounded by the news. Jesus Christ. Dead?

The cop holds out a card. "Here's Officer Hopkins's contact information."

My arm feels like it's battling a riptide when I reach for the card. "Thanks."

"I'm sorry for your loss." The officer nods and then walks to his patrol car.

I stand in the doorway and watch him pull out of my driveway. Cars whiz along the highway. The sun is still shining. Life keeps moving along while I'm absorbing the news.

May 24, 2013. My pop's dead.

Murky snippets from my past fill my mind. Pop's disdain for the so-called educated elite mitigated any guilt he felt about running long cons. He joked about helping them out by teaching them a valuable lesson in humility. After stealing a pile of money from one, he'd target his next unassuming mark, dragging me along for the ride, all the while preaching the value of life lessons over school.

Many probably consider him the devil, but he and I shared some good times along the way, too. I remember him swinging me over his big shoulders so I could fly, or wrestling me on the rug—my only real physical contact until I was old enough to take notice of girls.

I'm sure some part of him appreciated having me around because, as a youngster, I was easily impressed. Even as I grew older, I never judged him too harshly—at least not to his face. He made a lot of mistakes, neglected me too often, and taught me lessons others would find appalling.

But, looking back, he proved I mattered to him by keeping me with him, which is more than Mama can say. He did the best he knew how. In the end, perhaps one can't ask much more of another.

Startled by the painful lump swelling in my throat, I raise my unfinished bottle of beer in the air in a silent toast to the old man. Who knew even a poor parent was better than no parent at all? After my final swig, I walk into the bedroom and sit on the bed, subdued.

While packing a few things for my trip, I recall the cop's comment. *Appears he may have been involved in some illegal activity.* Even from the grave, Pop manages to drag me into a legal hassle. Fitting end to our short life together, I guess.

~

Lake Havasu's surprisingly striking, set among desert palms and rocky canyons and outcroppings. Home of the reconstructed London Bridge, it's a touristy town. It doesn't take me long to note its aging population, a key demographic for a grift. This city provided ample marks for my pop.

For reasons I can't pinpoint, I delayed visiting the morgue until this morning. Who on God's green earth can work there? I can't fathom the mindset of a person who fancies working with corpses. Even just toiling away in windowless rooms all day seems depressing as hell to me. Of course, casinos don't have windows, but at least they're full of hope and activity and good-looking cocktail waitresses.

When I show up, the coroner folds back the body bag to reveal Pop's face. My stomach lurches at the appearance of his frozen, gray skin. He barely resembles the man I remember. No Cheshire-cat grin, no dimples or pronounced laugh lines. Aside from his pastiness, he's much older and thinner than I recall, suggesting these past few years weren't easy ones for him.

We'd lost touch two years ago after I'd caught him using me to perpetuate one of his frauds. Hadn't heard from him since. Seeing my formerly bombastic pop now lying silent and petrified has me squirming like a worm in hot ashes.

After I identify his body, the cops hand me a plastic shoe box containing his meager personal possessions and walk me toward some private room. How about that? Pop's whole life reduced to one small box holding a wallet, a watch, a phone, and a gold wedding band. Nothing else left behind to mark his existence—except for me, that is.

I suppose he doesn't deserve much sympathy, but my chest tightens as I finger the unfamiliar objects in the box. Not much in his wallet. No credit cards. Only a driver's license, a scrap of paper with my name and address, a folded strip of photos we'd taken at a carnival when I was probably ten or eleven, and some lawyer's business card.

The photo strip of our chipper faces causes everything, and everyone else, to temporarily disappear.

I don't have any pictures from my childhood, mostly because there were so few. An outsider looking at these pictures would think Pop was real happy that day. But I know he wore that smile like a costume, so it doesn't mean anything at all. Seeing myself with a big grin so soon after Mama left—now that surprises me.

Staring at the two of us makes my nose tingle and tears cloud my eyes. I cough and move to conceal my reaction. Pushing the box aside, I squeeze my eyes shut and press my thumb and forefinger against the corners of them to stop the tears. One of the officers clears his throat, so I return my attention to the business at hand.

"Sorry for your loss." Officer Hopkins taps his finger on the table a few times, then narrows his eyes. "How much do you know about your father's life, Mr. Hardy?"

Wariness instantly replaces melancholy. Hell if I'll end up charged as an accessory after the fact to any of his frauds. I may've pitted my skills against other card sharks running in Pop's circle, but I've never deceived innocent people. Of course, I never turned Pop in, either. For better or worse, he was my only family and I didn't want to see him rot in jail.

"Recently? Not much." I pick at nonexistent lint on my jeans. "We had a falling-out a few years ago."

"How about historically?" Hopkins leans forward, cocking one brow. "How much did you know about his comings and goings, his occupations?"

I proceed cautiously. "Wanna be more specific?"

"How'd he make money?"

"Here and there." I pause, considering what to reveal. "He never had a regular job that I can remember."

"I did a little digging and discovered you're living quite a high life out there in Malibu." Before I collect my thoughts, he continues, "Fancy house, fancy vehicles . . . How'd you come by all the money to buy those fancy things?"

The thinly veiled accusation starts a fire in my belly, but I'm not about to let him think he's intimidating me. Leaning back in my chair, I stretch my legs, cross my ankles, then meet his gaze with a steely one of my own.

"Why don't you tell me what you suspect?" I link my hands together behind my head.

"I think your father took advantage of people, stole their money, and ruined their lives. I think you know a little something about it, and maybe you were even involved in some of his activities."

His presumption slashes my pride. I take a deep breath to keep my rage in check.

"Not that it's your business, but I earned my money working in Vegas nightclubs and winning multiple six-figure poker tournaments." I lean forward in my chair without breaking eye contact. "Between the two gigs, I was pulling down megabucks for a few years, which I started investing after the markets crashed. The Dow's nearly doubled since then. Skill, discipline, luck, and timing. *That's* how I got the money to pay for my 'fancy things.'" I lift my chin. "I'm no thief."

Hopkins tries to call my bluff with a scowl, but he's got nothing on me. I know I've won this hand.

"If we check your father's phone records, they'll back up your claim about not being in touch?"

"Check whatever the hell you want." When I push back from the table and stand, I grip the back of the chair and give it a little shove. "Y'all are real swell guys, dragging me here without giving me a minute to make peace with this situation before hurling unflattering insinuations at me. I gotta say, the disrespect doesn't motivate me to cooperate with your investigation."

Woodenly, Hopkins replies, "Fair enough. We don't have evidence linking you to his crimes."

He gestures for me to retake my seat and then launches into the details of my pop's last scam. Turns out he pulled a Sweetheart Swindle—tricking some poor woman into falling in love and investing in his new "business venture," and then running off with the cash. Neither the cops nor the victim, Mrs. Morgan, recovered the thirty grand he stole. How in the hell he talked her, or others before her, into giving him that kind of cash astounds me.

His undeniable talent for spotting a patsy, combined with his handsome face, made women his easiest targets. The niggling sense of dishonor I've lived with my whole life because of him cascades over me, hot and sticky, like a warm coat of honey I can't ever shed. Humbled, I return my attention to Hopkins.

He informs me my pop was shot in an alley behind a bar late at night. Evidence suggests Mrs. Morgan's son killed him. Guess he tried to exact revenge before Pop pulled out of town.

"You don't seem surprised, Mr. Hardy," remarks the other officer, who has kept quiet until this point.

"I'm not."

"What can you tell us about your father's habits?" Hopkins raises his bushy brow again. "Do you know anything that might lead us to recoup Mrs. Morgan's money?"

"First, what's the deal with her son? Is he being held on homicide charges, or are y'all letting him slide because you reckon my pop got what he deserved?" I'm dismayed by my own wish to see justice served despite Pop's unclean hands.

"He's in custody now. We'll gather evidence and work with the local DA to determine what charges can stick. Your father committed a crime, but he didn't deserve to be murdered, Mr. Hardy. We believe in justice."

I stare into his icy-blue eyes, holding his gaze for a minute to determine his sincerity. He's not blinking excessively or averting his gaze, so I decide to trust him.

Satisfied, I slouch back into my chair and tap my toe a few times. "I'm not surprised you didn't find the money. Pop always covered his tracks. He operated under false names and paid for everything with cash." I shift positions and put my elbows on the table. "If he stuck to old routines, he either found a partner to split the take and he or she's holding the money, or he rented a storage locker somewhere outside of town, under a different name, and stashed the money there before tying up loose ends."

"That's helpful. Any ideas of an alias he might use?"

A smile spreads slowly across my face. I know one thing would never, ever change. My pop never forgave Mama's daddy for keeping her whereabouts a secret from Pop and me after she abandoned us. So, Pop deliberately used his name when hiding the booty.

He'd brag about it when he was drunk, figuring if he ever got pinched, at least he'd tarnish my grandpappy's good name. Of course, it started back when we still lived around Tifton, Georgia. People there knew the name Buford Sinclair. But with almost two decades and several states between now and then, I doubt the stain would spread that far. Still, I know Pop's obsessions.

I haven't thought of my grandpappy much since Mama took off. Now I wonder if he's even alive. Then again, that mean ol' bastard will probably live forever.

"Something funny?" Hopkins's voice snaps me back to the present.

"No, just recalling some things." I drum my hands on the table. "Check for rentals in the name of Buford Sinclair. Good chance you'll find what you're lookin' for."

"Thank you, Mr. Hardy. Anything else before you leave?"

"No, sir." Beleaguered by the inquiry, I'm itching to move along.

"Would you like to be notified of the charges and trial dates of Mr. Morgan, or talk to Mrs. Morgan?"

"No, thanks," I mutter.

I don't want to apologize to Mrs. Morgan for what Pop did any more than she probably wants to apologize to me for her son killing him. Pop taught me plenty, including not wasting my time on things I can't change. And Mama, well, her leaving taught me how to let go and move on. Apparently she didn't have the money, or the inclination, to take me with her or keep in touch, so I try to even the score by not thinking about her too often.

In any case, whatever becomes of Mrs. Morgan and her son won't make a real difference in my life. No need to prolong the circus or pretend my being here matters much at all.

I pick up the box of Pop's things and exit the station. The past twenty-four hours remind me of why I broke away from the game. Reliving my old life, even briefly, makes me feel dirty. Best not to invite trouble by kicking up my heels or allowing rose-tinted glasses to filter the grit from my past.

I sit behind the wheel of my car and stare out the windshield. Pop's box rests in the passenger seat beside me. With him dead, I've got no family—no ties at all. Just the things in this box. Normally I'm content with my solitary life, but now an unwelcome sense of doubt slides through my mind, cracking the walls I've constructed.

I roll the gold band over in my fingers and hold it up to the sun. Was it a prop, or is it his real wedding ring? Nah. He couldn't have been sentimental about Mama. All his preaching about keeping one's heart safe had come from her breaking ours.

I turn over the ignition, preparing to drive back to Los Angeles, when I realize I'm not far from Vegas. I may as well take a detour before returning home. Perhaps I'll play a few games in honor of Pop. He'd like that.

I'll get my adrenaline fix, eat well, flirt with a showgirl, and then head home. I nod in silent affirmation. Life's good. I can do what I want, when I want, without anyone's permission. And just like that, I hit Highway 95 North toward Vegas.

~

New York City

Lindsey

I appraise myself skeptically in the mirror once more before slipping out of the creamy-silk Amalia Carrara couture gown, careful not to prick my skin with the pins put in place for the final fitting. Smiling politely, I step out of the dress with the help of the seamstress while my mother finalizes the details of delivery and payment with the saleswoman. It still seems surreal. I'm soon to be a June bride—just before my twenty-sixth birthday.

My life's been an uninterrupted series of events falling neatly into place right up to this point. Now I've got my Ivy League education, a job at a high-profile fashion magazine, and a successful fiancé. Yet a nagging sense of dissatisfaction grows like mildew, steadily enveloping my spirit. Lately, the harder I throw myself into my work and wedding plans, the more clouded my thoughts become.

I sigh and wriggle my body back into my stretch-jersey dress, throw my purse over my shoulder, and stride to the front of the store to find my mother.

"You could use a little lipstick, honey, before you meet Rob," she suggests.

"I'm fine, Mom, but thanks for noticing." I wrinkle my nose. She rolls her eyes.

"Never hurts to look your best, especially when your fiancé is surrounded by attractive, ambitious female colleagues at Goldman." As if to emphasize her point, she reapplies her own lipstick and combs her bejeweled fingers through her fabulous golden hair. "I speak from experience. More than one of the women at your father's bank tried to tempt him. Don't expect other women to respect your wedding vows, and don't give Rob any reason to wander."

Her brittle tone raises questions, but this is neither the time nor the place to seek answers.

I set my bag on the counter, retrieve my lip gloss, and quickly apply it. Smacking my lips together in exasperation, I turn to my mother. "Better?"

Annoyed for capitulating, *again*, I blame her perfectionist attitude for why I revert to being a child in her presence. Almost everywhere else I have confidence, but with her I'm always yearning for approval that's never fully given.

"Yes!" She smiles and opens the door for me, then follows me onto the crowded sidewalk of Fifth Avenue. "So, where are you off to now?"

My phone trills, interrupting us. "Hold on." While I read Rob's text message, my brows gather. "Huh. Change of plans. I'm to meet him at the apartment. Apparently something's come up. I hope he's not canceling our trip this weekend."

"I'll bet he's planning a surprise for you." Mom looks delighted. She loves Rob for his maturity, his million-dollar pedigree, and his million-dollar salary. "Do you want a ride?"

"No, I'll walk." I kiss her on the cheek. "Thanks for meeting me this morning. I'll call you from the airport. Our flight leaves at six thirty tonight."

"Have fun, honey." She waves good-bye before seating herself inside the limousine waiting to whisk her off on the forty-minute ride home to Greenwich, Connecticut.

~

Strolling toward Central Park, I relish the gentle touch of a late-spring breeze against my arms. On my way uptown, I cut through the diverse parade of people, a grin on my face. Some don't enjoy the river of fast-moving crowds flowing through the granite-and-glass canyons of Manhattan, or the cries of street vendors competing with the traffic noise, or the aromas of the hot dog carts. I love the energy and prefer the bustle to the pristine, isolated estate of my childhood.

When I arrive at my Upper East Side building, the doorman nods and tips his head to greet me in the lobby. Waving hello, I go directly to the elevator. I burst into our apartment and call out Rob's name but hear no reply. I reach our bedroom to find Rob's suitcase packed and ready to go, on the floor beside the bed. My own, sadly, lies open, partially packed, and surrounded by outfits and accessories yet to be selected.

Crossing my arms in front of my chest, I mentally pick through the items strewn across the bed. Why am I making such a production of packing? Typically I'm not that particular about my attire, nor do I struggle with basic decisions. I pray the overwhelming details involved in planning my wedding are the basis of this recent mental paralysis. If so, I'll return to normal soon. If not . . . well, I really can't consider that option.

I stand at the edge of the mattress, lost in thought, until his voice breaks the silence.

"Lindsey?"

"In here!"

Rob finds me still standing, perplexed, at the foot of our bed.

Approaching me from behind, he encircles me with his arms before planting a kiss on my temple. "How's the dress?"

"What dress?" I scan the bed searching for a dress absentmindedly.

"The wedding gown?" He chuckles and cuddles me again. I spin toward him with a smile.

"Really beautiful. I hope you love it!"

Wrapping my arms over his shoulders, I properly kiss him hello and thread my fingers through the back of his hair. Rob eases himself away before slowly removing his suit coat and hanging it over the back of a chair. He sighs and I notice the strain in his deep-blue eyes.

"What's up, honey?"

"I need to tell you something." He rakes his hands through his wavy, black locks before bringing them together over his face and drawing in a deep breath. "Why don't you sit?"

Robert Whitmore III typically oozes confidence, charisma, and authority. Born and bred to be in charge by his father, one of the top M&A lawyers in New York, he takes to his role well. Now, however, he's pacing the room while averting his eyes.

My internal alarm clangs violently as questions ricochet in my mind: a work crisis, a problem with the wedding plans, illness? I'm still seated at the edge of the bed when he finally looks at me.

"What, Rob? Spit it out." My hands fist in my lap. "Are you canceling our trip?"

"I wish it were that simple."

A pit opens in my stomach.

"That sounds ominous." I wait, my lungs stilled, while he fumbles for words. "Please, Rob, the suspense is terrible. Just tell me what's wrong."

"You know how much I love you. I really do love you, Lindsey. But," he starts, "I have a confession. . . ." He looks at me, his expression resigned. "I was with someone else a few weeks ago."

A low hum resonates in my ears as if I've experienced an abrupt change in altitude.

"What?" I blink, unable to process his remarks. Did I hear him correctly?

"When you went to Boston with your friends the other weekend, I went out with friends from work and ended up sleeping with a girl who was at the club. It was stupid, I was drunk—all the clichés—but it didn't mean anything, Linds."

He kneels before me, clutching my hands. When he looks up, his eyes and forehead wrinkle with regret. I stiffen, too astonished to think, let alone speak. Eventually, I find my voice.

"I went to Boston a month ago. Why are you telling me only now?"

He cringes at my accusatory tone, but I'm working on pure instinct. While awaiting his reply, I repress the nausea swelling and boiling inside.

"I promise it was only the one time," he starts, "but she called me this morning at the office with upsetting news. I need to, uh," he mumbles, before breaking off and rubbing his hand over his face again. "You need to be checked out by a doctor for chlamydia. Apparently you can have it a long time without any symptoms."

He stands up and bends over at the waist. Grasping his knees, he lets out a small whoosh of breath, obviously relieved by his admission. Accustomed to fixing problems once they're exposed, I know Rob believes telling me the unpleasant news is the worst part.

Fury replaces the sickness in my stomach. I jump to my feet, shrieking, "You had sex with some slut and now I might be infected with an STD? Are *you*?"

"I don't know yet. But either way, you need to be tested, Lindsey. It's easy to cure with antibiotics, but if left untreated, it can cause irreversible damage. I couldn't take a chance with your health just to conceal my indiscretion."

I lunge at him and pound my fists against his chest. He grabs my wrists after allowing two or three punches to land. I break into sobs, withdrawing from his touch as if he's burned my skin.

"How could you?" My body sways as my knees start to give. "Why? Why'd you do this to us?"

He holds me close and I momentarily melt into the familiar warmth of his body.

"I'm sorry. I'm so sorry. It meant nothing to me, Lindsey. I swear!" His cheek brushes against my hair and he kisses the top of my head. "It's not an excuse, but it was simply drunken stupidity. Tell me how we can put it behind us and move on."

"What?" I push away from him again, my mouth agape. "Put it behind us? This isn't something to sweep under the carpet. You risked our relationship *and* our health. If the tables were turned, you'd never forgive and forget."

His face blanches at the mere suggestion of my infidelity, but he recovers and considers my accusation. "You're upset, which you have every right to be. I'm sorry I hurt you. I've been sorry for weeks. Frankly, I'm relieved to have told the truth before we're married. Look at me—this will never happen again!"

In this instant, I don't recognize him or myself. My ears throb. I'm acutely aware of each heartbeat hammering in my chest, while my lungs search for air. Turning away, I draw a slow breath through my nose to steady my thoughts. A moment later, I force myself to face him.

I summon my strength and hide the depth of my heartache. "You bet it won't happen again. The wedding is off, Rob." My lips begin to quiver and tears mount in my eyes.

"Don't say that, Linds. Come on. I know I screwed up, but I haven't habitually betrayed you. I've loved you for years. I'm committed to being a partner and husband you can count on. For better or worse, that's the deal. This is my worst." When I don't respond, he applies guilt. "Don't break my heart, baby. I need you."

I recognize these moves. He's angling to win this argument. Smooth, savvy, and a great manipulator. Qualities that propelled his meteoric rise at work. I've been trained to respect these traits in a man, but suddenly, they seem vile and repulsive. The chiseled features I'd always found so handsome now appear hollow and grotesque. The worst, however, is his condescension—assured I'll forgive him as long as he begs. Misreading my silence as acquiescence, he moves to hug me. His contact awakens me from my trance and I bat at his arms.

Backing away, I whisper, "You can't love me. You don't know me at all."

"That's completely untrue." He spreads his arms wide, palms up. "I know you better than anyone."

"If you expect I'll marry you on schedule, after you betrayed me, then you *don't* know me." Despite feeling shaky, I continue, "And I don't know you, either. All I know now is I don't trust you."

Worry flickers across his face. "I love you more than I've ever loved anyone. You're the perfect girl for me." He slumps into the chair, studying me mournfully. "Please don't throw everything away two weeks before the wedding. Let's take the weekend to get some perspective. I believe in us. We can work through this together and be stronger."

Only two weeks until our wedding. What do I do about the guests, the gifts, all the plans . . . and the whispered rumors sure to follow a last-minute cancellation? I grab my stomach and ease back down onto the bed. Overcome with emotion, I refuse to meet his gaze. I'm conscious of his eyes searching out mine, waiting for me to speak.

Rob's phone rings, disturbing the heavy silence sitting between us. Of course, he answers it. Judging from his terse replies and his fingers rubbing his temples, I know he'll be returning to work. When he finishes the call, he turns to me and bites his lower lip.

"I've got to get back to the office to nail down a merger issue before we take off for Bermuda tonight," he says through a false smile. He sits beside me and rests his hand on my thigh, eliciting no response from me. "Lindsey, let's take the trip. We'll use the time to talk all of this through. Meet me at the airport?"

I view him as though he's one thousand miles away and hear myself say, "I need to call the doctor now."

"I love you." Apparently unwilling to risk probing me further, he takes his suitcase in his hand and kisses my forehead. "I'll meet you at the airport in a few hours and we'll work this all out. I'll do whatever you need me to do. I'm really sorry."

Despite my silence, the significance of his confession, and the fact that our future hangs in the balance, duty calls. Work has always been his first love and priority, so I'm not surprised when he leaves. Once the apartment door closes, I allow myself the freedom to cry out loud.

I slide from the bed onto the floor and hold my face. Hot tears soak my hands. Everything I thought I knew just slipped through my fingers like water in a sieve. Hugging my knees to my chest, I rock myself and replay the past few weeks to determine how I missed the signs.

I've always secretly assumed that women who claim they've been blindsided by a cheater probably weren't paying attention. Is this karmic payback for my arrogance? Convinced he'd shown no change in behavior, and no sign of guilt or remorse, I begin questioning what other elaborate lies he might have told. How many secrets does he keep?

Lying on the floor, I take stock of the hours wasted worrying about wedding plans, anticipating and planning to prevent crisis, following the expected path and working toward the life I'd been taught to desire. None of my preparation prevented disaster from striking. Worse, I didn't even see it coming.

The humiliating blow bites hard, irreparably breaking my heart. On some level, I know no one gets through life without pain. Had I truly understood it, however, I'd have wasted less time trying to manage circumstances beyond my control.

In a small way, perhaps the glass shattering is a sobering opportunity to revisit my life choices. Three years with Rob. I've felt comfortable and content with him. Is that enough? Can I forgive him?

Even though he's several years older than me, we share similar backgrounds and educations, have the same taste in movies and books, and both want a family and life similar to what we've always known. He's never forgotten a birthday, anniversary, or other special occasion, always treated my parents well, and been kind to my friends. He must love me if he wants to marry me. Does the positive outweigh the negative?

My open wounds sting in response to conjured images of him kissing and touching another woman. It's too soon to make a permanent decision, but I can't marry him in two weeks, if ever.

Eventually, I pick myself up off the floor and pack the suitcase on my bed, plus two others, now caring very little about what ends up inside them. On my way out the door, I take off my three-carat, colorless, cushion-cut diamond and place it on the entry table with a note that reads simply, *I can't marry you in June. I need time.*

CHAPTER THREE

Malibu, California
June 2, 2013

Levi

The noisy racket coming from my bathroom wakes me. I squint at the sunlight flooding through the open sliding-glass door of the bedroom. Familiar cries of seagulls and the crash of waves on the coast greet me, reminding me I'm not in Vegas anymore. Shoving aside a mostly empty glass of tequila, I roll over and squint harder at the clock on the bedside table. *10:48* in bright green numbers. Morning.

I flip the lid off of an Altoids tin and pop a cinnamon mint in my mouth, then notice the box of my pop's belongings sitting on the table. Neither the poker tables nor the women of LA have been able to erase the images of my pop in that morgue. Throughout the week I've been plagued by sudden bursts of gloom, just like now. I pinch the bridge of my nose to brush the feeling aside. More clattering in the bathroom catches my attention again.

She'll be coming out of there soon. Turning back over, I prop my head up on my hand and try to recall her name.

Comfortably naked as a jaybird, she halts in the doorway when she notices me watching her. Sexy, but she's just another Barbie doll. Straight, blonde hair; blue eyes; unnatural proportions. You'd think a *smart* girl chasing fame and fortune might try to distinguish herself, rather than imitate others. Then I decide smart people don't want fame—fortune yes, but fame's a life sentence in a fishbowl. No sane person would choose to live that way.

"Mornin', doll." I smile, lifting one brow. "You want to shower before I take you home?"

"Sure." Barbie doesn't even fight the brush-off. "I'll be quick."

I drag myself up to brush my teeth, make the bed, and peel the dirty clothes from the floor. Grabbing a fresh pair of jeans and clean T-shirt, I carry last night's tequila glass downstairs to the kitchen. I've nearly finished my orange juice when she appears from around the corner.

"All set." She combs her fingers through her wet hair.

"Hungry?" I ask to be polite, although I suspect she'll decline, since few women out here eat very much.

"A little, actually."

Damn. Nothing personal, but I don't want to spend much of my day with her, or anyone else for that matter. Pop always warned me of the dangers of trusting folks—of letting others know my heart and mind. His conditioning keeps me wary. For better or worse, those younger years hardened and shaped me.

On the other hand, I'm pretty hungry myself.

"Okay, then. Go take a seat somewhere and I'll call you when it's ready."

"Cereal's fine," she offers.

"Not for me it isn't." I smile and shoo her away.

Working quickly, I chop a red bell pepper, an onion, and fresh spinach, then toss them all in a hot sauté pan. While they heat, I whip eggs together with some milk. I pour the frothy egg mixture over the vegetables in the pan and cover it so the frittata can cook. After setting two plates out and heating some water for tea, I pop a few slices of bread in the toaster. I set the crisp toast out with butter before I call Barbie back to the kitchen.

"Wow, this smells amazing." She holds her hair back and sniffs the frittata. "Where'd you learn to cook?"

"I like to eat well, so I had to learn." My stomach rumbles in anticipation of the savory meal. "Enjoy."

"Can we eat out on your deck?"

"I guess so. Grab your plate."

I gather some things on a tray and follow her out to the deck.

Sunny skies and a lack of wind offer perfect conditions for eating outdoors, and for people watching. Saturdays at the beach are more congested than weekdays. Families scatter to construct sand castles and build other sand art. A few Pepperdine beach bunnies must have that new app that guides you past the barriers constructed by residents across the entrances to the public beach. The sorority scene's a plus in my mind, although at thirty, the maturity level of a nineteen-year-old girl holds less appeal to me now. Not sure why it matters, since I rarely see the same girl more than a few times. But I get bored with trivial conversation and find I'm growing less patient with each year.

Still, I admire the bikini-clad women from a distance. Flashbacks of my late teens pass through my mind like a slideshow, producing an unexpected smile. Despite not attending college, I'm no stranger to the sorority houses in Georgia, Alabama, and Florida.

"Nice-looking surfboard." Barbie gestures toward the corner of the deck where I left my shortboard yesterday. "Will you ride later?"

A quick scan of the shore shows that the mighty ocean's only offering ankle busters today—not enough temptation for me to suit up.

"Nah." I slice my fork through my frittata and take a bite. "Not worth it today."

"Huh. You're quite the man of mystery. You've got a hidden talent as a chef. You surf. I didn't see any pictures in your house of family or friends. And what's with all the books in the living room?

Are you a film scout or book critic or something?" She wipes the corner of her mouth with her napkin. "You never mentioned what you do for a living."

"Cooking's not a hidden talent if I share it, right? As for the books, I just enjoy reading." I evade the topic of my career.

"So, then, what's your occupation?"

"Work's for suckers," I joke, unwilling to share my history. I'd rather she think I inherited money, or some other such thing, than open myself up to a lot of questions about my past.

"You sound like you're not originally from LA. Is your family still somewhere in the *Say-outh*?" She smiles at her attempt to imitate my inflection.

And just like that, she destroys the little break from thinking about Pop I'd been enjoying during breakfast. "No family in LA."

She sips her tea, letting the silence stretch between us, and then arches one brow. "You don't talk much, do you, Levi?"

"Not when I'm eating." I wink, hoping to encourage her to finish soon so I can take her home before she starts grilling me for more personal details.

Her gaze wanders out to the beach as she taps her fingers on the arms of the chair. "We're not going to see each other again, are we?"

"I try not to predict the future." I wipe my mouth with my napkin. "But I wouldn't be sorry to bump into you again sometime."

"Gotcha." She inhales through her nose, then says, without sorrow or anger, "Well, I'm all set. Thanks for the delicious meal. Will you give me a ride me home now?"

Her lack of disappointment confirms we're alike; she values freedom and independence. In this regard, she's the perfect woman for me.

Except I'm not looking for the perfect woman.

"Yes, ma'am. Let's go." When she stands to collect her dishes, I wave her off. "I'll take care of all that when I return."

I motion toward the garage, then hand her a helmet and put on my shoes for the ride. She climbs behind me on my Ducati and wraps her arms around my waist as I turn south onto the Pacific Coast Highway.

~

Lindsey

Staring at the ocean while driving along the Pacific Coast Highway with my car top down, I catch sight of my bare finger gripping the steering wheel. I removed my engagement ring more than a week ago and, three days later, boxed up my belongings from Rob's apartment.

After storing nonessentials, I kissed my parents, my friends, my job, and New York good-bye. With the help of my trust fund, I rented a small beach house in Malibu for several months.

I've fond memories of Malibu thanks to my childhood visits with my dad's sister. The beach and mountains had always provided endless adventure. And although my mom called her kooky, I thought Aunt Sara's artistic spirit and unconventional friends were warm and welcoming.

She was so different from Dad, sometimes I questioned whether she was adopted. At times, I'd secretly wished to go live with her and be free to explore the world. Naturally, my mother could barely conceal her relief when Aunt Sara moved to Brazil ten years ago with some musician. Now she's living off the grid, so our visits are restricted to infrequent holiday FaceTime chats and e-mails.

Malibu won't be the same without her, but the distance should enable me to contemplate my future with minimal interference from my past.

Rob's deception rocked me, but it also allows me to reconsider the direction of my life. I only wish I didn't feel like I've jumped from a plane without a parachute.

My cell phone rings, interrupting my thoughts and Rihanna's raunchy song.

"Hello?"

"Are you there yet?" Jill asks.

"No. Navigation says thirty more minutes." I grin, eager to reach my destination. "Of course, in this traffic, who knows?"

"I still don't get why you had to leave New York to figure out whether or not to forgive Rob."

"The pitying stares. The daily pressure from my mother." I roll my eyes even though no one can see them. "I had to take drastic action."

"Drastic is right." Jill heaves an irritated, long sigh. "Seriously, is Rob's one-time fling worth blowing up your whole life?"

"His 'fling' called him at work." I feel the heat rush to my cheeks. "If she could find him there, she's probably not the random one-timer he claims."

"But he confessed before the wedding. Doesn't that count?"

"Jill, he confessed to safeguard my health, not because of a crisis of conscience." It's just so humiliating, and I'm still awaiting the damn test results. "I can't commit to a man who casually deceived me."

Why start a marriage as an insecure wife, incessantly worrying? I won't become one of those women who checks her husband's pockets and e-mails, who spends endless hours and dollars on my appearance in order to compete with younger women, or who turns a blind eye to duplicity out of fear of loneliness.

"I'm sorry. I know this sucks for you." Jill's tone softens. "Have you canceled all the wedding plans?"

"Rob's taking care of some of it with my mom's help. He owed it to me after all I did to plan everything." My heart pinches. "What a waste of time and money."

The sudden silence makes me question whether the call dropped, but then Jill speaks.

"Maybe this break is a good idea, actually. You've always killed yourself trying to please everyone. You deserve some 'me' time."

"Thanks, Jill." I smile, happy for the crumb of understanding. "Hey, I've got to pay attention to my navigation because I'm getting closer. Talk later?"

"Bye!"

The sky-blue home's tucked into a nest of palm trees and flowering shrubs. I spy the broker sitting in her car talking on her phone. As I approach her car, I notice her stretched skin and unexpressive forehead. She's spent beaucoup bucks fighting her forties. Apparently, some things are identical on both coasts.

After introductions, a quick tour, and instructions about the alarm system, appliances, and so on, she hands me the keys and a bottle of champagne and then leaves me alone.

An hour later, my emptied suitcases and boxes are stowed in the closet. I scatter a few personal items and photographs throughout the home. Strolling through each room, I hug myself.

The house is eighteen hundred square feet of airy perfection. Its white stucco living and dining rooms, each with pitched beamed ceilings, open to a nice-sized deck, decorated simply with lounge chairs and terra-cotta potted plants. From there is a gorgeous view of the ocean and nearby pier. Upstairs, a corner fireplace and glass sliders adorn the master bedroom, which opens to a private deck with the same view as the one below.

Everything about this house is a startling contrast to any place I've ever lived. Standing on the balcony outside my new bedroom—a bedroom I'll be sharing with no one—I observe the activity on the beach. Unlike New England shores, it's not swarming with people. The blazing late-afternoon sun slowly lowers toward the glimmering horizon. My first West Coast sunset in years. Too bad I'll be watching it alone.

Although it's Sunday, I'd bet Rob's working. Is he thinking of me? Does his stomach churn, like mine, at the recognition of what we've lost? Will he sit alone tonight, or will he drown his sorrows in a bottle or another woman's bed?

Disgusted by my speculation, I distract myself by going inside. Opening my laptop on the dining room table, I click through my e-mails. Wedding vendor notices, spam, another message from Rob. Nothing I want to deal with right now. I shut down the computer and collapse onto the comfy sofa, procrastinating making the inevitable call to my mother.

Determined to wear my big-girl pants, I finally pick up the phone and make the call.

"Hello, Lindsey."

"Hi, Mom. Thought you'd want to know I'm safe and sound." I tug on the ends of my hair. "The place is just like the online photos. You'd adore it."

"Glad the trust fund is going to such valuable use."

Her sarcastic remark hits the bull's-eye. My chest heaves. Over the years we've rarely argued, and I've never been one for combat.

"If you and Dad didn't want me to have the money, then why'd you bother giving it to me in the first place?" My forehead wrinkles upon hearing my own ungrateful, selfish retort. I appreciate how lucky I am to have been handed a safety net.

"Don't think we don't regret it now." Her brittle voice grates my eardrums. "You're supposed to be smarter and stronger than this, Lindsey."

"It is smart and strong to reconsider my options rather than rush to marry a man who's proven himself a liar." Her silence fuels slight elation at possibly having made my point, until I hear her sigh.

"You'll never find a relationship without bumps—serious bumps. Life's hard. Marriage takes work, compromise, and forgiveness." She softens her voice. "Rob made a terrible mistake, but he's apologized. You've sunk three years into that relationship. Together you have everything necessary to build a beautiful life together. I doubt you'll find a man more suitable than him."

Flabbergasted, I spit out, "Really? I can't do better than a cheater?" My eye twitches, so I take a deep breath. My mom doesn't realize this hiatus is about more than Rob, but if I tell her how I feel, she'll only be insulted and angrier. "I don't want to fight, Mom. Please stop insulting me, okay?"

Silence.

Her heavy-handed coercion angers the hell out of me. It also makes me question whether Dad broke her trust, too, and how, but I don't have the nerve to ask.

They'd always seemed normal, like other parents in our neighborhood. Dad worked long hours, traveled extensively, and left Mom to manage all things involving the house, the social calendar, and me. I'd never witnessed them argue. In fact, neither ever displayed much of any kind of emotion. Oddly, both were physically affectionate toward me and, until now, had been my biggest cheerleaders.

"Mom?"

"Fine, Lindsey." Her tense voice quiets again.

"Well, I'll call you tomorrow. Maybe then we can talk about the future instead of the past." I wait, hoping for one encouraging word before hanging up.

"I know you think I'm being unreasonable. Your father and I love you and want what's best for you. I know you're hurt, but you're being impetuous. Choices made from emotion, rather than reasoned thought, aren't usually the best."

"Good night, Mom." I end the call battered because, in truth, I can't refute her final point.

Rob and I had played out a pattern of general ease, friendship, and respect, similar to that of my parents. We didn't argue in front of others, break up and make up in equal measure, or engage in displays of public affection. I'd assumed it meant we were perfectly matched, but maybe the lack of emotion indicated a lack of deep passion. Is that why Rob strayed? Am I too predictable?

I pour myself a glass of champagne and wander out to the deck. Sinking into a lounge chair, I recline and consider a new beginning. Tiny, fruity bubbles tickle my nose, but even the postcard-worthy orange-and-pink sky can't lift my mood to match its vibrancy.

How is it possible to have been engaged, begun a career, and be nearly twenty-six, all without knowing who I am or what I want from my life? It's unacceptable. Pathetic even. I've obviously been more concerned with winning approval than pursuing my own desires.

And unlike Aunt Sara, my parents conditioned me to replace dreams with decisions based on fear. I miss being easily inspired and believing anything's possible. I want that back. That's why I came, and I'm not going home until I find it.

CHAPTER FOUR

June 3, 2013

Levi

Being alone hasn't helped me sleep any better than the comfort of being curled up next to a soft, warm body did this week. My room is still dark when I roll out of bed to go outside to get my morning paper. It's quiet; only a few cars driving along the Pacific Coast Highway. Then again, it's not even six o'clock in the morning. When I bend over to get the *Journal*, I notice a red BMW 6 Series convertible parked next door. Nice wheels. But I'm bummed someone finally rented that house.

That vacant property had afforded me extra privacy. I love this beach, but the houses are almost flush to one another. The downside of all the windows offering ocean views is seeing bits and pieces of your neighbor's activities each day. At least my house is more elevated, making it harder for them to see me than for me to see them.

I hope my new neighbor likes his or her privacy as much as I enjoy mine.

I've spent my adult life relaxed and comfortable in my solitude—at least I did up until last week. But lately images and memories of my pop are throwing me off my game. Perhaps the brutal nature of his death's haunting me.

Not that I'm surprised by the turn of events. You can't play with people's lives and not expect blowback. Given enough time, Pop was sure to cross the wrong person. He'd been convinced he'd be a little smarter and faster than the next guy. But you don't have to be a statistics guru to know no one indefinitely outsmarts everyone.

Yet, the norm of a grifter's life—the rush of the unknown, the thrill of a chase, and the excitement of an against-all-odds victory—has an addictive quality. My Vegas trips are becoming more frequent to satisfy my appetite for adventure. Unlike my pop's games, though, the only person harmed by my ill-advised habit is myself. With my expertise, that doesn't happen too often, however.

Queasiness unfurls when I consider the idea of Pop looking down the barrel of a gun knowing he was gonna die. Did he think of me? And now I'm alone . . . really alone. I cut him out of my life, but the finality of never being able to talk to him again suffocates me. If ever the turn of phrase "deafening silence" applied to my life, this is certainly the occasion.

My throat tightens as I digest the circumstances of his death without distractions. If he hadn't carried my name and address in his wallet, how long might he have remained unclaimed? Will anyone shed a tear over his demise? Will that be me one day, dying alone and, for all intents and purposes, leaving no one and nothing behind? Do I care? Maybe I do and that's why I can't sleep anymore.

Ah, to hell with this pity party. I've got shit to do. Life to live.

I set up shop on my deck to browse the *Journal*. An hour later, I refill my coffee and go stand at the railing to peek at the morning activity on the beach. I stretch my torso, holding my hands clasped behind my head. It's still early, just before seven. Not much happening, so it's easy to spot the girl on the beach not far from my house.

At first she's facing the ocean. Her almond-brown ponytail and lean, athletic legs make me eager for her to spin around and give me a full view. When she finally turns sideways, I notice her cheeks are stained pink. She's got a strong jawline and high cheekbones. Unlike the Barbie from yesterday, and the many other underfed, plastic-surgery guinea pigs in LA, this girl's naturally pretty.

When she approaches my house, I scowl. Why's she coming my way? Does she know me? Something about her is vaguely familiar, but I can't place her. One might write it off as "one of those faces," but she's memorable, and I'm good with faces. Perhaps I've seen her in the local markets or bars. Must be it.

When I realize she's actually heading toward the house next door, I'm relieved and slightly intrigued. Leaning my forearms against the railing, I watch her start up the steps to her own deck. A pleasant hum reverberates through me, so I indulge the feeling.

She must sense my stare, because she glances up, causing me to freeze in the spotlight of her owlish, golden-brown eyes. After regaining my composure, I nod.

"Howdy, neighbor. Nice mornin' for a run."

She halts for a second, blinking almost as if she's seen a ghost. Recovering quickly, she tips her chin and offers a thin smile before continuing inside. My brow lowers at the slight.

Frickin' ice princess. Can't even stop and say good morning to a new neighbor? Does she think I'm coming on to her? She doesn't have to worry about that from me. I've established rules, and neighbors make for bad bedfellows. If she's frigid, that's fine with me. I'm not looking for friends. I'd best be getting back to my work anyway.

～

Lindsey

Oh. My. God. Is *he* really my neighbor? He's more mature, but still impossibly gorgeous—those piercing eyes and that gritty accent. I'd wasted a week obsessively watching him work while plotting to win his attention.

Does he remember me? Doubtful. He's probably played out dozens of similar scenes, at dozens of resorts, with dozens of women. I meant less than nothing to him, but his orchestrated rejection left a lasting impact on my young heart.

It figures he caught me after my run, when I'm sweaty and disgusting. I already stick out here among the Amazon blondes. Still acting like a coward, too, ducking away from him as quickly as possible.

What were the odds I'd ever see him again, let alone end up his neighbor? A zillion to one! I should go purchase a lottery ticket, selecting the numbers of today's date and my new address.

Unbelievable. I finally free myself from my gilded cage in New York only to end up next door to *him*. How will I enjoy this neighborhood if I'm always checking over my shoulder for his sneer? Worse, what if he remembers me? Won't he have a good laugh?

I predicted he'd end up poor and alone. Instead, *I'm* alone, depressed, and living on my parents' generosity. Shame pulses through me. Maybe a long shower will wash away my searing discomfort.

No such luck. My thoughts return to him. How'd he end up affording to live in Malibu? Did he actually go to school? More likely he robbed a bank or is house-sitting for someone. Oh, one can hope he's just here temporarily.

Remembering our ancient conversation brings into sharp focus the dismal shape of my life. I've been parroting my parents' opinions and beliefs as my own for so long, I'm hard-pressed to separate them from my own.

How haughty and condescending I was to lecture him, to purport to know anything about life. Now, years later, we end up at the same place despite vastly different paths and plans. For all I know, he's better off than me.

He's probably acquired a purpose. Maybe he even opted for a few of those anchors he'd sworn off. An unexpected curiosity seizes me as I envision his equally beautiful girlfriend—or wife! Wife.

I could be someone's wife. My body slumps in response to visualizing Rob. Much as I hate to admit it, I miss him, or at least I miss the idea of *us*. I steady my bouncing knees. What am I doing here? What's this hiatus going to accomplish? Were my parents right about my hasty decision?

Instinctively, I reach for my phone to call Jill. She'll be awake now and walking to work.

"What's up?" she answers.

"You will *not* believe it!" I hold my forehead in my palm.

"What?"

"Remember when I went to Sanibel for Christmas break our senior year?"

"Yes," she answers.

"Remember the bartender I told you about and how he treated me?" *Levi*.

"Oh yeah, the super-hot one who seduced then rejected you?" She giggles.

"Not funny, by the way." I sniff.

"Come on. Kinda funny now, right?"

"Not really, Jill, considering he lives next door to my rental!"

"No way!"

"Yes way," I reply sullenly. "Can you believe it?"

"That's incredible. How'd you recognize him?"

"Oh, his mesmerizing, evil image is forever etched in my mind. I'm pretty sure it's him." Privately, I surmise his face is etched in the memories of many women, for many different reasons.

"Did he recognize you?"

"I doubt it. We didn't talk. He called hello from his porch when I

returned from my morning run. I responded by bolting into my house."
Her laughter on the other end of the line makes my mouth twitch.

"Sorry. That sucks. But he probably won't remember you, so act
normal. You can do that, right? Act normal?"

Right? Her light, mocking tone coaxes a fleeting smile from me. Then
heaviness settles back into my chest. "Jill, what am I even doing here?"

"What do you mean?"

"I mean, why did I think coming back to Malibu would solve my
problems? What am I doing?"

"Running away."

"I'm serious."

"Me too."

"Is that what everyone thinks? I couldn't handle the breakup, so I
ran away to hide?" Jill's hesitation gives me my answer.

"Who cares? Do whatever it takes to be happy."

"So, that's a yes, basically," I say without enthusiasm.

"Do you want me to tell you what you want to hear, or speak the
truth? But come on, you've only been in California one day and you're
already throwing in the towel. Explore the area. Give yourself time,"
she encourages.

"You're right." I wrap my hand around my ponytail. "It feels weird
being here without Aunt Sara or any friends. And now I've got an
unwelcome neighbor."

"I don't know, Linds. Unwelcome?" I could practically hear her
brows wiggling through the phone. "A sexy neighbor may be the
perfect diversion."

I suck in my breath. "Jill, I'm not looking for a new man. I
should be marrying Rob in a few days. Just because I'm hurt doesn't
mean all that love disappears overnight. And I haven't totally given
up on the relationship, either. Contrary to everyone's opinion, I
didn't *run away*. I came here to think."

"Sorry," she says. "Have you spoken with him yet?"

"No. I'm still too angry." I don't admit to the hours spent sifting through the little details of our relationship to unearth clues to his deception only to come up empty-handed. "Like I said yesterday, he only confessed when forced. It's like he has no integrity. I can't pretend that fact isn't significant. If I take him back, won't he just feel free to do it again?"

"I doubt forgiveness would be viewed as a free pass to cheat again." She pauses. "By the way, did you get your test results yet?"

"I'm supposed to hear back today."

"I'm sure you're fine. Try to relax. Hey, I've got to run to a meeting. Talk later?"

"Sure." I sigh. "Maybe you can come visit?"

"Sounds fun. Bye!" The line goes dead.

Jill's being at work reminds me it's Monday. Unlike her, I don't have to rush to the office. Quitting the magazine is a welcome change even if it is a horrendous career move.

When I first took the writing job, I'd hoped to empower women by getting them to focus on inner beauty. It sounds ridiculous now, since the managing editor and publisher ultimately dictated content. And who was I kidding? No matter how often we claim outer beauty isn't important, we still want to be at least as attractive as the next woman.

But despite its flaws, my job gave me an identity. I'd put on a great outfit, go to my office, work with a team, and feel a rush of pride each month when an issue appeared on the stands. A pleasant routine but not an intrinsically rewarding one. Much as Rob's preoccupation with mergers and acquisitions annoys me, I envy his passionate commitment. He really loves his work. I want that fire for myself.

Of course, *that* requires having a better sense of my own interests. I suppose that's part of the reason I'm sitting here in Malibu, too. I've come here to find myself. How trite.

Seagulls' cries capture my attention. What a difference from the ambulances, horns, and truck engines I'm used to hearing outside my window. I walk to the open door and smile when greeted by an ocean breeze. Determined to begin my internal exploration, I take a quick trip to a local drugstore for some beach essentials.

～

An hour later, I return home with a new folding chair, sunscreen, and a stack of magazines. Outfitted in a bright pink-and-orange tie-dyed bikini, I fill my eco-friendly bottle with ice water, grab my towel and magazines, and brave the beach—white skin and all.

In anticipation of the rising tide, I set up in the sand near my steps. I inhale the salty sea air and grin. The sun's warm rays enhance the decadence of sitting surfside on a Monday. Donning my sunglasses and hat, I insert my earbuds, crank up my iPod, and settle in to see what subjects other magazines are publishing today.

While reading a depressing article about another insider trading scandal, I notice *him*, in my peripheral vision, descending his steps. As he pads toward the surf, I study his well-defined, V-shaped physique, all of it accentuated by his shorty wetsuit. Carrying a surfboard under his arm, he jogs directly to the water, drops a water bottle in the sand, and then tosses his board in the ocean. Once he paddles beyond the waves, I return my focus to *Forbes*.

From behind the veil of my glasses and hat brim, I steal glimpses of him surfing and swimming, and then chide myself. Yet I can't refrain for long, just like when I first saw him in Florida. Good grief. Obviously, I should switch to a more captivating magazine.

Psychology Today looks promising, with marriage-centered themes promoted on its cover. Maybe an article or two will help me sort out my situation with Rob. Closing my eyes, I picture him canceling all of our plans. Did it sadden him? Is his remorse genuine?

Forty-five minutes later, I'm seriously rethinking my choices. These dreadful articles force me to question my own behavior and responses, rather than simply blaming Rob. He cheated, not me. Don't I deserve the freedom to cast him in the "black hat" role? Must I consider what kind of partner I've been, and whether my actions or neglect contributed to his straying?

My eyes snap shut as a huge part of my brain silently screams *bullshit!* But perhaps I expect too much. Or could it be our love isn't the kind of love required for a *lifelong* commitment?

Frustrated, I look out to the sea and notice the tide has encroached upon the shore to the spot where my neighbor dropped his water bottle. Disliking him doesn't mean I should let a cozy-covered plastic bottle go adrift and pollute the ocean. I trot across the sand and bend to retrieve it. As I straighten up, I catch him watching me while floating on his surfboard.

I hold up his bottle and point to it, gesturing that I'm moving it back from the rising tide. He doesn't respond. Shocker. Shrugging, I carry the bottle approximately six feet inland before dropping it in the sand and returning to my chair and magazine.

Not long afterward, he emerges from the water. Salt water drips from his hair as he pushes it away from his face, reclaims his bottle, and starts guzzling. He's still delectably hunky with his bronzed skin, wet hair, and sinewy arms and legs. My stomach flutters a bit, so I look away as he ambles toward me.

Against my will, my pulse quickens. Hoping to avoid eye contact, I glue my eyes to the pages in front of me and feign deep concentration. God, *please* don't remember me! My heart stops when sand hits my calf as he throws his board down near me and sits, forcing me to engage in conversation.

"Thanks for rescuing my bottle." His congenial smile reveals his dimples and rekindles my adolescent desire. The timbre of his voice makes my body resonate, like plucked guitar strings, fueling utter self-disgust. I attempt to repress both sensations.

"No problem." I glance at him from beneath the brim of my hat.

"You renting this house now?"

Clearly I won't escape this conversation without eye contact.

"Yes, for a little while, anyway." Hating awkward silences, I continue, "Do you rent that one?"

"Me? No. I bought it in foreclosure three years ago. Great deal." His pleasant expression reveals no shame or remorse.

Raising my brows, I tartly reply, "Not so great for the previous owner, I guess."

"No, not so much." His brows rise in observation, not anger. "You say that as if I did something wrong."

"Well, it's a shame some people profit off others' unfortunate circumstances."

He grins, quirking one brow upward. "Someone's usually profiting off of another's misfortune. This time I had a full house and these folks didn't. Someday it might be the other way around." I see the glint of challenge in his eyes.

"That's cynical."

"No, just honest." He studies my reaction. "Guess you've been lucky enough to avoid a bad hand so far."

I avert my eyes. This conversation's frighteningly similar to our first discussion. Eager to change the subject, I nod in agreement and avoid prolonged eye contact.

He turns toward me but doesn't extend his hand. "Well, neighbor, I'm Levi."

Suddenly I'm very thankful we never exchanged names in Florida. I rest my magazine across my legs.

"I'm Lindsey."

"Lindsey." He rolls my name over his tongue and flaunts a

provocative smile before noticing the magazine cover. "Are you a shrink, or are you getting married soon and making sure he's really 'the one'?"

His disdainful inflection tempts me to use the word *anchor* in my reply.

"Neither."

I choose not to risk jogging his memory with another dispute about marriage. He looks at me as if he senses my dishonesty.

"You know, I swear this isn't a line, but have we met before? There's something familiar about you."

Oh no. In the space of two seconds, blood drains from my face and races to my toes. Can I lie? I gulp to buy time when a woman's voice behind us suspends my internal panic.

"Hey, Levi, what happened last weekend? I thought you were coming to our little block party," she coos.

I twist around to meet a midthirty-something woman in a bikini and lots of bling. She's obviously sizing me up and evaluating my relationship to Levi. A current bed buddy of his, perhaps? She's not my idea of his type—as if I'd even know his type.

"Sorry, Elena. Something unexpected came up." He offers no further explanation, but his courteous expression falters before he takes another sip of water and stares at the ocean.

"What happened, someone die?" she teases, pressing for details.

He winces before resuming an unexpressive countenance. "Yes, actually. My pop died."

Elena and I both react in shock. Given her surprise, I gather they're not romantically involved, though not by her choice.

"Oh gosh, Levi, I'm so sorry. Really, I didn't mean to make such a dreadful joke. Are you okay?" As she sputters apologies, her obvious discomfort gains my sympathy. "Can I do anything for you?"

"No, thanks," he replies. "I'm fine."

He digs his heel into the sand without looking at either of us.

"I'm so sorry, and so embarrassed," she mumbles.

Eager to rescue her from her distress, I jump in.

"Hi, I'm Lindsey Hilliard. I moved into this house over the weekend." I tip my head toward my little blue cottage.

"Oh, so you two are new neighbors?" Her tone lacks enthusiasm for my arrival. "I'm Elena. I live a few doors up. Where are you coming from? Are you married?"

Why must I dodge recurring marriage questions today?

"I'm from New York. I came alone."

Levi studies my face while I speak with Elena. I shift in my chair, feeling overheated.

"If you have questions about the area, let me know," Elena offers. "I'm happy to introduce you to the neighborhood. I've lived here for years. Lucky for me, I won the house in the divorce." Her inauthentic smile reveals lingering pain, but she recovers and addresses Levi, whom she obviously covets. "I'm truly sorry for your loss, Levi." She faces me. "Nice meeting you, Lindsey." Her hand flits a little wave before she struts toward her house with a somewhat exaggerated feminine gait.

Levi rises, thankfully distracted and no longer interested in our prior discussion.

"Well, I've got some work to do." His previously pleasant mood fades as he bends to pick up his surfboard. "Enjoy the afternoon."

"I'm sorry, too . . . about your dad." I bite my lip.

He pauses and examines my face. He looks like he might say something important, but then reconsiders. "Thanks, Lindsey." Without fanfare, he trots up the steps to his house.

My magazine remains glued to my legs while I consider what I've discovered about him. I'm completely intrigued at how he went from being a poor, uneducated bartender to a wealthy homeowner.

Although we've had only two brief encounters today, he's less sarcastic and dismissive than I remember, though still obviously closed off.

Regardless, a smile breaks open. He said I looked familiar, which means I made a lasting impression in Florida. Maybe this is my second chance to prove I'm not the spoiled little rich girl he thought I was back then. Maybe, if I'm willing to put in some effort and risk another rejection, we can even become friends. I could use a friend out here.

I resolve to pluck the more courageous Lindsey from yesteryear and drop her in the present.

CHAPTER FIVE

Levi

Since the day my mama left, I've never lowered my guard or shared personal business with anyone. So I can only assume my piss-poor sleep this week led to my telling those women about Pop's death.

Both gawked at me with their doe eyes, offering condolences. Well, I don't want or need their pity. Regret taunts me while I spray off my board and lean it against the outer wall of the house.

I rinse the sand from my feet before going inside to peel off the wetsuit and wash away the salt water. As I enter the shower, Lindsey's face pops into my mind. I can't shake the feeling we've met before. She'd be tempting if she weren't my neighbor. Just as well, since she makes me feel a bit unsteady. Soap and hot water ease the tightness from my skin and help me shed my edgy feelings.

While I'm dressing, I see the box containing Pop's things again. I curl my fingers around the phony Rolex before inspecting it up close. It's a superb fake, but the weight's wrong.

How many hands did he shake while wearing it? Closing my eyes, I imagine him in the early stages of a con. He'd oh so subtly pull back his shirtsleeve, checking the time while revealing the "expensive" watch to perpetuate the myth of his own success. I know what he did is wrong, yet I smile at my daydream—at my memories of him playing the big shot.

Removing the Sinn U1 from my own wrist, I strap on his watch in its stead. Its iciness reminds me of the morgue. My nose tingles at that particular image, but I don't shy away from it this time. In my own home, I can experience my feelings without consequence, unlike that first year after Mama left, when I'd ended up in brawls, defending myself against schoolyard taunts about my family. Didn't take too long to learn to mask my emotions, and that habit sure pays off at the poker tables.

I flip open his wallet and withdraw the business card—Harper & Associates. Considering how little Pop kept, someone at that firm must be significant. I dial the number and wait for the receptionist to connect me with Mr. Harper. After a minute, an old Southern gentleman speaks.

"Mr. Hardy?" His warbled inflection transports me back to Tifton, Georgia. He's a good ol' boy, just like me.

"Yes. Hello, Mr. Harper. I'm Levi Hardy. My pop, Jim Hardy, passed away last week and I found your card among his personal items. I thought I should check to see if you represented him recently."

"I'm sorry for your loss, Mr. Hardy. Yes, I did represent him." I hear a low chuckle over the phone. "Your pappy's quite a character. I'm glad you called. I have some things to send you. Can you give me your address?"

Things to send? Red flags wave through my mind. "What kind of things?"

"His will, an insurance policy benefit claim form, and a sealed envelope, addressed to you. He appointed me as executor, but you're his sole beneficiary. I'll need some information and paperwork from you so I can file the proper documents with the courts and handle his estate."

Consumed by curiosity, I provide Harper what he needs and end our call. For a few moments, I try to predict what's coming my way. I admit, I'm somewhat suspicious about the contents of the letter. But mostly, I'm shocked Pop had a will and an insurance policy. Did he put those things in place decades ago, anticipating the possibility of leaving me orphaned? Guess even he sometimes realized I'd be alone in the world whenever he died.

Mama's my only family now, if she's even alive.

I remember, at first, Pop told me she'd taken off on an extended vacation. Once he realized she'd abandoned us for good, he tossed all her photos. She became persona non grata in our lives. My remaining memory of her physical appearance is a hazy image of a scrawny, pale, blonde waif of a woman with chilling blue eyes.

For a long while, I figured I'd done something to drive her away. With time and age I grew resentful until I just became numb. Still, to this day, the bite of her rejection haunts me, causing me to question what inherent defect made me so unlovable to my own mother.

Occasionally I've considered trying to find her. But I don't even know what I'd want from the woman other than to know if I've got siblings. I've mixed feelings on that subject, too. Siblings might be nice. But blood related or not, we'd be strangers. I'd likely resent them because she chose to raise them instead of me. It's as good a reason as any not to go searching for her.

I don't need her anymore, and I'm not sure I care to learn why she left. The answer might be even more painful than the act itself.

In any case, her leaving proves Pop's theory about trusting folks. Best to keep my distance from the start.

I remove the Rolex and grab my own watch before returning my attention to the financial markets. It's a slow day. I'm comfortable with my current market positions, so I don't expend too much time in front of the computer.

When I open the refrigerator to rummage for lunch, I realize I'm low on my dill mayo and basil butter. Maybe I'll hit the farmers' market to pick up a new crop of herb plants.

≈

In addition to the typical mint, oregano, rosemary, sage, and thyme plants, I purchase Italian and Thai basil, anise, arugula, Asian and regular cilantro, chives, curry, and dill. I load the baby plants and bags of potting soil into the back of my Jeep and return home. Once I've organized everything, I finally begin replanting the herbs in the ladder racks on my deck. You must carefully untangle the roots without breaking them if you want the plants to thrive.

Within thirty minutes of working under the blazing sun, my sweat-soaked T-shirt clings to my chest. I pause to remove it and cool down. I'm enjoying a cold beer and potting the dill when I hear Lindsey yelling from below.

"Are you planting flowers?" Her voice hangs between amazement and laughter.

I lean around the side of the shelving unit and spot her standing with her hand shielding her eyes. She's straining to see what I'm doing. I feel my face pinch in disgust at her suggestion and nosy behavior.

"No, I ain't planting flowers." Damn, my grammar slipped. I take a deep breath before I finish my reply. "Herbs."

"Really? Can I come see?" She starts down her steps without waiting for an invitation.

Presumptuous little thing. I'd thought a large family would make an annoying neighbor, but she might be worse. Wish she weren't so damn cute. It's distracting and impractical.

What's her deal? First, she's cool. Then she's polite, but reticent, on the beach. Now she's not shy at all. Of course, Lord knows people from New York are used to being up close and personal—and pushy. Too bad she's changed out of her bikini. Then again, she also looks mighty fine in her white shorts and ponytail.

"Wow, that's more than a dozen plants." She hovers over me, inspecting my work, her hands on her hips. "Why so many?"

Her thighs are at eye level since I'm on my knees. A spark of awareness sneaks up along my neck. Using my body to reestablish my personal space, I sit back on my calves and glance up over my shoulder. "I crave a lot of flavor."

"How domestic." She smiles, and it's genuine, because her eyes crinkle, too. A guy could get a little lost in her enormous, shining eyes and, again, I'm struck by a sense of familiarity. "You garden *and* cook?"

Disquieted, I return my attention to my plants. "Yes, I cook."

"I don't. Well, maybe I might. I haven't really done it enough to know whether I do. We always ate out in New York."

"We?" May as well discover more about her since she's butting into my life. "You leave someone behind back there?"

Knowing people speak more freely when they can avoid eye contact, I focus on my plants. She hesitates, apparently uncomfortable with her slipup. From the corner of my eye, I notice her stroking her ponytail. No doubt about it, she's hiding something.

"I left a lot of people back there. My point is I've never done much cooking. Where'd you learn? Are you a chef?"

A chef—that's funny—so I chuckle. "No. Cookbooks and the Food Network are my teachers. The prep's relaxing, and I prefer my own food to what's served at most of the local joints."

She bends to sniff some of the plants, then stands upright. "New York has an amazing variety of restaurants on every block. You can eat someplace different every night of the month. I'll miss that, I think," she muses as I finish potting my last plant.

Repressing a sarcastic quip about her ability to return to New York anytime, I'm troubled by the way she gets under my skin. It's unlike me to be jumpy around women. I'm not particularly fond of the reaction. Her presence awakens a hankering I want to escape while I still can.

I stand and hold my hands out to her with my fingers spread widely to display the filth. "I'm moving inside to wash up."

"Oh, sure." She waits for an invitation to stay. I turn and use my elbow to open my slider without extending an offer. Just as I'm about to make a clean getaway, she shocks me with a proposition.

"Hey. If I bring some wine, will you teach me to cook something later?"

My eyes narrow slightly while I consider her request. I grow suspicious whenever someone pushes in on me. She's not coy, like Elena. Her fidgeting hands reveal nervousness. Is she just lonely here without the gang of friends she left on the East Coast? My wavering causes her cheeks to turn three shades of crimson.

I rest my forearm against the doorjamb above my head. "I'm more of a beer drinker."

She stops fidgeting and her lips break open to reveal a wide, toothy smile. "Oh, fine. I'll bring beer, then. And don't worry, I don't have any food allergies."

Food allergies? Who is this chick and how'd she rope me into cooking for her? Although somewhat surprised by her meddlesome behavior, I suppress my discomfort. I admit, I kinda admire the way she deftly manipulated me.

"What time should I come back?" She clasps her hands behind her back.

I shrug. "Seven or so, I guess."

"Great! Looking forward to it."

When she twirls around to leave, I observe her backless halter top. She's got muscular shoulders. Tennis, I'd bet. I shake my head. I sense Lindsey's dangerous to me, but I don't know why.

Rules, Levi, stick to the rules.

While I'm washing my hands, images of her face, round eyes, and bare back all converge. I glimpse a hazy recollection of a younger Lindsey on a beach. Suddenly, I stand erect, my own eyes widening. Florida. New Year's Eve. The audacious, spoiled little girl with a crush on me.

"I'll be damned," I say aloud.

I *knew* she seemed familiar. Hell and damnation. If I remember her after all the girls I've met, then she surely remembers me. Now that I recall, she never answered me earlier when I'd asked if we'd met because Elena had interrupted us.

So, what's her dinner invitation really about? Is she plotting some kind of revenge? Granted, I didn't pull any punches that night on the beach. She'd handled herself pretty well. Her lip barely quivered as she tossed an insult my way before storming off.

I knew my little stunt had cut her. I didn't set out to be cruel, only wanted to teach her a lesson about being condescending to strangers. If she'd kept her judgments to herself, I wouldn't have pushed her off her pedestal.

On the other hand, I owe her thanks for her crack about my grammar. If you sound dumb, people assume you're dumb even when you're not. Often being underestimated comes in handy, but I needed to be able to control it. I've reduced major slipups, although I still screw up, especially when I'm irked.

If my old friend Lindsey's devising a game for me, I'll play along. Tonight could be interesting, depending on her goal. It'd be better if I knew what she's hoping to accomplish. Oh well, it'll be entertaining to simply wait for her plan to unfold.

My smile deepens in anticipation of the evening. This is the most unexpected amusement I've had in a while, actually. Maybe Vegas isn't the only place to achieve a thrill.

I find myself whistling for no particular reason at all.

~

Lindsey

At seven, I review the variety of specialty beers nestled in my small, ice-packed cooler, thankful he doesn't truly remember me. To be fair, I'll extend him a clean slate, too. He's less cocky than the young guy who strutted around the resort with a bored smile on his face. If I'm being honest, I was impolite to criticize his job and his choices back then. In truth, his embittered remarks that day made me better appreciate my own good fortune.

Tonight is a chance to close that door and begin anew. To discover more about him, and maybe even something about myself.

How strange. I'm here at an emotional crossroads and he's here, too, sure to challenge my beliefs. Is it fate? Is Levi some kind of a lightning rod for me?

Before leaving my house, I tousle my hair with my fingers, then sigh and scowl. No matter how pretty I may look, he will always look better. Even so, I'm not in the market for anything other than friends. My heart's still tangled up with Rob. So, why's my body buzzing before I've even sipped any beer?

Picking up the cooler, I journey through the sand and wind, my hair blowing in every direction. I climb up Levi's stairs and knock on the screen doorframe.

"It's open," he calls from inside.

Hmm, he won't greet me at the door? *Well, it's* not *a date, Lindsey!* Stepping into his living room, it's obvious he's never sought any woman's decorating input.

The decor is exclusively black leather and wood. Whites and dove grays color the walls. It's minimalist—almost antiseptically stark—and very tidy. The severe style conflicts with his relaxed appearance.

I wind my way to the kitchen to find him standing at the sink rinsing salmon. His hair, unlike mine, looks professionally messy. Soft-looking, old jeans hang low on his hips, snug against his thighs. His gauzy white shirt, unbuttoned to midchest, exposes a hint of his well-defined pecs.

Employing yoga breathing to reduce my heart rate, I snap my gaze up to his eyes. My cheeks must be some shade of fuchsia now. A bit of guilt-tinged astonishment washes over me for being so tempted despite my lingering love for Rob.

"Hey." His eyes narrow as he puts the fish down on a paper towel and lays his hands on the counter. "I thought you came here to cook."

His clipped tone takes me by surprise.

"I did." I place the cooler beside him on the counter and open the lid to display the impressive selection of beer. "Look! I chose an assortment since I didn't know what you like." I force a smile to ease the tension, then wave my hand above the bottles like a game show model.

But he's still frowning, not peering in the cooler. "Are you wearing a silk shirt?"

I glance down at my top. "Yes, so?"

He rolls his eyes at my apparent ignorance and pats the fish dry. "As long as you don't get your panties in a bunch if you get oil, water, or whatever on it, then I don't care."

"Oh." My eyes widen and I grimace, embarrassed by my ineptitude. "I didn't think about it. I told you, I don't cook."

He cocks his head to the left and stares intently at me. A few times today he's watched me this way, as if he's able to hear my thoughts.

Sighing, he bends over to open a drawer, pulls out an apron, and tosses it at me. "Here, this should help."

As I tie the apron, he picks through the beer bottles. I know he's impressed when he nods and raises his brows before opting for one of the Belgian beers.

"What's your preference?" He finally smiles and, I admit, I love those dimples.

"Anything light." I take what he hands me.

"Okay. Let's get started. This'll take about forty minutes or so, depending on how quickly we work."

Levi's organized his counter into prep stations, each with special containers and kitchen tools, including a large variety of high-quality knives and All-Clad cookware. During the next several minutes, he demonstrates all the steps, from cleaning the salmon to timing the other items. I notice his elegant-looking fingers move effortlessly from task to task, while mine fumble and mishandle nearly every-thing. Genuinely frustrated by my inability to properly chop any-thing from the cilantro to the avocado for the salad, he maintains a polite, if slightly impatient, attitude.

Folding parchment paper into pouches to wrap around the pre-pared salmon sends me over the edge. Naturally, he finds humor in my frustration. I suspect he purposely made this difficult to discour-age me from imposing on him again.

Determined not to let him enjoy my floundering, I refocus. I rejoice once we put the fish in the oven and I'm left to dry the cleaned lettuce. Levi pours chicken broth, rice, and butter into a pot.

"So, you actually find this relaxing?" My inflection's self-mocking.

"Yeah, it's methodical, rhythmic, and the end product's mighty satisfying."

Levi's phrasing and arched brow suggest he intends the double entendre. He leans against the refrigerator, his arms crossed casually in front of his chest, watching for my response.

I shrug. "Seems frustrating to me, but I guess the more you do it, the easier it gets."

The unintentional innuendo of my own reply causes me to blush, so I glance away for a moment. His stillness unnerves me.

"So, do you like music?" I pray he won't play heavy metal for the next two hours.

"What would you like to hear?" He picks up his iPhone and begins scrolling through his playlists.

"Whatever you enjoy." I aim to be conciliatory, to loosen his demeanor. "Your house, your music."

"Huh, so now you *don't* want to tell me what I'm supposed to do?" His intonation's half-joking, half-serious, and he's grinning.

Since I've barged my way into his home tonight, I guess I had that one coming, so I play the good sport. "Yes, I'll allow you a little discretion once in a while, but don't get used to it."

Heat reaches my face when he pins me with his bedroom eyes. Levi's very quiet, but I can tell his mind never rests. He attaches his phone to the Bose speakers, surprising me completely by playing David Gray's ultracool *White Ladder* before cracking open his second beer and sitting beside me.

"So, Lindsey, what brings you to the West Coast? You mentioned leaving a lot of people behind. Why?"

Even if he doesn't recall rejecting me years ago, I'm not about to admit my fiancé cheated on me.

"I need to make some changes."

"Obviously." He raises one brow. "Why?"

"Does it matter?"

Sitting back against a kitchen stool, he folds his arms in front of his chest again and watches me, waiting. Finally, he speaks.

"Yeah, it matters. You'll make different changes if you're searching than you will if you're running."

Wincing in response to his surprising commentary, I look off to the side. I know I'm running, and now he probably knows it, too. Bothered, I steer the conversation around on him.

"You sound pretty sure of yourself, like you have personal experience."

"With change?"

"Yes, or running."

His face wrinkles like he's laughing at a private joke. Rather than volley with me, he lifts his cute butt off the stool and returns to the stove to sprinkle something green in the rice.

"I know we chopped that up. What is it again?" I ask.

"Tarragon," he replies, before turning off the flame.

I watch him dress the salad, retrieve the wrapped salmon from the oven, and plate everything. Mesmerized by his graceful movements, I eventually realize I've sat there observing without helping.

"Oh, sorry." I stand up to help. "What can I do?"

"Just sit down at the table. Somehow you got me to cook *and* serve you dinner tonight." His grin reveals something akin to respect, as if I did it on purpose. "That's a first for me."

"I honestly didn't intend to do so."

"Sure you didn't." His voice is laced with playful sarcasm.

"Well, at any rate, it smells great—citrusy."

"Thanks."

Pride emanates from behind his hard-to-read eyes, and I'm glad I complimented him. We begin eating. Foolishly, I pick up the conversation where it had ended before he'd returned his attention to the kitchen.

"So, running or searching?" I ask.

"I've been at both ends of that spectrum, but never for long. Mostly I'm just living."

"What's that even mean? We're all living." Before he replies, I stop midbite to utter, "Yum, this is delicious, Levi."

"You're wrong."

"Why, you don't like it?" I frown in disbelief.

"No, not about the fish. About living. Most people aren't living. They're planning, remembering, or regretting."

"Not you? No plans, no regrets?"

"Some, but not many." He gulps down a healthy swallow of beer. "But I'm not the one who up and ran away from everyone I know."

I avert my eyes. "No, I guess you aren't."

He falls silent and finishes his dinner, waiting for me to say more. I pick at what's left on my plate, contemplating how to ease the friction without divulging the shameful details of my flight from New York.

Perhaps switching to a neutral topic is my best option. "So, what do you do here? I mean, where do you work?" I quickly learn my mistake.

"You mean, what's my *real* job, since I'm not a chef and all?" Now he's definitely expecting a specific reaction from me, which makes me a bit uneasy.

"Yes, what's your profession?"

Another of his secretive smirks flickers over his face. He pauses for a beat and then leans very close. In a whisper reminiscent of the one on the beach years ago, he asks, "Lindsey, do you want to play games all night?" His warm breath brushes against my ear and I shiver. Is it possible to feel turned-on and afraid at the same time?

"What games?" I sit on my hands to conceal my nerves. Does he think I'm trying to get him into bed?

He pulls away and tilts his head. "What games? You invite yourself over to learn to cook, but you don't really want to cook. You refuse to answer any direct questions about yourself, yet try to get me to admit personal things. Those games," he accuses.

"I'm not playing games." I feel a scowl seize my face. "It's called conversing."

"Really?" He inclines nearer to me, clearly disbelieving.

"Yes, really." I'm openly defiant now, confused by his accusation.

"Let's see about that." He locks on my eyes, trapping me. "Have we met before?"

I consider lying, but in the context of his odd expressions all evening and the directness of his question, I realize I can't escape the truth. I sit in silence—my mind absolutely blank—as I consider explaining why I didn't mention it sooner.

"You don't have to answer. I've remembered where we met." He stands and collects our plates. "So, cooking class is over. I don't know if you got what you came for tonight, but thanks for the beer."

"Got what I came for? Levi, I just wanted some company. I thought it would be better not to dredge up unpleasant history."

"Lindsey, you've refused to be honest with me all day. Your reasons are irrelevant." He gestures toward the back door. "You know your way home, right?"

His stony face and dismissal erode my already limited filter. "Still dismissive and condescending, I see."

"Still a confused little girl, I see," he spits acidly before turning his back to me.

I watch him scrape the excess food into the garbage before he places the plates in the sink. When he refuses to face me, I sigh.

"This was a mistake. I shouldn't have come."

I move to collect my cooler. As I reach for the handle, his hand firmly clamps on top of mine. He rubs his thumb across the top of my hand, sending a shiver up my arm.

"Yes, it was a mistake. Never play with people you don't really know unless you're sure you can get what you want." His hazel eyes turn so icy they look blue. Then he lets go of my hand.

Unaware I'd been holding my breath, I release a quiet whoosh. Maybe I hid the truth, but I didn't have a malicious agenda.

"There's something wrong with you, Levi. You're paranoid. I didn't come here tonight to torment you."

"Really? You wanted to hang out even though I'm so unpleasant and all? Rude, sarcastic jerk, actually, if memory serves."

Although astonished he recalled my cutting remarks, I stammer, "I'd hoped you'd changed, but you're still . . . unkind." I pick up my cooler and stomp toward the back door. When I hear him snicker, I whip around to face him.

"How's that funny?" I fume.

He examines me silently, infuriating me more.

"Seriously, tell me. What's so entertaining, Levi?"

"You amuse me. It's like I'm watching someone punch into the wind."

What a shame God poured a dark soul into such a beautiful container. My head droops and I behold him, not in resentment, but in sad resignation.

"You keep finding humor in bringing me to my knees. It's not enough that I left New York and came to a strange town with no friends, no job, and no idea of what to do next. Of course I had to end up next door to the one guy in the world who made me feel the smallest I've ever been made to feel in my life."

His brows shoot upward after that remark. His abashed expression gives me the courage to continue. "I was horrified when I first recognized you this morning. But then, to my surprise, you seemed human. When you didn't remember me, I'd hoped we could write the past off to immaturity and become friendly neighbors. Apparently my judgment really sucks. Since we're stuck here together for the time being, let's do our best to ignore each other from now on, okay? Thanks for dinner."

I yank the door open and step into the darkness before pulling it shut behind me. I'm trembling; whether it's from the chilly breeze or the confrontation is debatable. I run down his stairs and back home.

His back porch light goes dark as I open my own door and lock myself safely inside. I set the cooler down, wrap my arms around my chest, and blow out a long breath. How'd I walk into that situation? *Walk? I forced my way in on him.*

It's disappointing to find him to be as elusive and cold as I remember. Why'd I even want to spend time with him? I hate knowing I subjected myself to someone so hurtful just to avoid being alone.

Wait until Jill hears this tale. She'll really think I've lost my mind. Maybe I have. I hear my mother's voice echo the words *I doubt you'll find a man more suitable than Rob.*

CHAPTER SIX

Levi

Jesus, Lindsey's an emotional basket case, suggesting *I* did something wrong tonight. She's the one playing games: pretending not to know me, forcing me to cook for her, prying into my private life without invitation, calling me paranoid—and then acting indignant when I called her on her own behavior. She chose to leave her friends and family, and she sure shouldn't expect me, or anyone else, to fill in those gaps for her. I'm no babysitter.

She made her choice, now she needs to deal with it.

I practically attack the pots in the sink, all the while twisting and tilting my head and neck to loosen up. My shoulders are drawn tighter than suspension cables.

She's still a princess, assuming people owe her something. Everyone at home must kiss her little neurotic ass. Well, I sure as hell won't coddle her. It makes no difference to me what she does, where she goes, or if she figures out her shit or not. I'm not about to hold her hand while she cries.

Of course, tonight her velvety hand felt good beneath my own. My eyes squeeze shut in dismay at my finding one second's pleasure in that exchange.

After cleaning the kitchen, I turn on the TV to find *Shawshank Redemption* playing on cable. Great movie, although I'd never stoically accept punishment for something I didn't do, the way Andy Dufresne did. But I respect how he keeps his cool, structures a long play, and frees himself. He's a real leader.

My temper's too quick to lead. That, and I don't trust anyone enough to rely on them. I've seen too many people burned, by my pop and others. My mama? Well, if you can't rely on your own mama's love, what's it say about people—about love?

I bet Lindsey trusts everyone. She must, or she wouldn't have come here after I humiliated her years ago. Maybe putting herself back in the line of fire with me makes her brave. Brave or stupid. Maybe brave people are stupid, because smart people don't sign up for pain twice.

Made me feel the smallest I've ever been made to feel. My chest tightens. Christ, I can't believe I hurt her so deeply in Florida she recognized me on the spot. The funny thing is, I'd wanted to kiss her and more that night on the beach. It'd been a struggle to follow through with my ploy to piss her off. Those eyes of hers . . .

Leaning my head back, I stare at the ceiling. Guilt leaks from my conscience and slowly drips into my gut. I didn't set out to punish her tonight, either. Only meant to protect myself. After all, she did pretend not to remember me. Who knew she hadn't been planning to sucker punch me?

So, maybe she's a nice girl. It doesn't matter, because I'm not interested in complications. Unfortunately, I can't shake the vision of her trembling lip and misty eyes when she ran off tonight.

Ah, hell. I snatch a sheet of paper from my desk and dash off a note. Grabbing an envelope and tape, I wander over the cold beach to her deck. All of the lights are off downstairs. I consider knocking on the glass but decide to tape the note to her back door instead.

When I return home, my house seems unusually cramped. I need to go out to blow off steam and take my mind off the evening—off Lindsey. Why not ride my bike up to Duke's for last call.

It's a Monday night, so the bar's nearly empty when I arrive. I'm alone for about five minutes before I've got company. Two young girls send me a drink, so I oblige and join them. One is from Texas, the other from central California. Two more blonde Barbie dolls, like so many others. They're a little too young—college seniors—and sexually aggressive flirts. Before I finish my beer, they suggest a three-way. That's some kind of wet dream for many guys, but not my style. I've never had a steady girlfriend, but I'm also not a dog willing to bed anything, at any time, any place, and any way.

An alluring image of Lindsey wearing shorts and Converse sneakers emerges. I shake my head in surprise. Disturbed, I thank the coeds for the beer, then push off to go home.

The thick fog dampens the air—gray air to match my mood. Sweeping my hair away from my eyes, I fasten my helmet and start the ignition. I love this big red bike, so powerful. The day I bought it was a fine day. Shifting into gear, I begin rolling through the parking lot. The horny coeds spill outside and wave to me while they walk to their car.

I'm humming to myself and pulling onto the PCH when a shadowy figure startles me. Snapping my head left, I see an oncoming vehicle materialize from thin air. In motion slowed to the microsecond, the front end of a speeding van with broken headlights hurtles toward me.

My thoughts scatter in a million directions. My heart pounds with the rhythm of conga drums, but my body's frozen and uncooperative while my ears throb with the roar of white noise. I gun my bike, but I'm not gonna make a clean getaway. Holy Christ, I'm about to die.

~

When I wake up, flashing red lights swirl around me. I vomit, and the stench makes me want to vomit again. Searing pain overwhelms me. I'm afraid to look at my body, certain it's scraped to shit and has bones poking out of my skin. I've no sense of time while a blur of activity, lights, and noises whirls around me. My head feels as foggy as the night air. Paramedics fit me in a brace and carefully load me onto a gurney. From inside the ambulance, I witness an officer talking to the girls from the bar.

I overhear another cop question a paramedic about my blood alcohol content. Great, are they hoping to pin this on me? Is the damn driver injured, or worse? Will I end up in jail? I didn't have more than three beers counting the ones I drank at home. Jesus, I'm still nauseous and every twitch feels like a blade slicing up my spine. Unable to focus, I start to close my eyes, then everything turns dark.

I come to again under the bright lights of a hospital emergency room. People bombard me with questions, seeking information. I'm so damn confused, I can barely answer. A doctor tells me I suffered trauma to my spine and they need to operate—something about spinal fusion. Bile rises in my throat again. Am I paralyzed? My blood freezes. Instinctively, I flex my feet. Hot relief floods my veins when my toes move. Damn, I think I'm crying.

I try to concentrate on the details of the proposed surgery, consent, and next of kin, but everything's fuzzy and jumbled. The lights are too damn bright. Unintentionally, I slip back to sleep.

I awaken again before the nurse preps me for surgery. Trembling with uneasiness, I scan the sterile environment, which seems devoid of any smell. I've never had an operation before, and this one might leave me in a wheelchair. Everyone tells me to relax, talking to me as if we're friends, but I don't know these people. What if something goes wrong? What if I end up paralyzed? What if I die? Will anyone care?

I'm exactly like Pop—alone, unclaimed, and loved by no one. Almost thirty-one years old and this is all I am, all I have. Although I acknowledge it's not much, I don't want to die.

I stare at the ceiling and take deep breaths. Despite my solitary lifestyle, I've never felt so completely isolated. The doctor instructs me to count back from ten, so I begin.

"Ten, nine, eight, seven . . ."

$\sim$

Lindsey

It's taking me a while to fall asleep. Levi's a porcupine, prickly and defensive. What made him so suspicious? He's an enigma, too, with his expensive beach house but apparent lack of education or career.

His living room housed hundreds of books on its shelves, and he's not the type to display them for show. Does anyone even visit the guy? From what I can tell, he's a loner. I remember he kept to himself in Florida, taking his breaks alone while reading or smoking. At least he appears to have quit his cigarette habit.

For his many faults, he sure cooks well. Potting his herbs . . . What guy does that? Yet despite his many flaws, something about the air of sorrow around him tugs at my heart. He'd deny it or blame it on his father's death, but I think it goes deeper. Something in his life caused him to be so quick to distrust and so content to be alone. Regardless, I'm sure I'll never learn his secrets.

Unlike Levi, most of the people in my life are conventional and homogeneous. My parents sequestered me in posh schools and clubs to ensure my life would remain whitewashed, and I dutifully followed their plans. The results were rewarding at the time. Now I'm not so sure.

After college, I met Rob at happy hour through a friend of mine who worked for him at Goldman. During our conversation, we discovered our mutual love of tennis, both of us having played competitively in high school. I recognized in Rob everything I'd been coached to prize. Ambition, intelligence, good looks. He'd fit neatly into my schooled vision of the future, so when he'd asked me to join him the next day for tennis and lunch, I agreed without much consideration.

During the next three years of dating, family vacations, parties, and promotions, we rarely spent free time apart. Our romance culminated in a sweet and simple proposal on a fall day in Central Park. The betrayal scorched me and flew in the face of everything I had understood about him. I doubt I'll ever truly trust him again. Thank God the STD test results came back negative today.

Despite our problems, in many ways our relationship defined me, and without it I'm adrift. My throat aches from remembering everything we shared. Tears sting my eyes.

I drag myself from the comfort of my bed for a glass of water. Red and blue lights slip through the small bathroom window and dance on the ceiling. Seized with curiosity, I peer through the glass to Levi's driveway and see a police car parked in front of his home. Did he get arrested? Perhaps he's a drug dealer. It would explain his wealth and why he's tight-lipped about his career. Meddlesome, I know, but I can't resist investigating.

Wrapping myself in a robe, I clutch it tightly against my chest to brave the windy night. As I make my way outside, the cops turn from Levi's door and walk toward their squad car.

"Excuse me, officers, is there a problem?"

One of them approaches me. "Ma'am, do you know Mr. Levi Hardy?"

"Yes, why? Is he in trouble?"

"There's been an accident. He wasn't entirely conscious at the scene. We're trying to determine whether he has any family, or anyone here, to be notified."

My knees soften upon hearing the dark intonation of the officer's voice. Is Levi dying?

"Ma'am, do you know if he has a family?"

Dazed, I finally respond. "He doesn't live with anyone. His father died recently, but I don't know much more about his family. He's not originally from California. He's from the Southeast, but I don't know where. I'm sorry I can't be more helpful."

"Okay, ma'am, thanks. You can go back inside."

I'm cemented in place and shivering, watching him amble away. "Wait—can you tell me what happened?" I need more information. "Is he alive?"

"He was alive when we arrived, but his body's pretty broken up. Witnesses report a dark van or SUV without headlights came out of nowhere and clipped his motorcycle. He was thrown onto the pavement and his bike's totaled. Unfortunately, the other driver fled the scene."

The graphic brutality of the officer's description arrests my thoughts.

"Do you know where they took him?"

"Santa Monica UCLA Trauma Center," the cop offers.

"Okay, thanks."

"Good night." He nods politely before returning to the other officer and driving away.

Once inside, I lean against my front door for a minute. My imagination projects vivid pictures of Levi being thrown from his cycle, his body splayed across the highway like an abandoned rag doll. Did he have any forewarning? I hope not. It would be too awful to suspect you're about to die.

Shaking my head to erase the ugly images, I move to the living room to locate my phone. Of course, I'm not family, so I doubt the hospital will provide me with information. In fact, I only now learned his last name.

This recognition causes me to return the phone to the counter. There's nothing I can do tonight except pray. His friends or family should step in, assuming he has any. Why do I care? He's done nothing but insult me at nearly every turn. Yet, in each encounter, I sensed a better man hiding beneath the layers of contempt and distrust. Then again, maybe that's just what I want to see—an inside that matches his beautiful outside.

Torn by conflicting emotions, I pour myself a glass of wine. The minute it passes my lips, I feel the sedative effect take hold. *Please help me forget Levi and Rob, at least long enough to relax and sleep.* Standing motionless with my wine, I stare at nothing in particular.

Life's unpredictable and ever changing. Last week, the unthinkable happened to me and rearranged my world order, throwing my life into total disarray. But by some remarkable coincidence, it led me to this house, located next to Levi. Now his life's been horribly altered, too. Am I a bad-luck charm, or is there some mystical purpose to my being here with him?

It makes no sense, I know. Yet, in this moment, it makes perfect sense to me. Maybe I'm desperate to attach meaning to these recent painful events in our lives.

When I clear my thoughts, I notice something taped to my living room slider. A chill ripples through me. Who trespassed on my porch? I race to turn on the outside lights. After confirming nobody's there, I unlock the door and remove the envelope. Inside it, I find a handwritten note.

> *Lindsey,*
>
> *I'm sorry I made you feel small, then and now. In both cases, your unreserved nature made me uncomfortable. In retrospect, maybe that's just what folks from New York do— barge in, I mean. Anyway, I see you're a nice girl trying to meet new people, so I apologize for doubting your motives. However, I'm not someone who collects close friends, so the "polite-but-distant neighbors" plan is probably best. Let's put tonight, and the past, behind us.*
>
> *Levi*

I reread his missive several times. Is this his idea of an apology? He's basically calling me pushy. In truth, thanks to my lack of filter, he isn't the first to accuse me of "barging in" with unsolicited advice and opinions. He's right. I've always imposed my company on him.

Why am I drawn to him, aside from the obvious physical appeal? And even so, why's he so disinterested in friendship with anyone, not only me? Well, it's immaterial anyway, since he's instructed me to butt out. I toss the note on the dining table and shut off the lights. Based on our obvious incompatibility, I should keep my distance.

It's almost one o'clock now and I'm desperate for sleep. I want to call Jill, but it's after three in her time zone, and this isn't an emergency.

Despite my vow to disengage, I can't stop wondering if Levi's alive. The thought of him inspires a stream of confused responses. We're not friends. I barely know him, but it sickens me to imagine his untimely death. Please, God. Don't let him die.

CHAPTER SEVEN

Levi

Groggily, I open my eyes and survey the hushed, dim recovery room. When it dawns on me that the surgery's over, I wiggle my toes. Once again, tears of relief dampen my eyes. I'm thirsty as hell, but when I attempt to reach for the call button, my arms feel weighted down.

Seeds of alarm sprout due to my lack of control over my own body, let alone my circumstances. A deep, primitive fear of being powerless emerges, making my heart race.

"Hey," I croak. "Anyone out there?"

No one responds, so I yell louder.

"Hey! Somebody. I need help."

Frustrated by the delay, I struggle to reach my call button again. A heavyset old nurse with a grim face finally appears.

"What do you need, Mr. Hardy?"

"A glass of water," I bark. "And I want to see the doctor. Something's wrong. I'm having trouble moving my body and my arms."

"You're just coming out of major surgery and we've given you heavy painkillers." She checks my IV. "It takes time for your body to recover from the trauma. Try to relax and rest. The doctor will come see you when he's free."

"I don't want to relax. I need to see the doctor now. I don't feel right." I stare at her, but she's not intimidated. My sense of impotence stuns me. "Can I at least have some water?"

She leaves the room and returns quickly with a small mauve water pitcher and a plastic cup. She places the pitcher on the tray beside my bed and hands me a half-full cup.

"Here you are."

I take it from her and mutter my thanks.

"When can I talk to the surgeon?" The room-temperature water soothes my parched throat. "I'm telling you, I don't feel right."

"I'll see what I can find out. In the meantime, you need to relax. This will help." She hands me a small pill before she turns and leaves me alone. Guess my cantankerous mood motivated her to sedate me. I set the pill on the tray and shove everything away.

Hours later, I'm transferred to a double-occupancy room, shared with a man who underwent surgery yesterday. I'd prefer private accommodations, but I'm stuck. My new roommate's a chunky, middle-aged, cheerful Hispanic fellow. His side of our space resembles a gift shop, filled with brightly colored balloons, flowers, and cards. The nurse introduces Carlos and me. I'm in no mood for chitchat, so I dip my chin and grunt hello.

When the nurse engages me in a clumsy dance to help me into bed, she inadvertently causes me to twist at my waist. The rotation sends a shock wave of pain to my core. My gruff yell startles everyone. I bat my arms at her, wanting to lay blame for my pain. I know it's not her fault I'm here, but I need to vent my outrage somewhere.

Once settled in my hospital bed, I discover a moderately comfortable position to alleviate some of the pain. The nurse hooks me up to monitoring equipment and a morphine drip before leaving the room.

"You look real banged up. Sorry for you." Carlos speaks with heavily accented English. "What happened?"

I barely turn toward him, fearing the twinge of tenderness another gyration might launch down my back and legs.

"Car accident." Jesus, do I really have to talk? "No offense, Carlos, but I'm real uncomfortable right now. I'm not up for much talkin' just yet, okay?" I smile through clenched teeth. It's exceedingly difficult under the circumstances.

"Oh, sure, sure," he says. His apologetic smile reveals his chagrin. "Sorry. I'll keep quiet so you can sleep."

"Thanks." I close my eyes. My body's taut, anticipating agony. I'm curious about how much I'd be suffering if not for the morphine drip. I've never taken drugs, so I'm not keen on flooding my system with heavy painkillers. On the other hand, I'm unwilling to test my mettle without them, either.

～

Damn, it's impossible to get any rest in a hospital. If nurses aren't prodding you hourly, or the commotion from the hallway and nurses station doesn't disturb you, then your roommate's visitors will.

Prior to lunch, Carlos's family arrives bearing more drawings, love, and support. His wife, sister, and children fawn over him, lifting his spirits considerably.

They speak to each other in Spanish, assuming I can't understand them. But I do, thanks to several well-spent months attending Spanish-language immersion classes when I first moved to Southern California. I'd have been an imbecile to live here unable to understand half the population.

Carlos is considerate and reminds them to keep it down, but he also implies I'm neither especially friendly nor popular. In my peripheral vision, I observe his plump, merry kids. I wonder what it feels like, as a kid, to know you're safe with your parents. While I usually ignore notions of self-pity, it's more difficult when I'm confronted by happy families.

Family life with Pop was hardly what most would call comforting, but in our way we were connected to each other. Even when we weren't speaking, I knew he was out there somewhere and he cared for me as much as he could care for another person.

Once again, the weight of Pop's death sits on my chest. Then my thoughts drift again to Mama. Have I crossed her mind at all over the years? Did she stay away because she's ashamed to face me? Would she care if she knew what I'm going through right now? Well, hell—of course not. If she ever cared, she'd have found a way to reach me in the past twenty years.

I glance over and see Carlos's son kissing his face. Although I've never wished to be smothered with affection, a tiny part of me envies Carlos. He's not alone.

I am.

I've designed it this way, but it's sure going to make my recovery hard. Then again, no one's ever tended to me. Not since I was old enough to scrape my knees. I'm used to nursing myself and I'm not afraid. Tired, maybe, but not afraid.

The upside of my self-imposed isolation is I don't have to tend to anyone. You can't have it both ways, and I doubt I'd be any good at assisting someone else. Hell, I wouldn't even know how.

After Carlos's family departs, he leans toward me to apologize. "I hope we didn't disturb you too much."

Now I'm obligated to make small talk. I face him and force a smile. "It's okay. Nice family you've got there. You're a lucky guy."

"Yes, very lucky." He grins. "And you? Do you have a wife or girlfriend?"

"No, sir, and I don't expect company." I frown briefly, uncomfortable with the truth. The few folks I occasionally socialize with aren't likely to go out of their way to help me. Come to think of it, I doubt anyone will notice my absence for at least a few days.

Carlos's voice interrupts my musings.

"Ah, but why? You look like a guy who's got girls chasing you." He winks and raises his eyebrows, attempting to boost my spirits.

"Not the kind of girls who'll come here to check up on me." Unwilling to elaborate, I simply arch one eyebrow and grin. "Let's just leave it at that."

His frown catches me off guard.

"You find a nice girl now. A good girl with pretty insides." He affects a wise nod, as if he's delivered novel advice.

I grin rather than challenge his traditional views. What's the point? He's being gracious and I don't want to destroy his illusion of happily ever after.

Thankfully, our discussion's interrupted when a nurse takes him for a spin around the wing. I'm grateful for the privacy. Unfortunately it doesn't last too long, because before I can close my eyes, the doctor appears.

Now coherent, I understand I underwent a single-level postero-lateral spinal fusion that required a bone graft between the affected vertebrae and four titanium screws. The doctor claims I'm very lucky I didn't suffer any other major complications from the trauma. I don't feel too lucky, but at least I'm breathing and I'll walk again.

He explains a bit about the recovery and my limitations during the upcoming months. I'll be fitted for a brace I'll need to wear for a few weeks, and I can't bend, lift more than ten pounds, or twist for the next three months.

Our discussion wraps up with a mention of the long-term effects of the hardware in my back, such as the potential for future surgery due to the extra wear and tear on the vertebrae on either side of the graft, or the screws shattering or coming loose. I shove those miserable scenarios far from my thoughts.

"You'll remain here for two more days. We'll get you up and moving around a bit later today. Your chart indicates you aren't married. Do you have a partner or roommate at home to assist with your recovery?" He waits for my reply.

"No. I'll be alone."

"Well, how about parents or siblings?" He shoots me a pitying look. "Is there somewhere you can stay for the first couple of weeks while you'll be dependent on help?"

"No parents, no siblings. I'll be fine. I can manage."

"Can you secure a home-care worker? If not, you'll go to a rehabilitation facility for a week or two, until you can safely manage on your own."

I vigorously shake my head. "Look, Doc, don't imprison me in some rehab place. I'll be fine at home. I work from home. I need my things."

"We recommend avoiding stairs as much as possible for the next few weeks. You might want a cane for a while, and a grabber to help you pick things up off the floor. With all of the limitations I explained, you surely see that it's unwise to be alone at first. We don't want you back here again because you haven't allowed the graft to take."

I stare at him, unwilling to concede his point, yet unable to dissuade him.

"Let's see how the next two days progress. Perhaps you can arrange for some help." He writes a notation on my chart and nods at me before leaving my room.

Panic escalates at the thought of being confined in a rehabilitation center. Damn it, he can't keep me hostage. I can survive on my own. When I shimmy to sit upright, pain fans out throughout my core and legs, forcing me to privately acknowledge my house will present challenges.

I want my computer, a newspaper, and something decent to eat. Closing my eyes, I draw a few deep breaths. In desperation and anger, I wonder what the hell happened to the driver who fucked up my life.

~

Lindsey

The flat, gray sky perfectly reflects my current frame of mind as I make my way to the beach. Rob sent another e-mail late last night. He's trying to make me feel sorry for him now . . . like I'm hurting him by making him wait and wonder how I'm feeling. Amazing! *He* betrayed *me*, not the other way around.

I try to slough off my agitation while I stretch before taking off down the beach.

Morning runs here vastly differ from my typical Central Park excursions. Sand instead of pavement, blue water and sky instead of green grass and trees. The briny air and hushed sound of my feet padding in the sand soothe me while I trot along the shore near the waterline.

Today I'm aware of my life, my legs, and my choices. Instead of focusing on Rob during my run, I mull over Levi's note and accident. Did he survive? If so, how severe are his injuries? Although he's been bristly, I can't set aside my concern.

I suspect his polite-but-distant-neighbors attitude has left him without friends who really care about him. His isolation rouses my empathy.

It's not my nature to ignore someone's suffering. Jill used to always tease me about the many "wounded soldiers" whose hearts I've healed. Afterward, all my hard work usually waltzed off and ended up as some other girl's reward. Maybe Jill has a point. But I never help anyone in order to advance my own agenda; I just can't stand to watch someone struggling. If I can help, I do. At my core, it's who I am.

And of all the places I might have gone, and of all of the rental homes I might have selected, ending up next door to Levi *means* something. It must.

It can't be a random coincidence. There are no coincidences. Right? There was that book Jill's mom loved so many years ago, *The Celestine Prophecy*: Coincidences are opportunities in disguise to recognize, and exploit, to improve your life—or something along those lines.

Perhaps Levi and I are destined to teach each other something. Oh, God. Now I sound crazy, even in my own head. What valuable wisdom could he possibly impart? He's completely unpolished, gruff, and arrogant. Qualities I don't care to emulate. Be that as it may, I'll never know unless I try.

By the time I return from my run, I've resolved to visit Levi at the hospital. I'm certain I'll not be welcomed with open arms, but I'm not deterred. I'll bring him a book. A smile creeps across my face for the first time since last night. I know exactly which book to deliver.

~

I pull into the hospital parking lot and then my stomach flips over. What if Levi's facing a major setback? No one wants visitors, especially virtual strangers, while digesting life-altering information. God, that's assuming he even survived. My stomach lurches again, but somehow my clammy hands mechanically open the car door. Unconvinced my knees can hold me up, I cautiously step out of my car and make my way into the hospital.

Immediately I'm assaulted by the sterile odor. The lighting gives everyone's skin an ugly green undertone. Concerned visitors and busy employees move through the lobby area. It occurs to me I can't remember being in a hospital for any reason other than when my cousin Sara had her twins last year. That day had been joyous, unlike today.

A bored woman at the patient information desk shares Levi's room information. Relieved to learn he survived, I slowly exhale and begin making my way toward his room. I round the corner, pausing to rest my hand on my stomach and steel myself for what may turn into another unpleasant confrontation. As I approach his open door, I hear clipped voices emanating from within his room.

Levi's typically sexy voice is garbled, probably from heavy doses of painkillers. While I wait in the hallway, I overhear the debate between him and his doctor regarding a rehabilitation center.

Rehabilitation? Is he paralyzed? I remove my hand from my stomach and press it against the wall to my right. Coming here was a rash, self-indulgent idea. I should go. He's not going to be pleased to see me, and what will I say to him anyway? I'm wringing my hands when the doctor brushes past me on his way out.

Well, it's now or never. I'm trying to be bolder, so I may as well get on with it. Taking a deep breath, I plunge ahead and enter his room. Levi's eyes are shut and his hands are fisted by his sides. He doesn't hear me.

His helmet seems to have protected his face and skull pretty well, but his arms look bruised and swollen, decorated with angry red scrapes. I hide my pity to preserve his pride.

"Hey, Levi." I take unhurried steps toward the edge of his bed. "How are you?"

At the sound of my voice, his eyelids fly open and his brow knits.

"What're you doing here?" He stiffens. "How'd you find me?"

"Nice to see you, too." I smile to disarm him.

"Sorry. Hi," he amends. "But seriously, how'd you find me? Better yet, why?"

His head tilts slightly as he narrows his eyes. I'd braced for a cool reception, but I'm nonetheless set back by his apparent enmity. And he thinks *I* punch into the wind!

"The police came to your house late last night. I noticed their lights, so I went to investigate."

He nods, his face grimacing in acknowledgement. "Snooping. Yep, that sounds like you." His tone, however, has shifted to teasing, so I raise a brow and continue.

"Anyway, they told me about your collision. I'm not family, so I couldn't get information from the hospital over the phone. Since I'm a notorious glutton for punishment, I decided to visit. I assumed you could use some company." I hesitate, preparing for an onslaught of sarcasm. When he issues none, I continue. "At least I learned you're not a drug dealer, which is what I first thought when I saw the cops at your house so late at night." I flash a smile and wiggle my brows so he knows I'm joking—well, mostly joking, anyway.

He abruptly tucks his chin and widens his eyes, then sighs, shaking his head almost imperceptibly. His inquisitive stare feels like a spotlight, heating me up. "Did you get the note I taped to your back door last night after dinner?"

"Yes. An unconvincing apology, but I caught the drift."

He regards me for a moment, then responds in a flat tone, "I don't think so, or you wouldn't be here now."

"I got the message. Butt out." I nod my head once, for emphasis.

He narrows his eyes. "So you're ignoring my request?"

"Under the circumstances, yes." Evading his glare, I sit on the edge of the bed and fish through my large purse. "You like to read, right? I remember you reading in Florida. Last night I noticed all the books in your house."

"And?" He cranes his neck to try to see what I'm doing.

"Well, I brought you a book to read." I hand it to him. "Don't lose it, I have to return it to the library. I didn't think it would still be available in the bookstores. It's older." *Stop babbling, Lindsey.*

He inspects the jacket and his brows quirk upward. "This looks like a bunch of hocus-pocus. What magic life lessons are you promulgating now?" he asks skeptically. "Trying to force me to accept what's happened to me?"

"No." I pause. "Well, maybe. But that's not why I chose it." I decide to be honest. "Levi, isn't it incredible we've become neighbors? Truly. It makes me question whether it's predestined. Maybe fate wants me to learn something from you . . . or you from me. So, yes, I'm ignoring your note, and I want you to read this book."

He snickers and sets the book on his thighs. "You think *you* have something to teach *me*?"

He's clearly amazed by the prospect, and sporting the first authentic broad smile I've ever seen from him. Even beat-up and broken, he's more handsome than most men. His blithe reaction encourages me to continue.

"Obviously you've lots to learn about basic social graces, kindness, and trust. So, *my* purpose is pretty clear. What *you* could possibly teach me, now that's the real mystery. But I'm open to exploring what it might be."

He tips his head back when he laughs at my comment, exposing a hearty, deep chortle. Afterward, he snaps his gaze to me, narrowing his piercing eyes to fasten me in place with his stare. As if issuing a warning, he speaks quietly.

"You, Lindsey, have much to learn."

His confidence and heated stare send a delicious shiver surging through me. Luckily, his roommate returns, breaking the spell Levi cast before my daze becomes apparent.

When I introduce myself to Carlos, I notice the balloons and drawings on his side of the room. Levi's side is stark and cold, like him and his house.

An orderly brings lunch trays, but the food looks wretched. I perceive Levi's disgust. Aside from sampling the Jell-O, he pushes the cart away.

"So, Levi, tell me what happened," I say, switching topics in front of his roommate. "What are your injuries?"

He sighs, acquiescing to my determination. He crosses one arm over his chest while toying with the remote with his other hand. His defensive posture is rapidly becoming familiar.

"An idiot driving a car without headlights plowed into me on the PCH and fractured my spine. They stabilized it with some screws and a graft. Everything should start feeling better in four to six weeks and heal in six months to a year." He recites the summary without despair, but his glib tone rings hollow in my ears.

Despite his dismissive manner, I assume he's suppressing a storm of emotion. His stony facade may take years to chip away, if he'll even let anyone try.

"So, within a year you'll be practically back to normal? That's great. How long will you be here?"

"Two more days, but you don't need to come back," he preempts.

Shrouded by mistrust, he's difficult to read. My instinct tells me he's pushing back to protect himself, not to offend me. In any case, his behavior presents a challenge I must meet.

"No, I don't *need* to, but I bet you'd like some items from your house. A change of clothes, or your laptop?"

I watch him weigh the defeat of asking for a favor against living without his computer for the next few days. Sadistically, I enjoy his squirming, but only because I perceive it's not something he suffers often.

"I'd like some of those things, but you don't have to do it." He affects a bored countenance, presumably to maintain his own sense of control. "I'm not asking you for favors, Lindsey."

"Fine, Levi. I'm offering without being asked." I'm slightly agitated now, at him and myself. "Would you like some things from home, or not?"

Tapping the book against his legs twice before answering, he replies without looking me in the eyes. "Yes, thank you. That's real nice of you."

He coughs to cover his discomfort. Considering his current predicament, I don't rub his nose in my small victory.

"Okay. Write down a list of what you want and where I can locate it. I'll bring it back later today. Do you have a key hidden somewhere?"

"They're on the tray over there." He motions toward the table tray and jots down a short list of items.

"Great. I'll do this while you read." I wink in jest.

He flashes a friendly smile, revealing his dimples once more. "I'll need my glasses," he says, pointing to the list, "to read this book."

"Glasses, huh? You didn't need those in Florida," I remark.

"Seven years age a person, but thanks for reminding me."

Before leaving, I again notice the mush served up as lunch. Levi and Carlos deserve better.

"I know you're a picky eater. Can I bring you something for dinner?"

"I've cooked with you, so I'm not so sure that's a wise idea. You might bleed to death from mishandling the knives."

I cock my head in reply. "You misunderstood. May I order something from a restaurant you enjoy and bring it to you? Maybe something nearby, so it holds well?"

"I'm not supposed to eat solids today," he says. "Soup?"

Suddenly he's not uncomfortable asking for favors? Hmm. Food is Levi's Achilles' heel.

Carlos interrupts us to recommend a nearby restaurant that might have a decent selection of soups. He's a kindhearted person who doesn't deserve the misfortune of being saddled with Levi as his only companion. I'm sure he'll be eager to return home after another twenty-four hours with Mr. Personality. Once I convince him to allow me to bring him dinner, too, I take my leave.

As I near the door, I don't glance back, but say aloud, "You're so welcome, Levi," and then I depart. Curious to hear his retort, I wait outside the door for a second to listen. Levi's silent, but Carlos speaks.

"She's very nice. You were wrong saying no girls would check on you."

"She's not a girl, she's a neighbor. A bossy one," he mutters, but his voice sounds appreciative for a change.

"She's pretty on the outside and the inside," Carlos remarks. I hear Levi grunt an acknowledgment and turn on the TV.

He's *surly* on the outside, but I've glimpsed bits of gentleness underneath his bluster. Maybe I'm as naive as Jill thinks, but my gut tells me I'm right about some painful part of Levi's past making him withdraw in self-defense.

I'm determined to break through his shell, unless it's too late for anyone to crack it open. I can't control him or his behavior, but I can do what I know is right. Being helpful is always right.

CHAPTER EIGHT

June 7, 2013

Levi

The cops can't locate the hit-and-run driver since no one can adequately describe the vehicle model and color, or offer plate information. I doubt I'll ever see justice. It's probably some uninsured jerk anyway. At least he or she mustn't be injured or isn't filing baseless claims against me, so perhaps I should count myself lucky the idiot disappeared into the night.

My bike's totaled, however. I've already gotten the go-ahead from my insurance company to order a replacement. Damn, I loved that bike. I hope the new one rides as well.

On top of these letdowns, the past two days have been near hell. I despise the hospital—the odors, commotion, roommate, and food—and can't wait to sign my discharge papers. At least this morning I finally shed the damn tight, itchy circulation stockings. The white spandex contraptions were hot as hell. And at this point, I feel so trapped and uncomfortable here I might just welcome a blood clot.

For whatever reason I'm sure I don't know, Lindsey's stopped in each day with decent food, creature comforts from my house, and her company. She's strictly adhering to the high-protein diet the doctor recommends to help the graft heal. Believe it or not, her genuine motive appears to be her silly idea about our fates being intertwined. That or she gets her kicks from helping people. Although she deliberately antagonized me with a large, yellow smiley-face balloon—yes, a smiley face—which she tied to the bed railing, claiming *something* on my side of the room should smile.

She's harder to read than most, but it's possible I'm just unaccustomed to reading honest, open people. Most folks I've met are looking out for themselves, not bending over backward to help a stranger.

Her vivacious optimism's infectious to everyone in her orbit, and even I have succumbed somewhat to its power. She's been cheerful to the staff and calls them all by name. Carlos loved her instantly and I bet Lindsey hated to see him go home yesterday.

I've never met a whirling dervish like her before, and I equally dread and relish her visits. If I'm not careful, I'll get sucked into the quicksand of my growing preoccupation with her. Lindsey's determination knows no limits.

When she learned about my dilemma with home care and rehabilitation, she insisted on aiding in my recovery at home. While I'm grateful to avoid the rehab center, I drew the line when she suggested I stay at her house. I need to be in my own space. She also suggested I rent a hospital bed so I can avoid the steps. She's too quick to run wild with any small concession. I want to sleep in my own goddamned bed.

I'm hopeful, after a couple of days of checking on me, she'll see I'm okay and leave me to my own devices.

∽

"Hey there! Big day!" Lindsey floats into the room carrying a lunch bag and a duffel. She's glowing today, all too appealing in her peach-colored sundress and sandals. Placing the duffel beside me on the bed, she hands me a flavored seltzer and a broccoli and cheddar quiche. Better yet, she brought me pecan pie, which I love. I expect she assumes all Southerners love pecan pie, and she's probably not far off the mark.

"Thanks for lunch." I flip the tab on the seltzer and take a large bite of the quiche.

Her takeout meals have been a real saving grace. If I'd been stuck eating hospital food, I'd have lost ten pounds.

"Sure." Lindsey grins and sucks in her breath, preparing to share something unpleasant, I'm sure. "So, don't get all weird on me, but I went into your bedroom and brought you a fresh change of clothes. It seemed like sweats would create the least friction against your incision."

She begins unpacking my underwear and clothes from the duffel bag. Good God, she went through my underwear? I bet she messed up my drawers, too.

"Do you need help getting dressed, or can you do it yourself?" She smiles, completely unfazed by my discomfort. I think she uses that smile as a shield, or maybe as a weapon. "Remember, you shouldn't bend."

"Hell, Lindsey, I can put on my own pants." I groan, partly mortified, and partly affronted by the invasion of privacy.

"Only trying to help." She holds her hands up as if she's being arrested and rolls her eyes. "Fine, try it yourself. I'll step outside the room."

Once she's in the hallway, I sit up. With enormous effort, I swing my legs over the side of the bed. While wrestling with the underwear first, trying to swing it down and catch it with my toes, pain shoots through my back and legs. I bite through my discomfort because there's no way she's helping me when I'm naked. Somehow I manage to get it on without really bending.

After a meager victory with the Calvin Kleins, I admit defeat and call her back in to help with the rest. To her credit, she returns without saying "I told you so," but her grin tells me she's enjoying her power trip.

Agitated by my ineptitude, I hold the socks up. "Couldn't bring flip-flops?"

"You might drag your feet and trip over flip-flops, Levi. I can't lift you by myself if you end up on your ass." She cocks her head, ready for any challenge, so I say nothing.

Removing the socks from my hand, she kneels down to put them on me the way one might help a small child. Next, she helps me strap the back brace on. Finally, she grabs the sweats, bunches each leg up at the heel, and pulls them up over my knees like those girly tights.

Although she's being careful not to be too touchy, her fingers brush against my feet and legs while she works. I admit, the intimacy's arousing and unsettling. I've got to define the boundaries. Lord knows what latitude she'll take if I ever lower my guard.

$$\approx$$

Within the hour, we're driving home in her ragtop with the wind whipping through our hair. Thankfully, she brought a couple of pillows to help support my body. Fresh air and a view of the ocean—heaven. After being cooped up for so many days, I don't even complain about the jarring pain in my back when we hit bumps in the road.

I've missed home. When we arrive, Lindsey comes around to the passenger side to heave me up and out of the reclined car seat.

"Can you manage the steps by yourself, or should I take these things inside first and come back for you?"

"I can manage, Lindsey. I'm not paralyzed."

"Okay, Oscar the Grouch. Why are you so unwilling to accept my help?" She shakes her head and moves away, clearly intending her question to be rhetorical. "You should be more gracious."

Without complaining further, she follows behind me for the agonizing minutes it takes to climb the half flight of steps to reach the main living area.

"Remember, the doctor said only take the stairs once a day for a couple of weeks. So, rest here on the sofa this afternoon. Once you're upstairs, you'll be stuck there."

Man, she's as high-handed as ever. But after the brief experience of the half flight, I know I won't be going up and down the steps too often anyway. I glance at the split cushions of the sofa and wonder whether I can comfortably lie on them all day. I'd never admit it, but maybe Lindsey's hospital bed idea wasn't bad. I dread lowering my body onto the sofa. As if reading my mind, she holds out her arm to ease me down.

Once I'm settled, she repositions the coffee table so I can access my laptop and the remote. She exits the room and returns with several bed pillows and a blanket. As she props me up and tucks another pillow under my knees, I'm touched by her bigheartedness, and reach for her hand.

"Thanks. Sorry for being grumpy." I mean it, but I can't look her squarely in the eye. "I appreciate all your help."

The outer corners of her large eyes crinkle with her smile. She slaps her hands to her cheeks and opens her mouth into an O. "Oh my. Being nice didn't kill you!" She snickers at her little joke, then says, "You're welcome."

When she returns from taking my bag upstairs, she's carrying the accumulated mail, which includes a cardboard shipping box.

"Should I open this package?" She holds it up. "It's heavy."

"Who's it from?" I don't recall ordering anything online.

Lindsey reads the return address and printed packaging tape. Her face bristles before settling into a miserable expression while her hands gently rub the sides of the carton.

"It's from a mortuary in Nevada." Her eyes soften. "I'm so sorry, Levi. These must be your father's ashes."

"Go on, open it." I stare at the box, wide-eyed. My body is stock-still as I hold my breath.

She lifts a smaller plastic box from inside the container and pushes it toward me.

My pop's in that tiny box. I can hardly breathe. When Lindsey nudges it a little closer, I shake my head, unwilling to touch it.

She pulls it onto her lap. Her eyes glisten and she clears her throat. "Where would you prefer I place it until you get an urn? On a bookshelf?"

"Closet's fine."

"Are you sure?" She frowns and tilts her head as if she's misunderstood.

"Yes."

She straightens herself and then wanders to the front hall closet with the container.

"Wow, you're really organized. I thought your clothes closets and drawers were compulsively tidy, but here, too?" I hear her making space for the box.

My jaw clenches at the thought of Pop's ashes being here in my house. I've barely wrapped my head around the fact that he's gone, and now what's left of his flesh and bones is sitting on my shelf. I swallow the lump in my throat before Lindsey returns.

I sort through the mail and note an oversize envelope from Harper & Associates. When she returns, she spots the junk mail pile and takes it to the kitchen to toss out. Her phone rings while she's in there.

"Hi, Mom." Silence.

"Sorry, I've been busy this morning." Lindsey's voice loses its bounce. More silence.

"No. I haven't decided what to do about Rob yet." She sighs, submitting to her mother's apparent interrogation.

"Nope, haven't searched for a job yet, either." Pause.

"Yes, Mom, I know." Another pause.

I stretch my neck to catch a glimpse of her, but it hurts my back, so I withdraw a smidge. She's holding the phone to her ear and her other hand's plastered across her forehead.

"Aren't I even allowed a full week to do nothing?"

Her resentful tone increases my curiosity about the other end of the conversation.

"I told you. My neighbor was in a terrible car accident and I've been helping out. I've been preoccupied."

Now she's leaning one hand against the counter while holding the phone away from her ear. I can't help but smile because she looks cute all pissed off.

"Oh, I didn't realize compassion and empathy should only be extended to people we know well." Her acerbic tone could peel the paint from the walls. "My bad."

Hmm, the girl can bark when she's mad. Guess her mother disapproves of Lindsey wasting time helping me. Fortunately, it hasn't stopped her yet.

"No." Silence.

"Yes, you're right. I know. I know I have decisions to make." Silence.

Lindsey's bent over the counter now with her chin resting in her palm. I hear her exhale a deep, exasperated breath.

"I'm sorry. But seriously, why are you being so hard on me? We've never fought so much as we have these past few weeks. Please, I'm not alone now. Can we talk later? I'll call tonight. Love you."

When she returns, I pretend to be absorbed in my mail. Interestingly, she caters somewhat to her demanding mother. I smile wryly. The almighty Lindsey inherited her bossy streak honestly, and even *she* answers to someone, at least on occasion.

More interesting, however, is a certain someone named Rob. Is he a boyfriend? Why'd she leave? In any case, her mother obviously wants her to return. A covetous twinge of spite unfolds within me.

"Levi, if you're settled, I'll head home." She's distracted now, all traces of buoyancy erased. "What would you like for dinner?"

"I'll fix something, don't worry."

Once again, her palm flies to her forehead. She breathes a long sigh, then snaps.

"Any food you had here has gone bad. Plus, you shouldn't lift things or stand around bent over, chopping food. Please, just make it easy for me. If you write down a list, I can swing by the grocery store later to get you some prepared snacks."

It's the first hint of resentment I've witnessed, and I want to make it go away for both our sakes.

"I'll eat whatever you want to eat. Thanks."

She arches her brow, confused by my sudden cooperation. I'm awaiting a smart remark, but she simply nods.

"Thanks. I'll come back later. If you need me before then, call my cell, okay?" She thrusts her pointer finger toward me. "Don't push yourself. Stay on the couch and relax. Don't try to be superman."

"Yes, ma'am."

She exits through the back door, leaving it open so I can enjoy the breeze.

Once I'm alone, I tear open the envelope from Harper. As promised, he enclosed a copy of my pop's will and an insurance form, together with another small envelope with my name scrawled across the front in my pop's handwriting. My damn hand trembles while I tear open the letter.

> *Levi,*
> *I know we parted on bad terms. I'm sorry I tried using you in my venture without your knowledge. If you're reading this, then we never mended the fence, but I'm no longer able to do so, either.*

I won't win any Father of the Year awards, but I did love you, boy. I'm real proud of how you turned out. I know it was mostly your doing, but I'd like to think some of the things I taught you paid off. That, and all them damn books.

Anyway, I know you don't need any money, but Mr. Harper will be sending you an insurance check and some other things. You're the only person I've cared about in this whole damn world, so I wanted to leave you something to remember me by.

The only other thing of real value I can give you is your mama. Her leaving filled me with rage. But age mellows a man. I don't know if she ever looked for you, but I'd made it hard for her with all the moving around, phony names, and such. At the time, I didn't think she deserved any second chances, so I didn't care if she couldn't find us. I admit I was too full of hatred then to consider how my decisions affected you. I still think you were better off with the clean break, but maybe you disagree.

I hired someone to track her down. As of 2010, she was married and living in Atlanta as Sue Ellen Sinclair Thompson, 760 Martina Drive. She doesn't know I found her, and I don't know if you want to see her, but I thought I'd do one thing right in my life. I know it burned you when she left. Maybe if you talk to her, you'll get closure one way or another.

I'm sorry for dragging you all around the country. I'm sorry I never gave you a decent home or a normal life. I hope you know you're the one true, good thing in my life. I thank you for sharing my many adventures and not judging me too harshly. You were a blessing, son.

Love,
Pop

My throat tightens and I shiver while holding my pop's final words to me. I clear my throat to dislodge the heavy lump stuck inside. When rereading the letter, I take the time to notice each word. In my mind, I hear his voice as if he's speaking to me. He had a hypnotic voice—deep and Southern and smoother than mine.

Frankly, I'm shocked he used his death to drag Mama into my head. Why would he think I'd ever want to see her, and why's he forcing the issue by giving me her address? Hell, now I can't even fight with him about it. That makes me madder than a wet hen!

I don't want to see Mama. Even if those years on the run made me hard to find, I've been using my own name for more than a decade. If she wanted to locate me, she'd have done so by now.

Not surprising she hasn't, really, since she never much liked my company. She'd shoo me away while she stared out the window, smoked a cigarette, or watched television. Lindsey's been more nurturing this past week than Mama ever was.

Why's Pop encouraging me to go to her? Did he know something more about why she left? If so, do I want to know it, or will it just make me feel worse?

I can't believe these are his final words and wishes. My heart rate's climbing, but I can't throw anything or go anywhere. I can't even get up and move around. I'm stuck here on this damn sofa with no way to escape my thoughts.

Sue Ellen Thompson—married in Atlanta. So nice to learn she started a new family as if I never existed. My stomach twists in an angry knot, and this tension is aggravating my back pain. I take quick, deep breaths, blowing steam through my nostrils. For more than twenty years I kept thoughts of a reunion at bay because I didn't know where she lived. Now Pop force-fed me that information and I'm choking on it.

I wish I'd never called the damn lawyer. And I don't want Pop's tainted insurance proceeds, either. No doubt he bought the policy with money stolen from the suckers he fleeced. I've had my fill of bad karma for more than one lifetime.

I throw the letter on the coffee table and close my eyes. All the years of locking my past away have been undone in a few short weeks. Pop's death liberated memories I now can't seem to escape. Can things get worse?

~

Lindsey

Last night Levi turned into a bear. He barked at me over every little thing, but I gave him extra latitude since the arrival of his father's ashes obviously affected him. Still I question why I got myself more involved with him, but he's so pitiful, I can't quit.

From what I've read online, injuries like his cause significant agony. Oddly, the pain is the one thing he's taking well. He never complains about the accident or his discomfort, but I've caught him wincing when he moves. He's not taking the full dose of his pain medication, either, like he's afraid of it or something.

As far as I can tell, no one's come by to see him—not even Elena. How does a person get to be his age without a close friend or family member in his life?

Jill advises me to read the writing on the wall and get the hell away from him. Based on what little I've told her about him, she's convinced he's either an asshole or some kind of reclusive psychopath, but I'm sure that's not the case. He's distrustful, but he's also capable of kindness, patience, and appreciation. He treated Carlos with respect and, once in a while, he's been awkwardly polite—almost shy—toward me. I think his bluster is his way of hiding any weakness.

In any case, my own mood's fallen today.

I woke up this morning crying on what would have been my wedding day. Instead of preparing to walk down the aisle in a few hours, I'm alone, distracting myself by caring for someone who'd probably rather I didn't.

Although I left my gown in New York, I did sneak the veil into my bags before coming to California. I don't know exactly what possessed me to grab it at the last minute, but I did. Maybe I wasn't ready to accept the undoing of all my wedding plans and bridal fantasies.

Now, standing in the middle of my new bedroom, I regard myself in the mirror, my fingers stroking the length of the fine organza as if I were getting dressed for my wedding march. If Jill were here, she'd be forcing me to drink champagne in order to forget about Rob. But I can't drink alone, especially at this early hour.

Removing my veil, I tell myself it wasn't meant to be. I toss it on my bed, then tie my sneakers and head out to the beach.

~

After my run, I slip into Levi's house to check on him. I see an ice pack on the coffee table, and the cane is propped up at the edge of the sofa. He's still dressed in yesterday's sweats, lying on the couch, staring at his laptop. He trades his own accounts, which explains why he works on New York time.

I wait until he glances up to acknowledge me. His dark-rimmed glasses make him look sharp and smartly sexy. Then again, he pretty much always looks hot. It's probably a good thing he isn't too charming or I'd be in big trouble.

"Did you eat yet?" I ask.

"No, you?"

"Nope. Want some French toast?

"You know how to make it?" He arches his brows in jest.

Whew, his disposition's improved since last night. "I'll manage."

Levi resumes trading while I rummage around his kitchen

searching for mixing bowls and skillets. Like everything else in his house, the cabinets are immaculate and well organized.

Even his refrigerator's freakishly clean. On its shelves sit a variety of small glass containers, each filled with unusual condiments. Opening the lids of a few, I sniff them to figure out what's inside. Turns out he's created homemade butter blends, mayonnaises, and mustards, with dill, basil, cranberry, and other items. The man is serious about his food.

I keep the strawberry butter out and then whisk together eggs, milk, and vanilla extract. Ten minutes later, I hand Levi a steaming-hot plate of French toast, with fresh berries on the side. His eager grin reflects pleasure and surprise.

"These look mighty tasty, Lindsey. Thanks."

"Sure. Milk, orange juice, coffee?"

"Milk, please."

I join him in the living room, although he remains taciturn as usual. His face tenses in physical discomfort, probably resulting from his awkward position on the sofa.

Between bites, he makes notes and reads his computer screen. I envy his focus and apparent enjoyment of his work. Throughout my life, I've engaged in a wide variety of lessons, traveled extensively, and been introduced to countless options. Despite it all, I've never found a calling or deep passion.

It goes beyond my lack of enthusiasm for the magazine staff position. I'm coming to realize my personal life also lacked a degree of passion. Life with Rob revolved around his extreme work schedule. I filled some of my free time with volunteer work on fund-raising committees. But mostly I pursued social activities like dining with friends, going to the theater, or sitting at home reading.

Although I've done nothing remarkable these past ten days, either, they've been eye-opening. I've been a good person throughout the years, but not a particularly introspective or engaged one.

It's disturbing to see myself as an empty shell instead of the modern, accomplished woman I thought I was. I suppose technically I'm accomplished, but now I'm aware of my lack of direction.

While taking care of Levi isn't particularly noteworthy, I've enjoyed being useful and needed—so that's something to consider.

"What's the matter?" Levi's voice catches me off guard.

When I look up, he's scrutinizing me in his mind-reading manner. He's very adept at it—a marked difference from Rob, who rarely picked up on my nonverbal cues.

"Nothing."

"Bullshit. You're brooding over something. What's wrong?"

"Nothing I care to discuss right now, please."

Levi respects my privacy with a nod and then returns his attention to his screen.

I pick up our empty plates to take them to the kitchen. Since he's such a neat freak, I thoroughly clean his countertops and return everything to its proper place. I'd do anything to avoid the apoplectic fit that would surely ensue if something were left out of place. As I'm hanging the dish towel to dry, my phone rings. Without looking at the screen, I answer.

"Hello?"

"Lindsey . . . it's me."

Rob! Oh, God, not *today*, not now. Without warning, a single, harsh sob escapes from my throat.

"Lindsey, don't cry, baby. Talk to me. I need to talk to you today. Please."

I slide down to the floor, with my legs pressed against my chest, to hide my crying from Levi. After a steadying breath, I hug the phone to my ear. I haven't heard Rob's voice in over two weeks.

"I'm not ready to talk." My voice cracks twice during that short sentence.

"I know, but I can't think of anything but you today. Everything's wrong without you here. I can't fucking believe we aren't getting married tonight." His voice is threaded with grief and tension. In this moment, if he were here, I'd collapse against him.

"Please don't swear at me, Rob. This isn't how I envisioned this day, either."

"Then why'd you leave?" I hear him draw a deep breath. "Come home. Let's fix this now, Lindsey."

After only a brief time away, I'm already lured to the familiar. Closing my eyes, I picture Rob in our apartment, on the sofa, in jeans and an oxford shirt. I could nuzzle into the clean, lemony-soap scent of his neck. Still, a tiny voice from deep within tumbles out of my mouth.

"Rob, how'd she know where to find you?" I hold my breath.

"What?" He's thrown by my lack of segue. "Who?"

"The random girl from the bar. She called you at work to tell you about her *condition*." It occurs to me he hasn't asked me about my health, so I decide not to share the good news I got from my doctor. Petty, but it's one of the few things I can control. "How'd she know where to find you?"

My question's met with silence, sinking my heart straight into my stomach. "She was at the bar, but that's not where I met her. Ava works at Goldman. She's Tim's new assistant. But I swear, we were together only once. She joined our group after work and we got drunk together. That's it."

Ava. Her beautiful name summons an unwelcome image of an exotic siren, one with long legs dangling over a desk amid ledgers thrown to the floor in the heat of passion.

"You're *such* a liar!" I shout, forgetting I'm not alone.

"I'm not lying. It meant less than nothing, Lindsey!"

His stern, resentful tone shocks me, but I'll not be intimidated. I hear Levi moving around in the distance, so I lower my voice before responding.

"When you told me about her, you omitted the fact you see her every day at work. Does she stay late nights with all of you, too? If it meant 'nothing,' why didn't you tell me the whole truth?"

"I knew you'd make a big deal of it. I can't get her fired, Lindsey. I'd probably be sued on some trumped-up sexual harassment claim if I tried. She's not my assistant, so I only see her infrequently. Most importantly, I don't care about her. I love you. I want you to come home now."

"No. I'm not coming home now. I may never come back to you. God, I really can't trust you. Unless I know exactly which questions to ask, you won't give me the full story. I can't live that way, Rob." I cringe inwardly at what Levi's overhearing.

"How long will you make me wait, Lindsey?"

"What?"

"How long? Do you expect me to wait around a month, the summer, until Christmas, what? Tell me the plan."

I'm aghast at his question and contentious tone.

"There's no plan. You weren't faithful when we were together, so I assume you'll pursue women while we're broken up. You do what you need to do, and so will I. If we're meant to be, then it will happen."

"So that's it? I can't believe you ran away and won't even give me a chance to fix things. What's that say about you? Yes, I did a shitty thing, but I'm begging and fighting for us. You cut and run at the first sign of trouble. Nearly three great years tossed aside like garbage."

My mind's racing while hot tears spill over my cheeks. Is he right? Am I a coward? Worse, have I used his mistake as an excuse to escape? Rob hears me sniffling and changes his tune.

"Lindsey, I'm sorry. I'm not really mad at you. I'm angry with myself. Nothing's the same without you. I'd hoped you missed me, as I'm missing you. I thought I'd convince you to come home.

Obviously, that's not happening." I hear him sigh. "I'll leave you alone to figure out what you want. I'm here when you want to talk. I hope you come home soon. I love you, baby."

Before I reply, his end of the phone goes silent. Spent, I sit on the kitchen floor, weeping. Within a minute, Levi's feet appear at the edge of the counter cabinets.

"Lindsey?"

He sounds oddly uncertain. An alien experience for both of us, I'm sure. Our eyes meet, then my face crumbles as the intensity of my crying increases.

"I can't bend down to you. Stand up."

He's authoritative, yet compassionate. When he reaches his hand down to me, I take hold of it to stand. He pulls me into an awkward hug, then slowly strengthens his hold, pressing me infinitesimally closer, while he strokes my hair and lets me cry. Despite my being mortified and hurt, his unexpected tenderness is peculiarly soothing.

"Aw, sweetheart," he whispers into my hair. His heavenly voice wraps around me like a dense fog. "I knew you weren't all right."

The warmth of his breath and term of endearment tease my hair follicles into tingling. In panicked response, I push away from the comfort of his body. He folds his arms across his chest, blocking me from changing my mind and going back for seconds.

"Better now?"

I nod, but it's not true. Rather than ask for an explanation, he simply waits for me to decide if I want to talk.

I'm puzzled. No one in my life lets me decide anything, ever. My head's still tilted downward when my eyes look up in shame.

"Sorry. I didn't mean for you to overhear that discussion."

"I didn't hear it all, don't worry."

I feel sheepish and heartbroken, and the waterworks flow again. He stands solemnly, allowing me the freedom to cry, share, or leave. Needing to fill the silence between us, I divulge the truth.

"Today should've been my wedding day. But a couple of weeks ago I found out Rob, my fiancé—ex-fiancé—cheated on me. I was so blindsided, I called off the wedding and left town to think. He claims he's sorry and it happened only one time, but I don't know if I can trust him anymore."

Levi's face remains impassive as he hands me a tissue to blow my nose, and another for my eyes. I stare at him while I wipe my runny nose.

"What? You don't have an opinion? Any advice?" I ask, then crush the tissues in my hand and toss them in the trash. "Not even a wisecrack?"

He watches me for another minute, holding my eyes steady with his. When he speaks, his voice is relaxed and calming.

"You seem to have enough people in your life telling you what to do. You're not a stupid girl and, in the end, my opinion and theirs don't mean a damn thing. It's your life. You're a grown woman. I suspect you already know whether you trust him. When you're ready to accept what you know and make a decision you can live with, you will."

He cocks his head slightly, then returns to the living room with the help of his cane, leaving me alone to think. Unaccustomed to being told to trust my gut, I'm out of my depth in the cold waters of independence. Have I subconsciously encouraged my parents, Rob, and others to make decisions for me so I could be blameless if things went wrong? Am I self-sabotaging?

Levi's implied confidence rattles me. Frankly, I'm still shocked by his brief display of affection. Are we becoming friends? Maybe he's simply repaying me for my help. Maybe I'd better slink home before I do anything to embarrass myself further.

CHAPTER NINE

Levi

I'm working when Lindsey decides to leave. Promising to check in later, she offers a pathetically false smile before slipping out the back. Today's the only time I've seen her leveled. When she mentioned she should be getting married today, she about knocked me off my feet. An unpleasant sense of possessiveness wrenched my gut, too.

So, Rob's her fiancé and, apparently, a cheating lowlife. I shouldn't rush to judgment, though, since I've never committed to any relationship and don't know how long I could be loyal. But based on my own experience with Lindsey, I'm certain she doesn't deserve to be deceived.

She puts up a brave front, but she's basically a little girl lacking sufficient confidence to manage her own life. How does someone so privileged, pretty, and smart end up with such insecurities?

It hurt my heart to see her curled up on the floor in a hot mess of hair and tears. Comforting a teary woman was a first for me. Oddly, I could've stood there for a long time, stroking her hair, if she hadn't broken free. She felt good in my arms. It's disquieting. Neither of us should get attached in any way. She's rebounding and I'm not boyfriend material. No strings—it's the only safe way for me. Lindsey's not a no-strings gal.

I shut down the laptop and consider her sorrow—her non–wedding day. Selfishly, I'm grateful Rob's a jerk. Otherwise, Lindsey and I wouldn't know each other at all. Also, I'd be completely alone in my compromised condition.

Of course, I realize the loss would be all mine. She'd likely be better off having not moved next door to me.

I haven't met many truly unselfish people in my life. She'll be a lovely bride for someone, someday. She won't find him, though, pampered girl, until she knows herself better. She's got a ways to go before that day arrives.

Enough about Lindsey, for Christ's sake. *Switch topics, Levi.* I've never been so preoccupied with another person in my life.

Yearning to sit outside after too many days indoors, I stare through the glass doors at the lounge chairs on the deck. They look comfortable enough for my back. I take my book with me as I lumber across the living room. Each step causes serious discomfort, but at least I'm walking. Could be worse.

When I push open the heavy slider, my back spasms in response to the muscle movement in my core. Damn. I couldn't move a muscle without screaming if I weren't taking pain meds. Maybe I should take the full dose, but I've read too many horror stories in those spinal surgery chat rooms. I'd rather suffer the pain than end up an addict.

Gingerly, I lower myself onto the chaise and open my book. The high winds have blown out the waves, so at least I'm not missing out on decent surf. However, it's impossible to read the flapping pages, especially since the narcotics make me drowsy. I rest the book against my chest and close my eyes to daydream under the tent of a clear, blue sky.

～

"My God, Levi!" Lindsey's admonishment startles me out of a deep sleep. "How long have you been out here?"

"What time is it?" I squint up at her, barely able to move my stiff body.

"Two o'clock." Her hands rest on her hips, a sight that's become quite common this week. "You're as red as a lobster. Did you wear any sunscreen?"

She lifts the book off my chest and gasps, wide-eyed, before bursting into laughter. I glance down to see a square white patch of skin inset in my now ruby-red chest.

"Aw, shit." I touch the delicate skin.

"Oh!" She revels in my error and reaches out to touch my sunburn, but pulls back just in time. "If you want to nap, why not sleep in bed?"

"I haven't been outside since Monday. I wanted some fresh air." I'm sure my face is burnt, too. "Didn't intend to fall asleep. The damn painkillers make me woozy."

"Sorry, you're right." She stifles her laughter. "I didn't mean to laugh. It looks funny, though. Do you have aloe?"

"In the bathroom."

"Actually, you should probably wash your hair and take a sponge bath, too. How should we do that? You can't get the incision wet." She's frowning now, contemplating the options. Paying absolutely no attention to whether or not I agree, she jabbers on. "I guess I could bring hot water out here and use it, and the hose, to shampoo your hair for you. If you lie on the lounge chair, your back won't bend or get wet. I can sponge you down the back and hard-to-reach places, like your feet. You can do the rest on your own. It's perfect because all the soapy water will evaporate. No mess!" She's nodding and surveying the deck, still ignoring me.

"You're not giving me a sponge bath." The mere thought makes me twitchy and sets my mouth in a firm line.

"Why not? You haven't cleaned up well all week, Levi. Trust me, your hair's never looked worse." She's smirking now. "Don't be embarrassed. I promise, I've no ulterior motive. As you know, my heart's otherwise engaged. Let me get shampoo and aloe. I'll be back in a jiffy."

She bolts off the lounge chair before I can lodge another protest. Her earnest lack of interest should elate me, but truthfully, her comment has the opposite effect.

I remove my back brace and lie on the chaise. She returns carrying the products, two towels, a large pot of hot water, and an empty Tupperware container.

"I'm jealous, Levi. I love when someone else washes my hair. That's the best part of going to the salon." She covers my chest with a towel to protect me from further sunburn. "Stay on your back, but scoot up here so your head's a bit above the end of the chaise. Close your eyes."

In a Tupperware container, she mixes hot water from the pot with cold water from the hose and then empties the warm contents over my head. Her free hand combs through my hair, evenly wetting it all. The sensation strips away my tension.

Once her hands are lathered up with shampoo, her fingers glide through my hair. She applies the perfect amount of pressure to my scalp, sending tiny currents of energy down my neck. I'd gladly stay in this paradise for hours, but, too quickly, fresh warm water rinses over my head. I'm so tranquil I could fall asleep again.

"Can you roll over, Levi?" She mixes another soapy batch in the Tupperware and wrings out a washcloth. Starting at my neck, she gradually works her way down my shoulders and back, steering clear of the bandaged area. "We should get these sweats off you."

I'm enjoying this blissful process too much to protest. She carefully removes my sweats and scrubs the backs of my legs and my feet. A startling erotic shock jolts through me, suddenly making me uncomfortable.

"Okay. See? Not so terrible, right? Let's get you up now. You can take care of the rest inside. I'll get you some clean clothes. Any preference?"

Using the extra towel, she quickly pats down my legs and towel dries my hair. It takes an effort to stand up—like I'm an arthritic old man—but once I'm up, I wrap a towel around my waist. When her fingers unknot the tangles from my hair, my reflexes kick in and I grab her wrist. Jesus, I may need her help, but I'm still a guy whose body reacts when an attractive woman's touching me.

"I can take it from here." I hide the evidence of her effect on me by turning toward the door. "Thanks."

"Okay. I'll clean this up."

I wave my arm in the air to acknowledge her remark. *Must get away from her right now.* Of course, it's no easy feat for me to get fully undressed, clean myself, and put on fresh clothes. I take my time, opting for a robe rather than ask for help with another pair of pants.

When I return downstairs, she's got her hands on her hips again.

"What now?" I can't imagine what made her mad when I wasn't even in the room.

"The doctor said steps only once each day. I said I'd get you some fresh things. Now you've already come down twice, and gone up once. Don't you want to heal?"

I roll my eyes. "Hey, you ain't my mama." Damn, grammar slip. Darkness settles inside me now that I've reminded myself of Mama and of Pop's letter. My attitude shift must be visible, because Lindsey blanches slightly before shrugging and ordering me to lie on the couch.

"How about turkey with some of this pink cranberry mayo?" she asks.

"Fine." I'm uneasy with her growing familiarity in my space, but am equally unwilling to surrender the benefits of her care and attention. She must've acquired this knack from her own parents. But I suspect all this fuss can make one soft.

I won't allow myself to become soft.

Lindsey sets my lunch on the table and promptly leaves the room. I assume she went to fix her own lunch, but then hear her climbing the stairs. She descends more slowly, like she's carrying something heavy.

"What're you doing?" I call out.

She appears, hoisting a laundry basket to her hip. "Laundry."

"Put it down." I scowl. "You're not doing my laundry."

"You can't lift anything, Levi. Do you want it to pile up?" She scowls right back at me. "I know how to do laundry. I won't ruin your clothes."

Next thing I know, she exits the room with the basket in hand. When she returns, I'm pissed.

"What?" She collapses in the chair opposite me. "Why's it a big deal?"

"Don't you have other things to do today? Quit using me as a distraction from doing whatever you came to Malibu to do."

She sits back, mouth agape. "I liked you better this morning. You sure can run hot and cold, can't you?"

"Don't turn this on me. Why's it so hard for you to be alone? If you hadn't moved in the other week, I'd be managing. Not that I don't appreciate your help. You've been real sweet, but I'm not comfortable with you all up in my business—or in my laundry."

She folds her hands in her lap and averts her eyes. I notice a subtle slump in her posture. When she finally looks up, her eyes are dewy.

"Jesus, Lindsey, don't go crying on me." I inhale and count to ten in my head. "Why are you crying? I said I appreciate your help.

Look, I'm not used to taking orders from anyone, or giving anyone free range in my home. You're coming and going, getting in my drawers and closets. It's freaking me out a little, okay?"

She nods. "I'm sorry, I'm only trying to help. As you've gathered by now, my life's a mess. Helping you gives me a purpose, and I need a purpose now or I'll really lose it. But it's not your problem. I know you're very private. I'll back off."

She's piqued my curiosity.

"What'd you do in New York?"

"What?"

"Did you have a job, or did you spend your days taking care of your boyfriend or your family or whatever? What was your *purpose* there?"

Lindsey's demure expression is almost apologetic. "I wrote fashion magazine articles."

"So why don't you do that here and now?"

She shrugs and frowns. "I could, but I'm not inspired. I didn't care about it very much."

"What do you care about? What drives you?"

Her forehead creases more deeply. Oh no, more waterworks.

"I don't know. That's the problem. I don't know what I care about—what I want."

Unfortunately for her, my patience for whining is limited.

"Hey, stop it. If you want to moan and groan about being unfulfilled, take it someplace else. Don't ask for sympathy from me. You have everything and always had everything. Plenty of people out there got nothing but real problems. They worry about how to feed their kids or overcome an illness or significant loss. Don't sit around wallowing in self-pity. You have an education, money, parents who care, a boyfriend who wants you back, and friends. Stop analyzing everything and quit trying to please everyone else. Just take a step, and then another. Eventually you'll be walking on your own."

Her face stills in shock. "Gee, Levi, don't hold back. How do you really feel?"

"Go ahead and deflect. But I'm not the one who doesn't know what I want in my life." As I say the words, I'm struck by the hypocrisy, considering, only two weeks ago, I'd begun to wrestle my own feelings of boredom and dissatisfaction. "I'm not perfect, God knows, but I don't let other people dictate the terms of my life, dictate what I should do or how I live *my* life. Consider what you enjoy and then build your purpose around that pleasure. No one else can determine it for you."

She's staring through me now. My sharp tongue probably wasn't the most effective approach, especially today, when she's vulnerable because of the wedding that wasn't. I'm about to apologize when she snaps out of her funk.

I brace for more tears, but her eyes are dry.

"You have a point, Levi. Something to consider. For now, however, I'm doing your laundry. I'll continue taking care of you until you can fend for yourself. I'm good at it and it makes me happy to be helpful. So, for now, you're my *temporary* purpose."

She nods in affirmation of her own statement, stands up, and stalks out of the room. Ten minutes later, she informs me she's leaving and will stop back later with dinner.

I surrender to her will. "Okay, Nurse Ratched."

Lindsey stops short and shoots me a wry look, one brow raised. "Interesting reference. If you'd prefer Nurse Nightingale to Nurse Ratched, then adjust your sour attitude. See you at dinner. Try to stay flat on your back for most of the afternoon, *please.*"

She tilts her head slightly, awaiting my retort, but I leave her hanging. She smiles, pleased by my silence. I shake my head and wave her off.

Her emotional spectrum exhausts me. Today I've played counselor twice to her tears. Sandwiched in between those events, I endured an arousing sponge bath that left me horny and frustrated. Ultimately, no matter what I say, she does whatever she wants anyway. I may as well not talk, because it makes no difference to her. Jesus, she's challenging.

I close my eyes and relive the pleasant sensation of her hands in my hair. Man, I'm in trouble.

~

Lindsey

Since Levi and I argued last week about his laundry, we've stopped bickering at every turn. We've fallen into a bit of a routine with meals, mail, and errands. He's more agreeable outdoors than when he's cooped up, so I've taken him to local parks for short walks each day. I even coaxed him to go to the Adamson House, which was always one of Aunt Sara's and my favorite places.

He continually eyes the sand and surf, but he's not ready for the strain they'd cause. He's still recuperating and hasn't even started therapy yet. Sometimes his body is wracked with throbbing back spasms after overexertion, but each day he seems to improve a little. Of course, he could be lying just to be rid of me sooner.

One thing I shouldn't have tackled is his laundry. He's very particular about proper folding technique. His method takes longer than mine, but I'll concede his clothes and towels stack more neatly.

I'm getting sick of seeing that robe, but he refuses to allow me to help bathe him or wash his hair again. It's too bad, because I enjoyed toying with his hair, and he actually relaxed when I did, which was a first.

Surprisingly, I've overheard calls from some of his friends. He's not quite the loner I originally surmised. Not surprisingly, he skirts the truth about his current circumstances and simply puts off "getting together" until some future date. Once or twice I overheard him speak in a soft, gentle tone of voice—playful—and it left me feeling curiously disgruntled.

I wonder about what kind of woman he's attracted to—physically and emotionally.

Not me, that's for certain. Not at eighteen and not now.

I tread on his every nerve.

That aside, there's been some upside to our situation. He's taught me how to prepare a delicious mussels-marinara sauce, as well as a mustard-maple glaze for pork chops. I know I did a decent job because he was complimentary and ate everything. Although cooking's not relaxing to me, I enjoy eating the final product. He's a proficient tutor, even from the sofa, though he's confounded by why I can't master the proper use of a knife.

At any rate, caring for him keeps me busy and, at times, even entertained. As I initially suspected, he often maintains an opposing viewpoint and holds nothing back out of kindness. He'll be excellent at administering tough love if he ever becomes a parent.

Levi's quite a conundrum. He lives in a space protected by a hardened outer shell, but then his odd charm impresses me when I least expect it. Every once in a while, I catch him studying me and smiling. Of course, he can whisk it all away in a flash.

We might be enjoying a discussion of an inspiring book, debating a current event, or drinking a glass of wine, but when I ask anything about his family, he'll shut down.

There's also a storm shift in his eyes whenever my mother's calls interrupt us. He'll abruptly withdraw and remain distant after I hang up with her. I think he doesn't like her, which seems silly since they've never met. All my friends love my mom, especially my male friends. She's beautiful and charming and has a way of capturing the attention of most men. I didn't inherit that gene.

∼

Midmorning, I stop in to check on Levi and am surprised he's not on the deck or in the living room. I creep upstairs and gently knock on his bedroom door. His failure to respond raises concerns. It's unusual for him to sleep this late.

When I peek in his room, he's sprawled across his bed. The rumpled sheets are kicked to the floor. My first thoughts have nothing to do with his health, and everything to do with a growing infatuation. From a distance, I admire his practically naked physique, his sleepy face at rest amid the pillows.

Sunlight spills over his body, illuminating the sculpted contours of muscle in his shoulders, torso, and thighs. My God, he sure hit the DNA jackpot. I lick my lips, then feel the heat rush to my face. But I can't take my eyes off him. A wicked part of me envisions jumping into that bed. . . .

Good God, I shouldn't be standing here staring at him while he's passed out. Guilt spoils my lusty daydream and I begin considering the situation.

He mustn't have slept well last night. He's slightly ruddy and sweaty but his room is not particularly hot. Perhaps the sun beating on him is too warm. I tiptoe to the windows to close the blinds before I exit his room and descend the stairs.

I should leave, but standing alone in his living room, I'm gripped by an irrepressible urge to snoop. Over the past few weeks, I've shared much about my family, Rob, and my friends. Conversely, Levi's revealed nothing about himself. In fact, aside from knowing that his father's dead and he hails from Georgia, I know nothing of his childhood or family.

I'm thirsting for knowledge. Mostly, I want to unearth the skeletons I suspect form the foundation of his enormous emotional barrier. My conscience screams to dissuade me but fails.

I survey the room. It's no exaggeration to say he owns hundreds of books. What's not surprising to me now is finding them organized alphabetically by title. His preference for order extends to everything. It must be a coping tactic, a way to maintain control of things to compensate for whatever it is he can't control in his life.

Scanning the shelves and tabletops, I see no evidence of his past or how he became successful. Most people I know boast of their achievements, but Levi never discusses his own. I asked him if he has a broker's license. He laughed but didn't elaborate. Self-taught—that's his basic answer to everything.

More puzzling is an utter lack of photographs. No friends, no women, no family. Not a single snapshot anywhere. It's as if he's appeared on the planet out of thin air. After ten minutes, I give up my fruitless search. Like the mysterious island in the TV show *Lost*, Levi doesn't want to be discovered.

I check my watch again and decide to leave a note asking him to call me when he wakes. When I open the desk drawer to search for a notepad and pen, I see a strip of photos. Bingo! I immediately recognize Levi as the little boy, and presume the man with him is his father.

He strongly resembles his dad, but Levi's features are more refined. It's remarkable how a few subtle differences in one's nose or jaw alter a face. When I return the strip to the open drawer, I see a handwritten note from his father. It's wrong on every level, I know, but I can't help myself. I read it.

It's vague, but the major points are apparent. My hand clutches into a fist at my heart. Abandonment, neglect, vagabond living. No wonder he's detached and mistrusting.

His young face smiles at me—an authentic smile. Was he happy despite those circumstances? He was beautiful then, as now. That beauty masks the deep scars derived from such instability. He must consider my trust issues with Rob child's play.

I'm decidedly unhappy to know his history now, especially the way I discovered the truth. My forehead breaks out in a cold sweat as the magnitude of my gross invasion of his privacy—the abuse of his trust—dawns on me. It's inexcusable. I strain to remember exactly where I found these items so I can put everything away correctly. He's so particular; he'll notice if anything's out of place.

Crap. I'm so disconcerted, I leave without dashing off a note.

～

Several hours later, I'm convinced I can hide my deceit. If I confess, he'll bar me from his house. Despite his having every right to do so, I can't risk it because he needs my help.

At six o'clock, I return to his dark house. Something's very wrong. I take the steps two at a time and enter his room without knocking first. He's out cold, exactly where I'd left him earlier today. When I turn on the lamp beside his bed, I notice the faint red rash covering his chest. I touch his forehead with the back of my palm. It's burning hot.

"Levi, wake up." He's unresponsive to a gentle shake, so I shake harder. "Levi!"

He mumbles something unintelligible while thrashing in his bed.

"Please open your eyes." My hand touches his damp cheek. "Levi, open your eyes."

His eyelids flutter and finally open, but his eyes aren't focused. He's still half sleeping. Slowly, it dawns on me: high fever plus rash equals infection. Oh, God!

"Levi, can you sit up?" Reaching under his shoulders, I struggle to sit him upright. I can't possibly carry him to the car if he can't support his own weight. He's stammering and pushing my arms away. Even in this sickly state, he's stubborn. I let him fall back against his pillows and then I call 911.

An ambulance arrives fifteen minutes later. Two young guys follow me upstairs.

"Be careful when you move him. He's had spinal fusion surgery recently."

Unfortunately, I'm unable to sufficiently answer the paramedics' questions about when the fever started, where the rash began, and so on.

The depth of my self-deception chokes me. All this time I'd been playing nurse and housekeeper to keep myself busy. I hadn't really been taking *care* of him. I never took his temperature or checked his incision for signs of infection. Levi was right. I've been using him to avoid addressing my own problems. If I had been properly caring for him, I'd have caught this sooner.

The ambulance pulls out of the driveway. I run to my own house to get my car. Shaking, I sit behind the wheel, taking deep breaths until I'm sure I'm able to drive safely.

∼

The crowded, noisy emergency room amplifies the chaos in my mind. A mother with a crying infant sits next to me, wedging me between her and an old man with a gash on his arm. Despite all the commotion, I can't stop worrying about Levi's fever. My concern for his health is then supplanted by my guilty conscience. I wish I hadn't snooped, or at least I wish I could forget what I now know.

I sit there immersed in self-condemnation for what feels like hours. After shifting my position several times in the uncomfortable vinyl seat, I wonder if this nightmare provides ample punishment for my despicable behavior.

I start pacing around the waiting room. I need to talk to someone, but not my mother. She wouldn't be any comfort. It's after eleven in New York, but I phone Jill anyway.

"Hey, what's up?" Jill sounds sleepy.

"Did I wake you?"

"Nope, watching *Letterman*. What are you up to?"

"I'm at the hospital with Levi. He's really sick, Jill. I think he's contracted a staph infection. His body is covered in a rash." My voice squeaks from the strain of speaking so quickly. "It's really bad."

"Calm down, Lindsey. I'm sure he'll be fine now that he's in the hospital. Did you call his parents?"

"No."

"Why not? If it's so dire, shouldn't they know?"

"No, you don't understand. His dad's dead, and his mom . . . abandoned him when he was little."

Jill's quiet for a few seconds. "Well, at least now we know why he's such a jerk."

Her terse remark slaps me in the face.

"He's not a jerk. He's obstinate sometimes, but he's also clever, observant, and even kind." Tears mist my eyes. "Listen, please don't tell anyone about his past. I only know because I poked around and found a letter from his dad. Levi doesn't know I know anything."

"Who would I tell? But why'd you spy?" Her tone suggests she's eager for lurid details.

"I don't know." My fingers rub my temples. "We spend so much time together, but he never shares anything personal. I took advantage of an opportunity to snoop while he was napping."

"Wow, do you like this guy now?" Her sharp tone's critical. "Guess you're getting over Rob pretty quickly after all."

"Levi has nothing to do with Rob." I dismiss her insinuations. "We're not involved, Jill. Come on."

"Lindsey, you're spending practically all your time tending to a man you proclaim as the most beautiful creature on the planet, you defend his personality quirks, and now you're panicking over his health. It's not an unreasonable jump to suspect you've developed feelings for him."

"It's not romantic. There's nothing romantic between Levi and me." As I say the words, I realize some part of me feels disappointed. The recognition scares me. "Trust me, he's eager for me to become unnecessary."

"That's him, but what about you? Are you eager to be free of him?"

"Well, it's no picnic taking care of him." An unbidden image of washing Levi's hair springs to mind. "But I hope, once he's recovered, we'll be friends. I like him. He's different from everyone I know. Unpolished, but with a unique sense of honor and integrity. Plus, he's so alone. He needs me. And now, knowing why he's so detached, I'm more sympathetic." My voice trails off and Jill sighs.

"Oh brother, you *do* like him. I hear it in your voice. Here we go again—another 'wounded soldier' to add to your ranks." She blows out a long breath. "Lindsey, he needs professional help with his kind of baggage. You can't save him. Why do you always try to heal everyone?"

"I do not. I'm not an idiot. I know I can't heal anyone. Why can't I care about him, as a person, without you or my mom or anyone else jumping to conclusions?"

"So Helene's not happy. No surprise there—she loves Rob."

"What about you? Do you love Rob, too?"

"Rob messed up, but he's not the devil, Lindsey. Have you talked to him since last Saturday?"

"No. I don't know what else to say to him now. I don't trust him. First he cheats, and then he tells me only half the truth about Ava, the slut. He's really thrown me twice now. I'm so confused. I love him, but how can I be with someone I can't trust?"

Before we finish our discussion, a nurse enters the waiting room and calls my name. I rush Jill off the phone and follow the nurse to the hospital wing where Levi's resting. We're standing outside his door when I unleash my questions.

"How's he doing? What's the rash? Is his fever breaking?"

She forces me into one of the chairs in the hallway. Her grim expression offers no comfort whatsoever. "Honey, in all likelihood your friend has contracted a serious staph infection. We're testing for MRSA."

"The superbug?" My eyes widen. I vaguely recollect several terrifying reports from a few years ago. If I recall correctly, the mortality rate can be as high as forty percent. My ears thrum. Additional tests are needed to determine whether or not it's affecting his organs. If I want to see him, I have to wear a face mask, gloves, and surgical dress. Her voice fades in and out as my brain struggles to grasp the facts and circumstances.

"He's fairly incoherent now from the high fever. But if you want to see him for a few minutes, I'll show you in."

"Yes, please."

I cover myself with the stiff, green hospital gown and cap and snap on the sterile gloves. The nurse hands me a paper mask and then leads me into his room. She checks his temperature and makes some notes on his chart before leaving us alone.

He's asleep. His skin looks pasty and damp. I feel numb, but eventually sit on the edge of the bed and touch his side.

"Levi, it's me, Lindsey."

He stirs but doesn't wake up. His body's throwing off heat like a potbellied stove. I wipe his damp hair off his forehead. Staring at him, it's hard to believe I've known this man for only a few weeks. It seems like so much longer.

"Levi, can you hear me?"

Lethargically, his eyes open. I'm not sure whether he recognizes me in my Kermit the Frog getup. At first he seems confused, but then he catches my hand.

"Lindsey." The outer corners of his eyes wrinkle as he smiles.

Relief slashes through my fear. I return his smile, forgetting my mouth is hidden behind my mask. Words fail me, so I touch his chest in comfort.

He lifts my hand to his lips. "Go back to sleep, darlin'." The tender gesture surprises me. *Go back to sleep?* What's he imagining we're doing? He folds my hand under his cheek and turns his face toward me, closing his eyes again.

He looks so weak and helpless. Tears mount in my eyes. I want the cool, confident Levi back. With my free hand, I sweep the hair off the other side of his sweaty face. He's scorching hot, but his eyes flutter open once more.

"Come here, pretty girl." He kisses my wrist slowly, sucking on it with his hot mouth while his thumb traces little circles in my palm. Even with the barrier of the prophylactic glove dulling the sensation of his thumb's rotations, his searing tongue sends my pulse rocketing and creates a gentle ache in places nowhere near my hand.

Oh, God, Jill's right. I do care for him—very inappropriately. And what of him? Is this behavior an expression of his subconscious desire or simply fever-induced delirium? My disloyal yearnings launch me straight into self-reproach.

"Levi, I'm leaving now. I can't stay. I'll visit tomorrow, okay?"

"Stay." He stops nuzzling my wrist and holds my hand against his chest. "I don't like it when you go." Closing his eyes, he drifts back into dreamland, leaving me to wrestle with my response to his words and actions.

"Levi, I have to go. I'll be back tomorrow morning."

Gently, I slip my hands free of his. He twitches slightly as he loses his grip on me. He stills again in a heartbeat.

I slink out of his room and run to my car in tears.

~

I'm amazed I made it home without getting in an accident. I don't remember a single red light or other car on the road. My mind is still overwhelmed with confused thoughts and desires as I drop my purse on the dining table.

Last week, I nearly ran back to Rob at the first sound of his voice. I miss my home, the energy of New York, my family and friends. If I return now, I could easily slide back into the familiar patterns and rhythms that always worked for me. I could take the leap of faith to trust Rob again. We'd elope and get on with our life. These past few weeks would hopefully fade from memory by Christmas.

But Levi energizes me. He keeps me on my toes. He doesn't pander to me, or tell me what to do or believe. He shoves me outside my comfort zone. It's simultaneously terrifying and awakening. And he's sinfully good-looking. Rob's handsome, but few men have Levi's extreme sex appeal.

Regardless of these attributes, Levi doesn't fit in my life. My parents would never accept him. Plus, the depth of his painful problems is intimidating. If he were interested in dating me—which I doubt he is—it would be too risky anyway.

He's thirty and unlikely to change. In fact, he prefers life his way. He's a recluse—no anchors. I can't get caught up in Levi. Until tonight, he's never shown any interest in me, and he's delirious now. Nothing he muttered can be taken at face value.

Stay. I don't like it when you go.

God, please don't let him slip into septic shock. Honestly, if he dies, I'll never forgive myself for not getting him to the hospital sooner.

I crawl into bed with a gigantic glass of wine. I've let everyone down: my parents, Rob, my friends, and now Levi. Most importantly, I've disappointed myself. How can I be so competent and yet incapable? *Quit analyzing everything. Just do something.* Maybe Levi's right, but how do I get out of my own way?

I put the empty glass on the nightstand and snuggle under my blanket. Staring out my window, I watch the moonbeams dance on the ocean until I fall asleep.

∽

"Tell me what you want," Levi commands me. He pins me against the bed with his body. His husky voice fills me with longing. He kisses my collarbone, causing me to twist my head to provide easy access to my neck.

My hands brush against his bare chest before roaming across the firm muscles of his shoulders and back. His hands tangle in my hair, while his warm mouth slowly, achingly works its way up to my jaw. Levi's breathing becomes ragged and wanting.

A slight moan escapes from my throat when his hot breath hits my ear. He quickly brings his mouth to claim mine with an urgent, demanding kiss. His tongue expertly slides around my own. Playfully, his teeth gently capture my lower lip before he resumes another deep kiss. Pinning my arms above my head with his right hand, his left hand travels down my neck and around my breast, where his thumb circles my nipple over the top of my T-shirt.

"Tell me what you want, Lindsey."

I'm falling into a sea of sensual desire as he pulls his head away and searches my eyes for an answer. His hands continue their unrelenting exploration of my body and find their way under my shirt.

"I want you," I admit. His eyes gleam with excitement, then he bears his mouth down on mine again with another scorching kiss. My own pulse races as he removes my top.

∽

I awaken alone, a sweaty, frustrated mess. Contrition crashes over me for being unfaithful to Rob. Yes, we're broken up and, technically, I've done nothing. Rob slept with someone and I ran away. But now, mere weeks later, I'm dreaming about sex with a man who doesn't mean "less than nothing" to me. Really, really hot sex.

I close my eyes again, but there's no recapturing the moment.

I'm a bad person. A selfish, disingenuous woman. *Lindsey, get it together!* I'm not about to rearrange my entire life because of this insane infatuation with Levi. The whole point of coming to Malibu was to follow Aunt Sara's lead and focus on myself, not to agonize over what is or isn't happening with the two men in my life.

I can get past this infatuation with Levi and move forward alone or with Rob, depending on what I discover. When Levi's out of the hospital, I'll pare down my visits. Polite-but-distant neighbors—it's what he's always claiming he wants anyway.

It's only six thirty. Hopefully a long run will clear my head.

CHAPTER TEN

Levi

"Mr. Hardy, I'm afraid I have some unfortunate news." The doc's somber tone sets me on edge. "Your fever's reduced and the rash is receding, which are positive signs. But we aren't out of the woods. We can't risk a recurrence by failing to address the site of the incision and what's inside. We need to clean the hardware in your spine to eliminate all sources of the infection."

Doc waits for my response, but I bite my tongue while I digest what's happening. Jesus, go back into my spine? The potential for a negative outcome with another surgery scares the hell out of me, but so does the astonishing speed with which this infection invaded my body. To top it off, my skin's itchy and I'm freezing cold.

"Doesn't sound like you're giving me a choice, are you, Doc?" I scratch my arm. I'm worried, but I'm not gonna advertise it to him or anyone else. "How soon?"

"I'll schedule surgery for tomorrow morning." He makes a notation on my chart. "Try not to be anxious. If you have questions, page me." He nods and then exits without further comment.

I shove the tray of disgusting scrambled eggs away from my bed. Even if I were hungry, the sight of the pale, rubbery lump would surely dampen my appetite. I'm pissed off. Not a great start to the day.

Where's Lindsey? I want to know what the hell happened yesterday. I can't remember how I ended up here. It's disconcerting that everyone entering my room today is covered, head to toe, in sterile clothes and face masks. I must be highly contagious or extremely susceptible to germs, neither of which is very good.

Damn, I hate hospitals. What'd I do to deserve these problems?

~

"Good morning, Levi."

Lindsey's voice wakes me from my nap. My brain's muddled, but I recognize her eyes even though her face and hair are hidden. Unfortunately, my dismal mood and clammy skin override any enthusiasm I feel for her arrival.

"Is it? Doesn't seem too good to me." She's not the reason for my bad humor, but she's here and I need to unload. Her brows shoot upward and I watch her hands find their way to her hips. Oh boy, here we go. "Don't light into me, Lindsey. I'm sorry I barked at you. Give me a break, would you? It's been a shitty morning."

Her eyes soften and she launches into a barrage of questions. "How's your temperature? Has the rash improved? Is the vancomycin working? What did the doctor say?"

She sits at the edge of my bed, taking a break from her rapid-fire questions, and rests her hand on my arm. Instinctively I flinch, but then relax and allow myself to enjoy the pleasure of her tenderly stroking my forearm.

"You look a little better than last night." Her voice cracks. "You scared me yesterday."

"Doc says the meds are working." I shrug. "Apparently my fever's dropping. But he's going back into my spine to clean the screws and check the graft for infection."

Lindsey's eyes fly open.

"Yeah, another surgery. Trust me, I'm not happy." I place my hand over hers. The tenderness shocks me, so I withdraw it and tuck it behind my head. "So, what happened yesterday? How'd I end up back here?"

"You don't remember *anything* about yesterday . . . or last night?" Lindsey's eyeing me like she's hoping for a specific memory to surface. Well, she'll be waiting a long time, because yesterday's a blank slate.

"Not really. I'd been sleepy, so I stayed in bed. I don't remember much more. You must've found me and brought me here."

"Not exactly. You'd been sleeping all day. When I returned in the early evening, I came to your room and noticed the rash and fever. It was really scary, Levi. You've no idea. You were incoherent." Her stricken expression oddly elevates my mood.

She cares about me. I can hardly believe it.

I refocus on her words while she continues her story.

"I couldn't move you, so I called the ambulance. They'd only let me see you briefly before they sent me home."

Lindsey's eyes start to water. More evidence of her genuine concern for my welfare. Warmth spreads through me, erasing much of my anxiety.

"Ah, boy, tears?" I lay my hand on top of hers, which is still gripping my forearm. "Come on, no cryin'."

"I thought you might die." She wipes her widened, red-rimmed eyes with her free hand. "The rash spread so quickly and your temperature shot up to brain-damage range."

"Don't tell me you'd miss me if I died? I'd assumed you'd be happy to be rid of me, since I'm so grouchy and particular and all." My joke elicits a gentle slap from her, but no smile.

"That's bad form, Levi. Not the least bit funny. Last night was awful."

I must agree. "Well, there's nothing funny about needing another surgery, either. Another chance for a mistake that might leave me paralyzed."

Immediately regretting vocalizing my concern, I look away to keep her from seeing my fears. When I face her, she laces her fingers with mine. The startling intimacy causes my breath to catch. I stare at our hands, fighting the panic urging me to yank free.

"Levi, I'm so sorry. I feel responsible because I didn't catch the signs sooner. I'm sure the surgery will be fine, just like last time. The infection's the more dangerous problem, but it sounds like they're getting it under control."

Not sure if she's trying to convince herself or me, but I shrug because what else can she or I say? She's never withstood a serious threat of paralysis. For me, it might be worse than dying. I doubt I could live the rest of my life needing help. Plus, no more bike, no surfing, and what about sex? Life without sex, well, that's simply too awful to consider.

Holding Lindsey's hand in mine, I know, if she weren't my neighbor, I'd want her in my bed—more than once. I won't seduce her, but it sucks thinking I could end up paralyzed and unable to do so if I changed my mind.

I close my eyes to focus on something else.

She slips her hand from mine. "I brought you some things to keep you occupied these next few days."

Opening her bag, she retrieves my computer, some headphones, my robe, a smoothie, and a new book. I'm humbled by her thoughtfulness over and over again. She takes damn good care of me.

"You keep treating me this way and I may stay sick forever."

I can't see her mouth, but her eyes glow as if she's sporting a big grin under her mask. She's too damn easy to please, despite her being a princess.

She pushes the food tray close to me so I can reach the smoothie, then tilts her head and watches me. It's pretty plain she's considering saying something she thinks might upset me. I'm not interested in being upset, so I ignore her and concentrate on the drink. Unfortunately, my peace doesn't last long.

"Levi, I know you protect your privacy, but last night I needed to contact your family and didn't know who to call. You've avoided sharing any information, but I need emergency contact names and numbers now."

"No, you don't." I put down the cup and cross my arms in front of my chest. Lindsey's eyes are still and cautious. She's fishing for information, but I can tell she has her own ideas about me.

"Yes, I do. Your father passed away, but what about your mom? Or do you have any siblings, cousins, anyone at all?"

My gaze remains steady and calm while I consider what to share. "Why're you so interested?"

"Beyond emergencies, you mean?" Her eye roll may have been visible from the moon. "How about fairness? We've spent a lot of time together, yet you remain a stranger. I've revealed everything from my humiliating situation with Rob to details about my parents and my home. You've given back nothing. It's not really how friendship works, one-sided like this. I deserve to know something about your family, about who you are."

Her demands and requirements of "friendship" tarnish all the heady feelings I've been soaking up this morning. No one knows anything about my family, such as it is. Lindsey thinks she wants to know me, but will learning the truth about Pop and Mama change the way she looks at me?

"Is that what we have, Lindsey—friendship?" I notice her flinch. "I recall telling you I don't really do friendship." *But I might, for you.*

"True, but in our case, you can't avoid it." Lindsey's head droops. A dejected, distant look clouds her eyes. "Anyway, why do you prefer such distance? I understand shying away from serious romantic relationships, but *no* close friends? Why?"

"It's the way I've always been. I didn't grow up in a neighborhood, going to a regular school. We moved a lot." I sigh. "When you grow up like me, it's easier not to get attached to anyone or any place. After years of conditioning, it's simply who I am."

"Why'd you move around so much that you couldn't enroll in school? Did your dad have some crazy sales job or something?" Her dubious expression suggests I can't skirt the truth.

"Or something. My pop wasn't a good man, at least not by most people's standards." Lindsey's eyes pop open a bit, but she waits for me to say more. She's learning to keep quiet. "Jesus, Lindsey. You want all the gory details?"

"Well, not if he killed someone or something. Don't tell me that!"

Now I'm stunned. Murder?

"Hell no! My pop didn't kill anyone." I feel my eyebrows skimming my hairline. "Boy, you set a low bar."

"No. *You* set my low expectation with your cryptic commentary." A single brow arches above her pretty eyes. "So, why do you think he wasn't a good man?"

My eyelid twitches, so I twist my neck around to relax. My past isn't something I'm comfortable sharing, but her wild ideas are even worse than the truth.

"I owe you for all you've done for me, but this is the only time I'll talk about it. I don't want you bringing it up again. Deal?"

"Deal." She sits back, bracing herself.

I push the smoothie aside. A minute or two passes while I consider where to begin.

"My pop conned people for a living. He'd use a false name, approach people with phony investment schemes, then take their money and run. By the time I turned twelve, I couldn't enroll in school because we were moving from town to town every several weeks or months. That, plus Pop didn't want any records to be traced back to him or his real name. So when I wasn't playing cards, I hid out in local libraries reading about whatever interested me, or what I figured I needed to learn to have a different life."

Surprisingly, Lindsey's unresponsive to my news. It's very unusual for her to conceal her emotions. Maybe she's trying to be reassuring. Warily, I continue.

"My whole world revolved around Pop. I didn't understand much about his 'profession' until I was a teenager. But even when I learned the truth, I didn't turn him in, because I couldn't send my only family to jail. So I bided my time until my eighteenth birthday and then I took off. I've lived on my own since then."

For an instant, I'm faintly relieved at having told someone the truth. Then panic strikes as I worry about how Lindsey will view my past. Fortunately, she appears sympathetic instead of disapproving.

"You must've been very lonely." She pauses, as if she's afraid to continue. "It makes your accomplishments that much more impressive."

Her lack of judgment relaxes me until she continues with the questions.

"That's another thing—how did you acquire so much without any formal education? Surely you didn't bartend your way into so much money." She winks, and the reminder of our first encounter coaxes a smile from me.

"Actually, I sorta did. Right after we met, I moved to Vegas, where I spent several years bartending at nightclubs and playing in poker tournaments in my free time. I lived in a dump and saved almost everything I made. After reading a dozen books about stock trading, I gave it a shot. Got real lucky with a few risky investments during the recession, and now here I am. Actually, most people probably don't realize the parallels between poker and investing."

"That's incredible. You must've been extremely disciplined. Come to think of it, you still are pretty disciplined." She grins, then her brows crease. She's looking at everything except for me. "So, where was your mother all this time? Did she die when you were young?"

"She's dead to me." My jaw tics.

"Again, cryptic."

"It really doesn't matter much why she's not in my life. It is what it is."

"So she's not dead."

I bury my head back into my pillow and squeeze my eyes closed, heaving an exasperated sigh.

"No, she's not dead. I haven't seen her since I turned nine. I don't care for her and she sure don't care about me." Shit. The grammar again. I open one eye and peer at Lindsey.

Oddly, she seems unsurprised by my admission. How's that possible? Maybe she's too stunned to react to everything she just learned. She picks imaginary lint off my blanket while she considers her next question.

"So, you push everyone away because you're afraid they'll leave like she did?" Lindsey's searching for a way in, but I can't let her in any deeper. I'm already in tricky territory with her.

"Don't play shrink with me. I *choose* how to live my life. That's how I want things. I keep friendly acquaintances with folks around town, but I don't get overly involved. It works for me. I'm not lonely. Unlike you, I don't suffer any heartbreak."

She leans close to me, speaking quietly. "You only think it works because you focus on the potential for pain at the expense of all the pleasure. Yes, I've been hurt by people, but I've also experienced the highs of loving and of being loved. It's a gift to be connected to something bigger than myself."

Failing to tamp down my own bewildered annoyance, I sneer. "Goody for you, but I'm not interested in being someone different. Don't try to change me."

With my final remark, her eyes dim. All of the light from inside snuffs out. She shrugs, causing a shudder to travel through me.

"Okay." She sighs and drops her head.

"Okay? So, the inquisition's over?" I reach for her hand. "You won't keep at me to open up and make friends with people?"

She views me, affectless.

"No. I hear you. No friends. No family. You want to be left alone." She removes her hand from mine and stands.

Something opens up and shifts between us. I don't like it. Nausea brews, and not as a result of my infection. In a split second, all of her affection vanished.

"Well, thanks for your honesty, Levi." She walks to the edge of the bed. "I should be off. You're not supposed to have lengthy visits with anyone. When's the surgery? I'll be here before and wait until I know you're all right."

Her tone's even and controlled. I prefer the domineering, cheerful Lindsey to this version, but the fact that I care at all alarms me. I've become too fond of her, and I feel her pulling away now that I've disclosed nearly everything. Knowing this can only end badly for me, I need to disengage before I risk any more of myself.

"Thanks, but you've devoted too much time to me and my problems. If I recall, you have your own issues to sort out."

Lindsey inhales a long, deep breath, glancing off and up toward the ceiling. When she looks at me again, her eyes are glistening.

"Get well soon, Levi. I'll see you . . . later."

She grabs her purse and dashes out the door before I can respond.

Suddenly, my chest is crushed by doubt. Did I just adhere to a valid stop-loss policy, or did I fold while holding a royal flush?

~

Lindsey

The nurse informs me Levi's surgery is scheduled very early tomorrow morning. He doesn't want me there. He doesn't want to be my friend. He doesn't want anything from me at all.

If I recall, you have your own issues to sort out. Yes. Yes, I do. I've spent the past several weeks pretending I'm on some kind of vacation. But it's not a vacation—it's my frickin' life. I'm no closer to making a decision about Rob, or anything else, than I was the day I left New York.

I arrive home flustered and antsy, but eager to take one step. Determined to do *something*, I call Rob at his office.

"Robert Whitmore."

"Hi, Rob, it's me." I hear a whoosh of air.

"Lindsey, what's wrong? What happened?"

"Nothing happened. Why?"

"I didn't expect to hear from you, so I assumed something happened."

I wince. Something did happen, just not the way he suspects. "I've been considering our last conversation. Part of me wants to pretend these past few weeks never happened, but every time I think I might be able to, I can't. I'm afraid. And I really hate you working with Ava. I'm sure she's told others in your office about her conquest. How can I face them? How can you?"

Ignoring my questions, he replies, "Come home. Come home and I'll rebuild your trust."

It's so tempting. He still loves me, but is it enough? What does his love mean? What do I need for myself and from him? And what about these feelings for Levi I'm repressing?

"Rob, why do you love me?"

"What?"

"Why do you love me?"

"Because you're you. You're beautiful and warm, we're compatible, you understand the demands of my career, and we want the same things."

"Do we?"

"Do we what?"

"Want the same things? I don't like how your job always comes first, for instance. I doubt I'd be happy living with your seventy-five-hour workweeks for the next thirty years."

"Who says I'll work here for thirty years? I'll be able to retire by forty if I want to, Lindsey."

"That's still more than a decade away, and you'd never retire so young. It's not in your nature."

"So, now this isn't only about my infidelity. Now my ambition's a problem? What else suddenly doesn't work for you?"

I can almost hear his jaw clench through the phone.

"I'm just reconsidering what being partners who can love and support each another for life really means. Trust is the cornerstone, but there are other things, too. Things I can't quite articulate."

I hear Rob's exasperated exhale. "How can I say this politely? You've been in LA for a month and you're already sounding very 'granola.' Have you been pretending to be happy with me all these years?"

"No, I was happy." I frown. "I thought I was happy. You're an amazing, talented, and persuasive man. But something's changed. Instead of worrying about pleasing everyone else, I'm thinking of my own needs. Maybe I'm not good for you, or anyone, until I figure out who I am and what makes me tick."

"I'm trying to be patient, but you're making it difficult. Why do you have to be in California to *find yourself*?" Rob's sarcasm bursts through his final words, which irritates me. "Can't you do it here in New York?"

"In New York, you and my parents constantly tell me what to think. You shape my responses. The geography's a buffer."

"I've never tried to control you. Don't lump me with Helene and Bill. That's not fair."

"Sorry, you're right. But I anticipate your expectations and conform my behavior to meet them."

"Then be honest with me, but don't run away and break everything apart."

"I need this time and distance."

"So we're back to square one. What else can I say that I haven't already said?"

"Nothing. I only wanted to hear your voice and let you know what's in my head." I bite my lower lip. "That's all."

He huffs. "Do you feel better now, or worse?"

"Better."

"Okay. Well, I don't, but I'll deal with it. I guess I don't have a choice." His resignation is apparent.

"Thanks for trying to understand. It means a lot, Rob. Really."

"What I understand is you're pulling away from everything you are and unilaterally changing us. I don't like it, but again, what can I do? I thought you left because of Ava, but obviously your doubts extend beyond her. Maybe it's you who doesn't love me."

Astonished, I blurt, "I do love you. But maybe love's not the only issue."

"You know what? That's enough. This conversation's going nowhere and it's pissing me off. We shouldn't talk again unless you decide to come home before I choose to move on. Until then, we'll each muddle through on our own."

His parting threat deepens the crack between us, creating a sinkhole. I realize he may well move on before I've reconciled my own feelings. But I suppose it's basically what I've done to him already. It'd be selfish to restrict his freedom after I've moved across the country. If we can't wait it out a few months, we really weren't meant to be together.

"I'm sorry I've hurt you, Rob. Despite everything, you hold a big part of my heart in your hands."

I hang up before he replies or I burst into tears. I sink back into my chair. Some of the tension I'd been carrying around these past two days dissipates. At least now Rob knows what I'm thinking, even if he mocked me. Of course, I concealed my growing attraction to Levi. The hypocrisy of my situation slowly tightens like a noose wrapped around my neck.

If Rob and Levi didn't exist, what would I be doing? What would I want to accomplish? Honestly, I always have been happiest when helping others. Maybe that's where I start; maybe my purpose is service. But what kind of service?

Do I want to reinvest the time and money to reeducate myself as a doctor, nurse, or therapist so I can help people battling illness or an emotional crisis? What if I undertake that commitment and end up hating the actual job?

Perhaps I can volunteer at a hospital or shelter for abused women or some other organization, and figure out if I've got the skills to assist people with serious problems. After all, the only volunteering I've done has involved working on fund-raising committees for my school's endowment fund and a local museum. Not exactly tough stuff.

This endless cycle of thoughts exhausts me, so I climb into bed early and pass out.

～

I forgo my morning run when I finally awaken. It's already eight o'clock. Levi's been wheeled into surgery by now, while I lie snuggled under my fluffy down blanket. I know he's terrified, yet I'm intentionally staying away. I feel like a brat for punishing him just because he hurt my feelings. His lashing out probably had more to do with my prying than with our relationship.

He'd bravely peeled back his carefully constructed mask for me, exposing the most painful, disgraceful truths of his life. I'd been so intent on finding answers, I failed to consider how dredging up those old injuries might affect him. Now, in his moment of need, I've let my pride supersede decency.

I've essentially proven to him, once again, he can't rely on anyone. Worse, he probably thinks I've abandoned him because of what he shared. I left him sitting alone all night, worried about paralysis. Remorse pricks my heart.

I need to go to him today, if only to show not everyone will desert him. I'll adjust my expectations of our friendship, but I won't withdraw it completely.

~

When I'm descending Levi's stairs with his mail in hand, Elena spots me. Oh, great.

"Lindsey, didn't expect to catch you on a morning walk of shame." Her jovial tone fails to screen the resentful shimmer in her eyes.

"Oh, no, Elena. He isn't home. I'm just picking up his mail for him." I hold up the envelopes as proof. "He's in the hospital."

Elena cocks her head. "What happened?"

He'll probably be livid with me for disclosing personal information, but to hell with him and his artificial walls.

"A few weeks ago he fell victim to a hit and run, resulting in emergency spinal surgery. He's in surgery again for a blood infection, but hopefully everything will turn out fine."

"Santa Monica Trauma?" Elena asks.

"Yes." I see the wheels turning behind her eyes as she plans the next move in her imaginary contest for Levi's affection. Jealousy pierces me when I picture her comforting him in my stead. "Elena, if you go visit him, don't expect a cheerful greeting. The surgery's very painful."

"Obviously you braved it. I've known him longer than you anyway." Her posture issues her challenge. "I'm as willing as you are to lend a helping hand."

I don't need to get in a turf war. "I'm sure he'll appreciate it."

Elena nods and marches home.

I decide to be productive until I'm sure Levi's out of the recovery room. Revisiting the idea of charity work, I research organizations focused on supporting the needs of children. Within seconds I have a list of sites to research. Google rocks.

After reading through several, I discover Child Advocacy Association, a national nonprofit organization that provides adult liaisons and advocates for children subjected to court proceedings involving abusive or neglectful parents. According to the website, volunteers don't need a legal or counseling background. The organization provides intense training to potential advocates, in addition to recommending dozens of books on topics from child abuse and cultural competency to diversity and advocacy skill building.

Speaking up on behalf of defenseless children would be extremely rewarding and life changing—for them and me. Imagine the lifelong bonds that develop throughout the process. It sounds like a perfect fit, assuming I pass the training and qualify to become an advocate.

Perhaps if I do this, I can freelance write on the side to promote the agency and its cause. Maybe I can even journal my experience and write a book about it one day, which could extend the reach of my assistance by raising awareness.

I get lost in my excitement, spending the next few hours reading more material and outlining a plan.

CHAPTER ELEVEN

Levi

The chirping alarm of some hospital equipment in the hall right outside my room makes me want to kill someone. I glance at the wall clock. Three fifteen p.m. I've slept for almost four hours. This surgery went a little quicker since there weren't other emergency conditions involved. I'm relieved it's over.

My fingers and toes are all in working order. This time I knew to expect the general lethargy in the recovery room, so I didn't panic. And the upside of my staph infection is getting a private room. Now I just wish Lindsey would show up.

She ignored me last night and didn't wish me luck this morning. I didn't expect her to show up at six this morning, but she didn't even call. It's not her fault. I drove a wedge between us yesterday, but then immediately regretted my remarks.

I think I've pretty much severed whatever bond we'd begun to share. Reestablishing boundaries and retreating into my safe zone ought to make me ecstatic. Instead, I feel cold through to my bones, like I'm walking through sleet.

Damn if she didn't tunnel her way through my barriers. I admit, she introduced a sorely needed lightheartedness to my world. Now I'll miss her. I don't know what to do with that feeling.

I could call her, but in the end it'd only postpone the inevitable hell I'll suffer when she runs back to New York. This kind of torment is why I've shunned relationships. Dependence or dejection—the only certain outcomes of intimacy. Neither seems a great prize.

Of course, she might not return to New York, at least not for a while. Visions of her smile and teasing glances taunt me, urging me to reach out. Well, I can't do it without knowing what exactly I'm reaching for. Her friendly company, or more?

I think these drugs are making me crazy. Or perhaps my near brushes with death this month have me reevaluating Pop's edicts against love.

I hear a knock at my door before someone enters. My body breaks out in goose bumps, assuming it's Lindsey.

"Hey there, Levi." Elena sashays into my room, as only she can. "It's me, Elena."

Good Lord, the woman even figured out how to fashion a hospital gown to show off her curves. What's she doing here anyway?

"What a surprise." Raising the bed into a sitting position, I proceed with caution, hoping to strike a balance between being too aloof and encouraging additional visits. Her company is all right, but she's too eager to build something between us that will never exist.

"Yes, imagine *my* surprise when I ran into Lindsey on the beach this morning and heard what happened. It's terrible. If I'd known sooner, I'd have offered to help. But now I know, so you can count on me."

The surgical mask obscures most of her face, but her eyes sparkle with hope and hunger. Pulling a chair right beside my bed, she sits down, pats my thigh, and then leaves her hand resting there. Restraining the urge to swat it away, I hope she'll eventually take the hint from my lack of response.

"That's real sweet, but I'm doin' all right. Lindsey's been helping, so I'm covered." A numbing sensation cinches my heart when I consider perhaps Lindsey won't be assisting me anymore.

Elena's not yet deterred, but her suddenly straightened posture indicates a temporary concession. Finally, she withdraws her hand from my leg.

"Okay, but I can still stop in and visit. Must get dreadfully dull, staying in bed all day. Or not?" She's teasing, but with genuine intent.

I ignore the flirtation. "It's boring. I miss the ocean."

"If it's any consolation, I haven't noticed many surfers out lately. Hasn't been great."

Elena spends the following thirty minutes chattering on about our neighborhood, a party she attended, and her love life—or lack thereof. I smile, but my mind drifts in and out of the conversation. Each time I hear footsteps outside my door, I hope it's Lindsey. My insides crumble as I realize she's not going to surface. Fortunately, Elena's so busy reciting her litany, she doesn't notice. Guess she's used to my quietude.

Then, at four thirty, Lindsey materializes. I inhale sharply when she enters the room. Reflexively, I reach for her, but then drop my hand to my side to conceal my reaction.

She greets Elena. Her eyes dart around the room without meeting mine. I guess she's unwilling to trust me after yesterday's discussion. I need to fix this situation because I dislike her distant conduct. Unfortunately, my mouth went dry the instant she appeared. Despite my every effort to remain detached, I've failed. Damn it to hell, I'm unable to manage my feelings.

"Hi, Levi. I brought you some dinner." Lindsey sets a container of soup on my tray. Its sweet aroma reveals it to be my favorite, butternut squash soup. "Did everything go all right? No more setbacks?"

Her worry gives rise to hope that lifts my spirit. But like a soap bubble floating upward, it's in constant jeopardy of bursting.

"No setbacks." My eyes move from her to Elena and back before I shoot one brow upward.

Lindsey's guarded, but addresses Elena. "Sorry to intrude on your visit."

Since Elena's occupying the only chair, Lindsey leans against the window ledge.

Thankfully, Elena isn't one to share the spotlight and chooses to leave. After slobbering over me with a grand good-bye kiss on the forehead, she tosses us her signature mini-wave and struts from the room. Once she's gone, Lindsey holds her finger to her lips to shush me while she closes the door.

Her odd behavior makes me smile. "Why'd you close my door?"

She frowns and sighs, tossing her hand to the side with her palm facing upward. "I'm preparing for you to unleash your wrath and prefer not to have everyone in the hall overhear us." Her hand then finds its favorite resting spot—her hip.

"My wrath? Huh." I grin. "About Elena's surprise visit, you mean?"

"Yes." She studies me. "Why don't you like her, Levi? Did you two have a romantic falling-out or something?"

Possessive curiosity. That thrills me almost as much as her feigned indifference. "No. I like her fine, just not the way she wants. I try not to give her false hope, that's all."

"Oh. Well, that's considerate." Lindsey's eyes register relief. "She ran into me when I was getting your mail early this morning—by the way, here it is." She tosses it on the tray. "Anyway, she accused me of slinking away on a 'walk of shame,' so I had to tell her the truth. Sorry."

"Okay."

Her brows climb up her forehead. "Really? No lectures, no admonishments, no more 'I just don't like people' speeches?"

Yep, my remarks yesterday upset her, as I'd guessed. Now she's keeping her distance, doubting me. Strategically, I know the only way to win this hand is to swallow my pride. "You didn't come back last night or this morning." I edge toward the abyss of exposing vulnerability. "I worried you might not be back again."

She presses her hand against her heart and bats her lashes with mock flirtation. "Did you miss me?"

"Yes." I keep my eyes focused on reading her.

"Oh." Her eyes widen. She stops playing and starts fidgeting. "Sorry. I thought you wanted some space."

Her gaze flickers. The air between us grows thick with unspoken sentiment. I'm close to yanking her back, so I push it a step further.

"So did I." I resolutely hold her stare. "But I was wrong."

Jesus, the urge to spring from bed and kiss her overwhelms me. Damn it. Worse, my powers of observation fail me. I can't tell if she's feeling any of the same yearning. My weakness for her clouds my senses.

"Levi, I'm not your mother. I won't turn and run when you least expect it."

As soon as the words leave her mouth, her hand flies upward to cover it.

The priceless expression on her face makes me snort. "It's okay. I'm not offended. In fact, I owe you an apology. Yesterday's discussion unearthed a lot of issues I keep buried, for obvious reasons. I never meant to suggest I don't consider you a friend, Lindsey."

My honesty's rewarded with her twinkling eyes. I'm quite sure she's smiling underneath that face mask. I wish I could see it.

"I don't know what to say. I'm proud of you for trying, Levi. I promise, you won't be sorry."

"We'll see," I tease. Now that the world doesn't feel so tilted, I can breathe easily. "Thanks for the food, by the way, and the mail. Mind if I eat?"

"Sure, but let me warm it in the nurses' microwave. I'm sure it's too cool now."

She jumps up with the container and leaves the room. When she returns, she demands an update on the infection and surgery. She appears to relax upon hearing my relatively good news.

"I should be sprung in three more days." I look at the IV bag. "But I'm gonna be on these antibiotics for a long time."

"This time you're staying at my house and we're renting a hospital bed." Her expression warns me not to speak. "No more taking chances. I'll be keeping a closer watch from now on."

Considering the miserable sixteen hours I've spent wondering if she'd be returning, I agree. I won't risk pushing her away again.

Plus, I'm curious to see the inside of her house. I know it's a rental, but I suspect she's particular and took her time to pick something she'd feel at home in, even temporarily. It'll be interesting to live with someone for a while. Ironically, I haven't had a roommate since Dan, in Florida.

≈

Lindsey

Elena visited Levi twice during his stay at the hospital. Her obvious lust only pushes him further away. I'm tempted to tell her the truth, but he'd probably kill me. No doubt she'll be stopping by once he's settled in my house.

He'll be wearing a PICC line to administer intravenous antibiotics during the next several weeks, so he's hiring a nurse to check him twice a week. Thank God. A trained set of eyes will recognize the signs of infection better than mine would.

The hospital bed arrived yesterday. It's set up in the living room by the sliding doors to provide Levi a nice view of the ocean, and easy access to a bathroom and the kitchen.

Under other circumstances, I'd be perfectly comfortable moving him in during his recovery. However, I haven't confessed the truth about my new roommate to my parents. I hate lying to them but don't want to go to war over it, either. I guess I'm a coward, or maybe simply pragmatic. I'm a grown-up and am entitled to some privacy anyway, right?

On the ride home from the hospital, I thank God the doctors were able to control the infection. Levi's still weakened, but his color's better, and the rash and fever have receded. When we arrive at my house, he postpones the tour and crawls directly into the bed.

Once he's comfortably stretched out, he scans the living room and grins. "It's cheerful in here, Lindsey. Suits you."

"When I saw it online, it looked perfect." I survey the living room in affirmation. "I really love it."

"Thanks for sharing your space with me. I know it's an imposition."

"It's fine. Of course, if you don't cooperate, then I'll ship you off to Elena's!" I laugh but am inwardly ashamed for picking on her. She's a lonesome woman, like me, trying to improve her life.

"She's persistent, that's for sure." He shakes his head wearily. "Not sure how to deal with her."

"Well, if you can't be honest, then tell her you have a girlfriend. That should stop her from hoping."

"She's never seen me with anyone more than once, not ever." He stares out the window, considering my idea. "I reckon she'd know it's a lie."

"Tell her it's me." As the words pass over my lips, my body temperature spikes. What the hell am I thinking? In a second moment of stupidity, I plunge further, hoping to make light of it all. "She'll believe it; she suspects it anyhow. I'll play along. But make sure she knows she's welcome to visit and be your *friend*."

A seductive smile plays on his lips. "How far are you willing to play along?"

His grin and flirtatious invitation make me tingly all over. Having him live here might be more than I can take. Is he teasing or testing the waters? Which do I want to be true? I can't decide, but one good turn deserves another. I'll not be the only one dancing on a hot tin roof.

"Well, I guess you'll have to wait and see," I pose coyly, then head for the hills. "You rest now. I'll run out to pick up some things from the store. Be back in an hour." I snatch the keys from the counter and bolt from the room before he notices the color in my cheeks.

~

I return to find Elena helping Levi into my living room from the deck. Apparently he's unwilling to follow simple instructions and lie still. She's holding one of his arms while he shuffles across the floor. I drop the bags on the counter and rush to his other side.

I snake my arm around his waist, careful not to bump his PICC line or touch his stitches. He rests his arm on my shoulder and bends his head down to bestow a gentle, warm kiss on my mouth. His lips linger long enough to make it seem real. A surge of heat rushes through my entire body. Oh, God, I'm in trouble. Although I suggested this ploy, my fingers involuntarily touch my lips in surprise. Our eyes lock in a mystified daze until Levi breaks it by winking.

"Glad you're home, sweetheart." This is the second time he's used that term with me this month, and once again, it disorients me.

Elena's eyes pop open and slide back and forth between us. I fumble to help him into bed and avoid her gaze. My insides have turned to jelly. Willing myself to regain control, I plant my fists on my hips and nag Levi.

"Are you really glad I'm home? Even though I'm about to lecture you about pushing too hard, too fast?" I roll my eyes and glance at Elena, hoping to be convincing. "Thanks for helping him, Elena. Can I get either of you something to drink?"

I hurry to the kitchen to unpack the bags. Gosh, I always speak staccato when I'm out of sorts. His tender kiss left me wanting more.

Shoot. I take two deep breaths and finish putting the groceries away. From the kitchen, I hear Elena speak.

"Well, I didn't realize you two had become so close."

I strain to listen to their conversation without getting caught eavesdropping.

"It kinda snuck up on us." He pauses. I can't see what he's doing, but then I hear him again. "We'd actually met in Florida years ago. When she moved in next door, we reconnected."

Alluding to our former acquaintance was a persuasive maneuver. Thinking back on that day so long ago, I can hardly believe where we are today.

"How amazing." Elena's voice sounds as uncomfortable as I feel. "Guess you can't interfere with fate, can you?"

When I reenter the room, Levi motions for me to sit beside him, so I comply. He wraps one arm around my waist and holds my hand in his own, his thumb mindlessly tracing circles in my palm again. I act nonchalant, but his caress is melting my spine. In my head I'm chanting, *This is fake, this is fake*, although I'd easily stay snuggled up with him for a while. The desire unsettles me, even as I fight against my body's response to his touch.

Elena lasts fifteen more minutes before "remembering" errands she needs to run, then politely excuses herself.

"Lindsey, you're a genius. That worked like a charm. She didn't touch me once after I kissed you." He's holding my hand and smiling like a kid at Christmas. "She's never kept her hands to herself before."

Who'd imagine he'd struggle to address something so simple with a woman? He's practically adolescent when it comes to genuine interpersonal skills, which makes sense considering he's had little to no experience with real relationships.

The intimacy of sitting on this bed with him arouses me, heating my body from head to toe. I withdraw my hand and climb off of his bed before I straddle his lap and attack him. Another quick trip to the kitchen's my only means of escape. I've never been so ruled by my hormones before. I don't like it. . . . Well, maybe I like it a little.

I need to take my mind off sex. Food's always been a good substitute. I pop back into the living room to ask if Levi wants something to eat.

"Sure. I'll take whatever's easiest." He smiles as if nothing unusual transpired. How dare he be so unaffected by our counterfeit affection. It'll be a long couple of weeks for me if I have to play that role very often.

"I have more squash soup. How about that?"

"Thanks." He opens a book and begins reading.

While I'm reheating the soup, Jill calls. I realize I haven't mentioned moving Levi into my house to her, either. After our last discussion, I've avoided further interrogation about my relationship with him.

"Hey, Jill." I force a casual tone. "What's up?"

"Just checking in. Are you still a wreck?"

"Oh, no. I'm better. Levi survived the infection and second surgery. He's home now." *Home.*

"So you're back to being a private nurse?" Jill's snide tone catches me off guard. "I thought you had bigger goals in mind when you took off for Malibu."

Did she really just judge me?

"Actually, I do. I've been looking into some nonprofit organizations and am considering becoming an advocate for abused and neglected kids. If I get through the training and enjoy the work, maybe I'll start my own little foundation one day with some of my trust fund money."

A beat of stunned silence passes before Jill speaks. "What brought this on? I never knew you had such a social conscience." She's upset with me, but I'm not sure why. In any case, I refuse to succumb to her taunts.

"I guess I should credit Levi, and you. He told me to stop whining, figure out what makes me happy, and then follow my heart. As you've always lamented, I'm happiest when I'm helping people who can't help themselves. So, I combined those ideas and am a little excited about the possibility of a totally new direction. I think it could even inspire me to write a book about the experience or the plight of so many children." I'm smiling to myself, but Jill's lack of support saps some of my enthusiasm. "Nothing is set in stone, but the idea of making a real difference in someone's life is very tempting. Novel, even."

"So, will you be doing this in California or New York?" Ah, now I understand her displeasure. She'd never admit it, but she misses me.

"I signed a six-month lease here back in May, but I guess it depends."

"Depends on what?"

"On lots of things. I kind of like being away from home. My mom can't pry or judge as easily with so much distance between us. The privacy lets me make my own decisions. Eventually I won't need the crutch, but for now it works."

"What about Rob?"

I groan at the memory of my last conversation with him. "Rob and I spoke earlier this week. It didn't go well. Now that I'm away from him, I'm spotting other problems with our relationship."

"Really? Like what—your hot neighbor?"

Jill's retort is a little too close for comfort, but still, on the heels of her other sarcastic remarks, this one makes me pissed. Why should I have to defend my love life to her, or anyone?

"No, Jill. Maybe I don't want to be a Goldman widow for the next ten or fifteen years. It could be lonely being married to someone you see only one or two hours on any given day. Also, despite what he says now, Rob wants me to be the supportive, doting wife. He's always expected me to be available on his schedule. To make his priorities *my* priorities. I'm not sure that's enough for me now—and if that's true, Rob and I wouldn't fit together in the long run."

I pause to fix a tray with Levi's lunch. "I don't know; it's hard to explain. I'm having second thoughts about everything. When I shared these concerns, he basically told me not to call him again unless I planned to come back. He also made it pretty clear he's thinking of moving on. I hurt him. He hurt me. It's not great."

While on the phone, Jill overhears Levi thanking me for delivering his lunch.

"Who's with you?" Her voice abruptly turns playful. "Is that Levi?"

"Yes, I'm fixing him lunch."

"Guess you didn't mention him to Rob, did you?" Her brash, sometimes intimidating manner prevents her from making a lot of female friends. I guess I'm able to tolerate it better than most because she reminds me of my mom. Both of them mean well, even when they're obnoxiously overbearing.

"No. Why have him jump to mistaken conclusions?"

"'Mistaken,' huh? Yeah." Jill lets her opinion hang suspended between us. The only thing keeping me from snapping back is two decades of her loyalty and friendship. Deep down—way deep down—I know she loves me.

"I want to see this guy who's stealing you from us," she demands. Before I can protest her ridiculous conclusion, she continues, "Take his picture and e-mail it to me right now."

"No! How embarrassing. Besides, he's eating lunch."

My remark piques Levi's interest, so he interrupts. "What's embarrassing?"

Horrified, I roll my eyes. "My friend wants to see you, so she asked me to snap a photo and send it to her."

His wicked smile suggests he's amused by the idea. "Hand me the phone."

He laughs at my stricken expression, but I comply.

"Hi, Jill. Before I send my picture, I need to know what I'm going to get in return." Silence, but he's smirking . . . like he's having fun. "Okay, fair enough." More silence is followed by a conspiratorial smile that spreads across Levi's face. "Hope you're not displeased, ma'am. Have a nice day."

Levi hands the phone back to me so I can take the photo. I mouth the words "What did she say?" He only grins.

"Jill, I'll call you back after I've taken the photo." I hang up annoyed, but snap a shot, check it—God, he's photogenic—and e-mail it to Jill before hitting redial. "Okay, Jill. Check your in-box."

"Lindsey, if he looks half as amazing as he sounds, I know you're never coming back to New York." I practically hear Jill's heart fluttering over the phone.

"I'm not so superficial." I frown.

"You know what I mean. Wait, here's your e-mail. Oh my God! You were *not* exaggerating." She pauses, then, as if musing aloud, says, "Maybe I'll visit before you do decide to hook up with him. I've always been available for a little no-strings fun, unlike you."

"You're welcome any time, friend." I play along despite every muscle in my body tensing. "Talk later."

The thought of Levi sleeping with Jill makes me physically ill. Of course, I've no right to stop them.

Levi holds his arm out, motioning for my phone with his hand. "Okay, show me Jill."

I'm shocked by his interest in this very girly exchange. Rob would never find it fun. I sit on the edge of his bed and scroll through the photos, searching for a flattering picture of Jill. I find one taken on my dad's boat. Her skin is bronzed, her blonde hair lightened by the summer sun, her deep-blue eyes dazzling, and her long, lithe body proudly displayed in a tiny bikini.

"That's her. All the boys love Jill. She was homecoming queen at our school. She's really pretty. Maybe you'll meet her someday, if she visits. She works for a hedge fund. You guys would probably have a lot to talk about, actually." Heaviness sits in my chest at the image of Levi and Jill cozied up, trading sexual innuendos while discussing investment strategies.

"She's okay. Not as pretty as you. Blondes all look the same. I'm sick of Barbie dolls." He promptly returns his attention to lunch after making his matter-of-fact pronouncement.

I roll my eyes, disbelieving the compliment, and the fact that Levi isn't attracted to Barbie dolls and Jill. Every man's attracted to them—women, too. Levi smiles at me and continues eating his soup.

I study the photograph and am hit with a pang of nostalgia for the lazy days spent on Long Island Sound. My dad is at his best on his boat—friendly, energetic, and engaged. A consummate host, stocking the galley with beverages, crudités, and the best cold fillet and horseradish sandwich bites available.

The few times I've spoken to him this month, he's been reserved. Unlike Mom, Dad doesn't browbeat, but his gentle admonishment is apparent from passive-aggressive lines like, "I'm sure you aren't simply spending time and money indulging your whims" or "You're probably overwhelmed with contacting agents and editors in Los Angeles."

"Where'd you go, Lindsey?" Levi's voice breaks my trance.

"Nowhere. Just thinking about this photo, my dad's boat . . . good times."

"Thinking you'd rather be there than here?" He speaks with cool detachment, but it's a loaded question.

Against every instinct, he's trusting in our fledging friendship. I'm sure he's wondering if I'm ready to ditch California to run home. Sadly, I don't have an adequate answer.

"I miss home, my friends, and, well, other stuff. But I have freedom here I don't enjoy there. I'm not willing to give it up yet." I glance out the window toward the sea. "I'll stay here for the rest of my lease term and complete the volunteer training. It's a national organization, so I don't need to make any decisions yet. One step at a time. Who knows where I'll ultimately end up?"

I make light of my situation, hoping to avoid a serious conversation.

He nonchalantly raises his brows, but his eyes veer into more distant territory. I don't want to hurt him, but I can't base my decisions on how they affect him. If I do, I'll end up in the same placating role I left behind in New York, with my parents and Rob.

As Levi says, we're all adults and need to take responsibility for the consequences of our decisions. I've been honest. It's all I can do.

CHAPTER TWELVE

July 29, 2013

Levi

I've lived with Lindsey for nearly five weeks now. Five of the most refreshing weeks of my life. Despite my back pain and inability to do much more than hang out and take short walks with her, it's been enlightening. Maybe it sounds stupid, but I'm pretty certain I know just about everything one could know about her at this point.

She chatters *a lot*, whether to me, or on the phone with friends or parents, or with the people from the nonprofit group she's getting all jazzed up about. Most of the time, she says something meaningful, but other times she's simply speaking aloud, almost narrating her actions and thoughts. It's frequent enough to make me wonder if she does it even when no one's around. When I do return home, I'm curious whether the silence will be heavenly or deafening.

She also doesn't spend much time on her clothes, makeup, or hair. Her clothes are pretty basic with hints of femininity—a ruffle here, a sequin there. I've seen her blow-dry her hair only once. She's a "girly tomboy," if there's such a thing, and it's one of my favorite things about her.

Her cooking has improved, though she still can't handle a knife well. I suspect she might end up enjoying the kitchen one day. The thought brightens me, since I introduced her to that particular pleasure.

At night, she insists on playing board games or watching reality-television competitions. She's slick with word games, like Scrabble, and often chooses better words, but I'm a more strategic player. We're both competitive, but my wins are sweeter because, unlike me, she pouts when she loses. She'd never admit it, but the fact that I can beat her Ivy League brain blows her mind.

Mostly, she's a truly jubilant person. She wakes up with a start, takes off on her run, and returns ready to go. The only time she loses steam is after her mother's calls. The damn woman destroys Lindsey's confidence with comments I never hear.

I'm aware Lindsey's not been honest about my living here. I'm not sure if she's protecting herself or her relationship with Rob, but it bothers me either way. I've no right to be upset, but it's the truth.

Unfortunately, I'll probably just be here a few more days. I'm getting around better and can take the stairs more than once a day. Of course, I must look like an octogenarian—moving at a snail's pace and bracing for a shock of pain that may or may not come—but I'm mobile. The grabber helps me get my shorts on, so I've ditched the robe.

I can shower now, too, which is great. It's for the best, since her washing my hair stirs up longing I can't afford to indulge.

As if on cue, I see Lindsey through the screen door, returning from her run. She stops to water her plants before coming inside. Bathed in sunlight, her skin shimmers. The tap of her foot indicates she's listening to her pop hip-hop music, one of the few tastes in music we don't share.

"Good morning." She's smiling and sweaty. "Did I wake you?"

"No." I nod at my open laptop. "Been working."

"Oh. Hungry?"

"Not really."

"Okay. I'm going to shower. See you in a bit." She marches right past the shoes she's left by the sofa, and the empty water glass she left on the table, and bounds up the stairs and out of view. I swear, my physical restrictions are all that have kept me from organizing her things this month.

A few minutes later, I hear the water running. I'm researching a tractor supply company, but visualizing Lindsey in the shower. *Jesus, Levi, stop it.* Thankfully, she's not one to indulge in long showers, so I'm able to concentrate on my work again in a short time. When she returns, she smells like grapefruit.

Each day, the urge to touch her grows stronger, which is another reason I need to move out.

"What shall we do today?" she asks. "Hit a park? You must be growing bored of the view in here."

I'm not particularly bored of the view, considering she's often part of it, but I don't argue with her. "Sure, but not too far. I don't want back spasms later."

"Then maybe we'll only go to the grocery store or something?"

I wrinkle my nose. Normally I enjoy the grocery store, but I'd rather be outdoors. "Maybe I can manage a quick lunch outside at Duke's?" It occurs to me I haven't been back there since my accident.

"You can sit in a chair for an hour without discomfort?" Lindsey's expression is skeptical.

"I can try." I shrug. "If it starts to hurt too much, I'll get up and walk the deck."

"Okay. But first I want to read through some of this training material and read another few chapters of *Invisible Kids*." She points to the book and pile of papers from the nonprofit group. "You still have work to do, right?"

"Yes, ma'am." I smile.

Lindsey and I sit in companionable silence, reading our respective research. Although we're not talking, it's nice to work alongside her. She's excited about pursuing this child advocacy thing, although the stories and statistics in that book upset her. I can't help wonder if my own history affected her choice.

No doubt she'll be a sharp and sympathetic ally for helpless children with lousy parents, but Lindsey's sensitive heart is bound to take many beatings in the process. I'm convinced she'll become too attached to the kids, but I won't undermine her enthusiasm by voicing my concern.

∼

Late in the morning, I shut down my computer, then shower before we leave for lunch. While dressing, I hear the familiar bass beat of Lindsey's music as the floor beneath me vibrates in time with the song.

I hide so I can watch her reflection in the living room mirror without being noticed. She's cleaning the breakfast dishes while dancing and singing animatedly. She knows all the words to the B.o.B song "So Good." Although she's not a talented singer by anyone's measure, she's enthusiastic. Her spirited facial expressions charm me.

She whisks her hands above her head when she belts out the refrain. Instead of being rattled by my spying once she sees me, she encourages me to join her. I shake my head, which draws a sharp look of disapproval, then dismissal. She finishes her singing as if I weren't in the room.

She's fun to be around, and each day I sink deeper into the dangerous waters of attachment. Worse, I'm drowning willingly.

∼

The drive to Duke's is brief, so my back doesn't bother me. It's a beautiful late-July day, and luckily, we nab an outdoor table. Joe, a bartender I know from years of drinking here, stops by to ask about my recovery. I introduce him to Lindsey and he jokingly warns her of my reputation.

Shari, a leggy server with wild, dark hair and green eyes, ends up waiting on us. Shari and I slept together a few times last year. It never meant much to either of us. We get along fine now and enjoy occasional harmless flirtation. However, with Lindsey there, I minimize the coy banter.

Shari, however, treats me the same flirty way she always does. I might assume she was trying to make Lindsey jealous if I didn't know this is how she treats most of the regulars. In any case, Lindsey pretends not to care. However, she stiffens every time Shari shows up or touches me. Fortunately, my back provides a great excuse for a quick meal, so the torment doesn't last long for either of us.

∽

"So, Shari's an ex-girlfriend?" Lindsey asks once we're in her car and she can elude eye contact because she's driving.

"I told you, I don't do girlfriends. But yes, you could say we know each other, biblically speaking. Is that a problem?"

Lindsey flinches and her forehead creases. "No. I'm simply curious about the kind of girls you find appealing."

"You don't find her attractive?"

Lindsey frowns. Shari's objectively attractive and very sensual. In fact, she's the polar opposite of Lindsey's kind of beauty.

"Of course she's attractive. She's very *friendly*. Why'd you stop seeing her?"

"Our kind of relationship doesn't have any start or end. It's one of mutual convenience and pleasure."

Lindsey's eyes pop open in shock, and I chuckle at her innocence.

Her voice becomes high and strained. "So, you mean, you two still get together now and again?"

Despite knowing I've no interest in Shari, I provoke Lindsey to see her reaction. "If she and I are mutually interested at some point now or in the future, then sure."

"Are you?" She shields her emotions.

"Am I what?" I tilt one brow up, still prodding her.

"Still interested?"

"Right now? You give me too much credit. I'm still healing, darlin'." I wink, knowing I'm grating on her nerves. I don't reveal Shari and Joe are supposedly dating, from what I've heard anyway.

"Oh, so in a couple of weeks, when you're all healed, *thanks to me*, then you'll run up here to drag her to your bed." Her sarcasm doesn't cover her jealousy, and I'm having too much fun to stop nudging her. "How lovely."

"I don't have to *drag* anyone into my bed." I cock my head and stare at her. "Why're you taking this personally?"

"I'm not!" She tips her chin up. "I simply don't understand it. I've only been with two men, including Rob. Both have been during prolonged, serious relationships. I can't imagine how you bed-hop and don't care one way or the other."

I'm stunned into silence. I knew she wasn't promiscuous but didn't realize how wholesome she'd been. Now I regret my remarks. If I admit I don't care for these women, her opinion of me will plummet further. If I pretend to care more than I do, I'd be lying. After some deliberation, I step onto the tightrope.

"So, you haven't had any friends, male or female, who've slept with someone they liked but didn't love?" It's not possible. Not in today's day and age, and not in New York City.

She sighs with reluctant acknowledgement. "Actually, this is yet another thing you and Jill have in common, although I suspect she's bothered by it more than she'd ever admit." Lindsey's glowering thinking about Jill, or me, or both.

"Well, I can't speak for Jill, but I've always maintained a friendly status with women I've slept with, assuming I see them again. I told you, I don't get involved with women who want something more than what I'm offering. If Jill comes to visit, well, you'd have to advise me on how to proceed there." I'm teasing, hoping to lighten the mood. She shoots me a look that tells me I failed.

"I thought you weren't attracted to Jill." Her eyes reflect betrayal, which is oddly gratifying. Seems I might not be the only one who's wading into dangerous emotional territory.

"Not true. I said she's pretty. Just said you're prettier. But you're not in the market for a casual fling, are you?" I ask jokingly, but I mean it, too. Now I've intentionally wandered toward the end of the plank. I watch her, hoping perhaps she'll amuse me with her response, but she doesn't.

"Not now, not ever." She stares at the highway. "Let's change the subject, since we don't see eye to eye."

"Okay by me." I lay my head back against the headrest and close my eyes. This whole conversation was a major miscalculation on my part. I'm not used to being on the losing end of any game.

We enter the house in silence and I immediately slide into the hospital bed. The ride and the chair at Duke's strained my back, but I don't complain because I suspect she'd be unsympathetic in her current mood.

I don't care what Lindsey says or denies—there's a ton of sexual tension between us.

But pursuing Lindsey would mean breaking all my rules, or changing myself into something I've never been. The only viable solution is to rid myself of this longing. I suspect it'll be easier said than done as long as I'm living in this house.

∾

Lindsey

I take my mail up to my room, unable to face Levi while I'm still seeing red. No wonder he suggested lunch at Duke's. Shari draped herself all over him. How'd she know he and I weren't dating, or did she intend to sabotage our relationship . . . friendship . . . whatever? She kept touching his hair, caressing his shoulders. Ugh.

She oozed sexual confidence. More awful, she's hot in the same carnal way he's hot. Meanwhile, Levi relaxed there, basking in all of her attention. I thought he didn't have close friends. *I have plenty of friendly acquaintances.* Friendly acquaintance my ass!

I'm burning with jealousy and curiosity, but can't ask more questions without tipping him off. He's right about me taking it personally, too.

Maybe we're not dating, but we've spent so much time together. I know he's shared personal details with me he's never discussed with her, or anyone. We're not physically involved, but that's less important than our emotional attachment, isn't it? I mean, really, how could he be satisfied with a purely physical relationship now?

Of course, he can't understand me, considering his limited experience in this arena. Our different outlooks and upbringings make us utterly incompatible. I should maintain some distance. Besides, I've no business indulging my desire until I'm one hundred percent resolved about Rob.

I've been cut off from him for two-thirds of the summer and haven't spoken to him since our last call. Would he be proud of, or unimpressed by, my foray into the nonprofit world? Probably the latter since Rob's most interested in money and power.

Perhaps that's why he sought intrigue with Ava. She works at Goldman, so she must share his ambition and professional interests. Has he spent more time with her, or any other woman, this summer? Will I ever be certain, one way or the other, about the right choice where Rob's concerned?

I sit on my bed and flip through my mail. My heart skips a beat when I come across a mail pouch from Rob. The e-mails had stopped after our last argument, so this package shocks me.

I tear it open to find a card and a framed photo of the two of us taken at a party this past winter. I recognize it as the photo I used to keep in our living room beside the sofa. My fingers trace his face, and my heart aches to see how happy I looked. I lay the frame on my lap and open the card.

Dear Lindsey,

It's been a long month here in New York. I've been thinking about everything you said, and what I've done. I've stopped writing because you need space, not because I don't care. I haven't given up on us. I'm hoping this picture will remind you of all the good things we share so you don't spend all your time out there focused on the bad. Maybe if you see it every day, you won't write me off so quickly.

I miss you. I love you. I wish you'd return to me.

Love,
Rob

I wipe the tear from my cheek and pick up the photo again. He's right, it does remind me of the good times. The love. The security. The life I had in New York.

Until this summer, everything had seemed relatively easy. Black and white. Now my life is so confusing and complicated. I'm not exactly happy, but I'm not horribly depressed, either. I have one foot in the past, one in the present, and my next step is uncertain.

I lie back on my bed and set the photo on my nightstand next to one of my parents and me. Is Rob still my future? I hear Levi moving around downstairs, which reminds me of our unpleasant conversation about Shari.

Darn it, my head aches. I need a nap.

~

I wake up around four o'clock and find Levi on the deck. It occurs to me he's fairly independent at this point. He's ditched the back brace. He still needs to rest often, but with the exception of driving and lifting heavier objects, he doesn't really need my help. Any day now he'll probably move out. The realization saddens me because, for the most part, I've enjoyed his company. With that in mind, I choose to ignore our earlier discussion when I go join him on the deck.

"Hey, what's up?"

"Reading." He holds up Laura Hillenbrand's *Unbroken*. I swear, the man's rarely separated from a book.

"I've heard that's excellent."

"I just started it, literally. It's supposed to give the reader a new appreciation for life and hardship."

"I should probably read it, then."

"I'll share." He smiles, and it gives me an idea.

"Or you can read it aloud. I love being read to."

I do. My dad used to read to me, even as a teenager. It's one of the few cozy activities I remember enjoying with him.

Levi's brows twist in an unusual expression. I'm certain it's the oddest request he's ever received from any woman. He shrugs.

"Okay, but I'm starting now. I don't want to read on your sched-ule 'cause it'll never get done."

I smirk while pulling another lounge chair right beside his. I lie on my side, facing him. For the next thirty minutes, he reads aloud. The harsh afternoon sun beats down on the deck, but the ocean breezes keep us comfortable. Occasionally, a child's laugh or a dog's barking cuts through the air and interrupts Levi. Nonetheless, I'm lulled into peaceful contentedness by the cadence and tone of his oh-so-very-sexy voice.

"Are you sleeping?" He slaps the book against his thighs. "If you're sleeping, I'm gonna be mad because reading aloud slows me down considerably."

"I'm not sleeping. I'm listening with my eyes closed." I open one eye and catch him studying me with one brow raised in doubt. "I swear! I heard every word."

"Okay." He closes the book and sets it aside. "I need a break. I'm thirsty and hot. I think I should lie in bed because my back's getting sore."

Inside, I pour us each a glass of his homemade sweet tea. I'm setting up the Scrabble board by his bed when my mother calls.

"Hi, Mom." I notice a shadow cross Levi's face.

"Hi, honey. I'm calling about your birthday. Dad and I are planning to be in Los Angeles next weekend and want to take you out to celebrate."

"You and Dad will be here? I'd love to see you, but let's ignore my birthday."

"Age is only a number, dear. Of course, getting older puts a certain perspective on your future."

I draw a deep breath, bite my tongue, and let her comment pass. "So, do you and Dad want to stay here with me?" If they come here, Levi will definitely need to move back home. I grimace at the thought.

"No. We'll be staying in Beverly Hills at the Montage. Your father has a meeting to attend Friday afternoon, so we'll fly in that morning. I'm tagging along to see you. I'll have the driver bring me up to your house when we land, and we'll join your father later for dinner. Unfortunately, we need to return early Saturday morning because of obligations here Saturday night."

"Wow, that's quick." Sadly, I feel relief rather than regret. "Should I make dinner reservations, or does Dad want to pick the restaurant?"

"We'll arrange everything. Do you have any new friends you want to invite?"

Levi's pretending not to pay attention to my conversation, although I know he's able to hear it. I'm sure my mother wants to meet him, but it would be a disaster.

"No, thanks. I'll see you Friday. Thanks for making the trip, Mom."

"I'll call you when we land. Bye, honey."

I pick up the Scrabble box, hoping to avoid any mention of the call. Of course, Levi overheard the reference to my birthday.

"Your mom's coming for your birthday? When's that?"

"August tenth, but they'll be here on Friday, the ninth. An overnight visit. It's best, actually, considering how unhappy they are with me lately."

Frowning, Levi grunts. "They should be darn proud of you. You're a good girl. You're kind, smart, and solicitous as hell where they're concerned." He shakes his head. "What more do they want?"

"They are proud. They just want me to be happy." I shrug. When I see the confused look on his face, I explain, "What I mean is they're worried about me more than they're unhappy with me. I've gone off the farm, so to speak, by disobeying them, quitting my job, leaving my fiancé . . ."

"Disobeying them?" He sits upright and flings his arm toward the ceiling. "You're twenty-six years old, almost, anyway. It's your life. Why do they get any say?"

"You can't understand because you grew up differently. It's not so easy to dismiss parents when they're involved in your life." His churlish expression warns me to proceed carefully. "They've given me their time, attention, money, and love. Don't I owe them some measure of respect, loyalty, and concession in exchange? They have my best interests at heart and often give me solid advice. I've usually been happy to comply. This is the first time I've needed to seek my own answers."

"*Owe* them. See, that's one of many reasons why I've steered clear of love. People feel 'owed' and 'owned' in relationships. Love goes hand in hand with expectations, so people compromise themselves for the sake of someone else's demands, dreams, or needs."

He's staring out the window. I'm not sure if we're still talking about me, or someone else. Does he feel obligated to me because I've been helpful? Is this why he's trying to forge a friendship despite his general lack of interest in one?

"Don't worry, Levi. I'm not expecting anything from you. Everything I've done, I've done without expectation. Don't panic. You don't have to force yourself to be my friend out of some sense of duty."

Levi stares at me without responding. He conceals his emotions so well; I rarely know what he's thinking.

I begin turning over the Scrabble tiles to break the silence. Unexpectedly, he grabs my hand and laces his fingers through mine. I hold my breath, affected by the insistence of his grip.

"I know you don't expect anything from me. When I leave here, I'll never do or say anything out of a sense of obligation, okay? Whatever happens will be authentic. It's the only way I know how to be."

Oddly, his words comfort me. I envy his secure sense of self—his fierce independence. He's carved out a life on his own terms, overcome great odds, and, contrary to my earlier assumptions, has a social life, albeit a shallow one.

Once he's healed, he'll resume his normal lifestyle, Shari and all. Remembering Shari sends a little shiver through me. I jerk my hand away.

"Good to know, Levi."

CHAPTER THIRTEEN

Levi

At first, returning home felt foreign. I'd been away for almost seven weeks. Lindsey changed the sheets on my bed and cleaned the house for me. Whenever I'm convinced I've seen the limit of her generosity, she goes a step further. She's the kindest person I've ever met and I've missed her company these past two days.

In just two months, she's blown into my life and reshuffled everything. My solitude now leaves me empty instead of comforted. My house now seems cold instead of peaceful.

I've seen her a bit, only because she's still running errands for me until I'm permitted to drive. I've purposely kept her at bay. Foolishly, I thought my life would return to normal once I came home and dived into my old routines. Not happening. I've simply spent most of the past two days consumed with thoughts of her. To top it off, I'm more aware of my aches and pains without her company to distract me.

No matter how I convince myself of the benefits of my no-strings philosophy, or of us being only friends, the truth is I want her—all of her. I want her heart and soul, her warmth and compassion, and her love.

It's a startling and completely uncomfortable need, but I want her to love me. It's unfair, too, because I doubt I'm capable of giving love in return.

I'm sure my confession has Pop rolling his eyes in heaven, or hell. But I'm no fool. She deserves better than me and she knows it. Hell, considering what she's learned about my parents, my background, and my love life, she'd probably run for the hills rather than give me a chance to break her heart.

Can't say I'd blame her, either. Also, while she hasn't mentioned Rob lately, it's not over between them, in my opinion.

Her parents arrive today, sure to hound her to return home, and to him. Although I don't stand a chance against them, I've decided I can't let her take off without any fight.

This past week I purchased the first birthday gifts I've bought anyone in decades. I ordered a Wüsthof chef's knife, a paring knife, and an apron. Although these things aren't romantic, they're sentimental, considering this whole thing between us began with a cooking lesson. I expect she'll appreciate the intention.

She intimated to Jill she'd be staying through her lease term, which gives me a few months to wrest her from her past. I need to start with these gifts and get them to her before her mother arrives. I feel like a ten-year-old boy trying to impress a girl.

When did I become such a pansy? Scowling at myself, I straighten my shoulders and make my way to her house.

∼

When I arrive, I knock on the screen door's frame as a courtesy before I open the door, call out her name, and step inside. I'm greeted, however, by a glamorous older woman with a blonde bob; sharp, pale-blue eyes; and patrician features, just like her daughter's. She raises one eyebrow.

"You must be Levi." She steps forward with her hand extended. "I'm Helene, Lindsey's mother."

Her polite smile is dazzling but lacks real warmth. Her eyes fix on mine, attempting to discern my character in a few heartbeats. She's shrewd, but she doesn't scare me. I already dislike the way she condescends to Lindsey, so I'm hardly interested in impressing her. For Lindsey's sake, I'll be polite.

"Hello, ma'am. Yes, I'm Levi. Sorry to intrude." I step back. "I didn't expect you to arrive until a little later. I only stopped in to deliver something to Lindsey."

Her gaze drops to the gift box, wrapped in pink paper and ribbons, held in my left hand. "How lovely. A birthday or thank-you gift?"

"Birthday. Haven't found anything suitable to thank her for everything she's done for me, but I will."

"I'm pleased to see you're recovering. I'm sure you're enjoying your independence again."

Her phony demeanor chills the room. The pale hair and cool-blue eyes remind me of Mama. What is it about me that makes mothers' blood run so cold? Guess I'll never know unless I insist on answers from my own—which pretty much means I'll never know.

Thinking of Mama makes *my* blood run cold. Lately it seems I've been thinking about her, Pop, and the past far too often. I blame Pop's death and Lindsey's arrival for thrusting Mama to the forefront.

Helene clears her throat, awaiting a response.

"It's great to finally be feeling stronger, although I'd be lying if I didn't admit to missing Lindsey's care. It's a pleasure to meet the woman who raised such a fine, compassionate person. I suspect she learned how to tend to others by your example."

From what I know of Helene, I've just lied through my teeth. But I needed to disarm her during this parry of ours. Her authentic smile convinces me she bought my line.

Lindsey is midway down the stairs when she sees me with her mother and stops short. Her eyes initially flash with alarm, but she contains her fear and smiles.

"Levi, I didn't expect to see you today." She slowly takes the final two steps. "Is everything okay?"

"I'm fine." I raise the gift in the air, then place it on her dining table. "I came by to drop off a little birthday present. Didn't intend to interrupt your visit."

I'm used to seeing her in shorts and sneakers, or a robe, so her conservative minidress and ultrastraight hair tucked behind a headband throw me. Guess she dressed up for her mom. The short skirt practically begs me to run my hand up along the inside of her thigh . . . all the way up. Ah, hell. I've gotta get out of here.

"That's sweet, thanks. You didn't need to buy me anything." Her eyes light up with curiosity as she tries to guess what would fit inside the box. "Can I open it now?"

"No, open it later. It's only something small." I wish her mother would disappear for ten minutes, but that won't happen. "I'll leave you ladies alone and talk to you tomorrow. Enjoy your afternoon."

I turn to Helene and affect a slight bow before stepping toward the back door to make my escape. "Nice to meet you, ma'am."

"Levi, you should join us for dinner tonight." Helene's offer ambushes Lindsey and me, and I sense Lindsey's concern from across the room.

"Thank you, but no." Part of me is disappointed to miss out on an up-close look at Lindsey with her parents. Seeing them together would give me the insight I need to advance my own agenda. "I'm sure y'all prefer some private family time after these months apart."

"Nonsense. I always make it a point to know my daughter's friends. Apparently, you've become someone I should get to know." Helene's smooth, and intent on her prey. "It's unlikely I'll have another opportunity to do so anytime soon. Plus, Bill will welcome another man at the table tonight. He hates to be outnumbered."

I'm not interested in being her quarry.

"That's very kind, but Lindsey probably wants to visit with you alone."

Without even looking at her daughter, Helene waves her hand dismissively.

"We'll have alone time this afternoon. Tonight, you'll join us. I insist. We're dining at Spago at eight o'clock."

I offer Lindsey an apologetic expression before accepting the invitation. Just then, the doorbell rings, thankfully interrupting the awkward silence and tension in the room.

Lindsey leaves me with the tiger lady and goes to answer her door. She returns carrying a large vase with three dozen long-stemmed red and pink roses, which she places on the coffee table before she reads the card. Helene observes me to determine whether I sent them, which I did not. I can guess who did, and now she can, too.

"How gorgeous, dear." She clasps her hands in front of her chest. "Who sent them?"

Lindsey shifts her weight to one leg and fiddles with the card between her fingers. "Rob."

"How thoughtful, especially under the present circumstances." She gazes at me, smiling, as she hammers the wedge. "Don't you agree, Levi?"

"Hmmm." I nod and don't dare utter a negative word about the manipulative SOB. "Well, ladies, have a pleasant afternoon. I look forward to meeting Mr. Hilliard." I nod to Lindsey and take my leave.

This night promises to be exhausting. Helene's openly challenging me, knowing I can't fight back without alienating Lindsey. She used my feelings for Lindsey to lure me into her trap, proving once again my pop's wise advice about the danger of letting your emotions run amok. Damn.

I need to approach this dinner like a poker game and leave my feelings at the door. Otherwise I'm bound to blow everything.

At seven, I shower, trim my whiskers, and dress in a jacket for dinner. After considering several strategies for dealing with Lindsey's parents, I decide to be honest. Truth is, they'll never approve of me anyway. I don't share Rob's pedigree and I'm geographically undesirable, too. Ultimately, it's all up to Lindsey, so I'll place my money on her good sense and the progress she's made these past couple of months.

∼

Lindsey

My mother's machinations today set me on edge. All afternoon I sidestepped her efforts to pump me for information about Levi. She also pressured me about Rob, but I remained silent on that topic, too. Admittedly, my resolve is weakening after mere hours with her.

She can be nearly rabid about getting what she wants. Despite her overreaching, I know she loves and misses me. I'm her only child. We did everything together for years. She thinks she still knows best what I need. I can't convince her overnight of my differing opinions. But however good her intentions are toward me, I dread how she may treat Levi tonight.

He's a cool cucumber. I'm fairly certain he'll handle whatever she dishes out. I'm only sorry he's been forced into this situation. Perhaps Dad's presence will keep her from baring her fangs. My stray thoughts are interrupted by Levi's knock at the front door.

The sight of him takes my breath away. He's dressed in white linen slacks and a crisp pale-blue shirt, paired with an unstructured, navy, linen-silk blend jacket. He looks as if he stepped right out of an Armani advertisement. I almost reach out to touch his refined five o'clock shadow.

How utterly embarrassing!

"Wow, you clean up well, Levi." My pulse thunders in my ears.

"Thank you, ma'am."

His eyes graze the length of my body, which is wrapped in a flirty, brightly colored Nanette Lepore dress. I've thrown on a pair of high wedge sandals and pulled back the front of my hair to reveal gold hoop earrings.

He clears his throat. "You look beautiful."

I realize Levi's never seen me dressed up, at least not since that night on the beach years ago. His obvious approval considerably improves my mood.

On the way to the restaurant, I'm uncharacteristically quiet. I can't stop fretting about how the evening will play out. My hands grip the steering wheel until my knuckles turn white. My left knee bounces continually. Of course, none of this escapes Levi's attention.

"Darlin', calm down." He squeezes my shoulder to reassure me. "Everything will be fine."

"I'm sorry she dragged you to dinner. I don't trust her intentions. She wants me to come home. She's likely to look for ways to make you squirm. We should have told her your back couldn't handle sitting through a leisurely dinner."

He pauses to consider my comments, then tilts his head. "Are you ashamed of me, or of what they might learn?" His eyes look guarded. "Is that the problem?"

My eyes widen in protest. "Absolutely not. No! This isn't even about you. It's about her dissatisfaction with me. You're merely collateral damage to her. You should have heard her today, rambling on and on about Rob and the roses and New York." I scowl at myself. "I hate how I revert to being a mouse in her presence."

"Sweetheart, settle yourself. No one's getting hurt tonight, least of all me. I know exactly what your mother's doing. I'm not an imbecile." He stares ahead, then turns to me and speaks softly. "You know she's not mad at you. She's under the misimpression she and I are in a competition over where you end up living. That's all this is, and it's silly. She assumes we can control your choices. As soon as she realizes that's not the case, things will be easier for you."

He's right. If only I can figure out how to cut the apron strings with Mom, this battle between us will end. Levi's confidence always empowers me. I love that about him.

～

The valet takes my car. When we enter the restaurant, my parents are already seated. I introduce Levi and my father. Levi kisses my mother's hand when greeting her. Before seating himself, he pulls out my chair for me. My father's already selected a bottle of wine, so Levi and I each take a glass and toast to my birthday.

At first, the conversation stays light. We discuss the restaurant motif, the menu, the weather, their flight, and other nonconfrontational topics. Dad and Levi end up conversing about the financial markets. I'm relieved because Levi can hold his own on this topic.

His Southern manners become evident when he stands each time my mom or I get up from, or return to, the table. I hope his conduct wins some approval from my parents. How can they not respect him, especially considering all he's accomplished?

The second glass of wine helps me relax. I slouch back into my seat and listen to the casual conversation, pleased to be wrong about my mother's intentions. Just as I blow out my last bit of tension, my mom jumps off the bench and gets in the game.

"So, Levi, your accent is charming." Mom sips on her wine. "Where were you raised?"

"Charming?" Levi chuckles. "That's one way to describe it, I guess. Most would call it a redneck's dialect. But, to answer your question, I'm from a small town in southern Georgia—Tifton."

"Oh, so you're far from home, too. Do you visit your parents often?"

"No, ma'am. My pop died recently. I haven't seen Mama since she left us twenty-plus years ago." I notice Levi's slight grin, which is likely springing from his surprising my mom with his direct and horrific answer.

I'm blown away by his casual admission, but wonder whether catching her off guard will be worth the high emotional cost of sacrificing his privacy.

"Oh my, dear." Mom glances at Dad for help while she backtracks and considers her next move. "I'm so sorry."

Dad jumps in, on cue. "Well, Levi, you've certainly overcome some difficult circumstances. It's impressive."

"Thank you, sir. I've learned to play the cards I'm dealt without complaining." Levi winks at me. "Whining never resolves anything."

Mom rejoins the conversation. "Good for you. I'm sure your mother would be proud to see you now. Have you ever tried to find her?"

I sharply inhale and drop my fork. "Mom, that's none of our business. Levi, you don't have to answer her." My throat tightens at my inability to cut her off.

"Lindsey, Levi was young when she left. Maybe there were circumstances he didn't know or understand. Not that there's much to justify her actions, but maybe talking with her would be beneficial." She nods at me assuredly and then turns to Levi. I sit helpless and appalled.

Levi watches my mother and me and then directs his answer to her. "Well, Mrs. Hilliard, I respectfully disagree. I appreciate your perspective as a mother. Speaking as a son, and specifically the son she abandoned, I can't imagine any benefit to finding her now. Nothing can change. It's done."

My mind flashes back to the letter containing Levi's mother's contact information. I've often thought of broaching the topic, but obviously Levi has no intention of reuniting with his mother. Despite the highly personal nature of this ambush, he's behaved with dignity. I could kiss him. And that thought makes me admit, yes, I really would like to kiss him.

Mom picks at her salad. Without looking at Levi, she zings him with one of her special judgments. "Well, it's certainly easier to avoid a potentially ugly confrontation than to secure answers."

With that statement, Levi inhales slowly and leans back in his chair. He examines my father through narrowed eyes. He must be curious about Dad's silence, but I'm used to it. "Trust me, ma'am, I've never shied away from confrontation. But I've moved on, so I don't need to confront my mama." His eyes dart to me and his grim expression becomes friendly. "Why don't we steer the conversation in another direction before Lindsey becomes uncomfortable. After all, this is her party, right?" He beams at me. "We should celebrate her involvement with advocacy for abused kids. She's very enthusiastic about the program. I've no doubt she'll be accepted into CAA once she finishes the training, which she has more time to do now that she's no longer taking care of me. After that, she'll be assigned her first case."

Levi's obvious pleasure sends my heart to my throat. My mother, however, tosses a trivializing hand gesture my way. "The nonprofit business? Yes, she's mentioned it." She swirls her wine glass twice and takes a sip.

"Lindsey tells me you do a lot of charity work. You must be pleased she's following in your footsteps." Somehow he managed to say that without making it sound like an obnoxious dig.

"No, Levi. It's completely different. I was a lawyer before I quit to raise Lindsey. I got involved with charities rather than go back to work because being her mother was my priority and Bill's job afforded me the option." My mom sighs. "I'm not sure why Lindsey needed to attend Columbia if she only ever planned to be a volunteer."

Levi's eyes darken with indignation at my mother's remark, but he restrains his temper. "You think she's wasting her education by using it to help the less fortunate and give a voice to those who can't speak for themselves?" He tips his head sideways to level one of his trademark stares at my mother. "Regardless, you aren't the first parent to spend too much money on an Ivy League education. I'm not convinced of the value of paying hundreds of thousands of dollars to have other people teach you what you can learn for yourself, or at least can buy at a lower cost. I suspect it's often egos driving the investment in the brand name of the college as much as the actual education the kid receives for that sum of money."

"Really?" My mom raises her eyebrows. "So you don't advocate continuing education?"

"I didn't say that, ma'am. I just don't think you need to spend a lot of money to get an education. I'm all for knowledge. But that's beside the point, which is Lindsey's current excitement. She'll be an excellent liaison and I'm happy for the lucky children who'll benefit from her compassion. Having Lindsey in their corner will make all the difference."

Without being aware of it, Levi momentarily takes hold of my hand. "I hope she doesn't get too attached to them and end up hurt when things don't go well, which is bound to happen on occasion. But she's a big girl, and a smart one, too. She'll figure it out in her own way, in her own time. Don't you agree, sir?" Levi releases my hand when addressing my father.

Dad's cornered. Levi's successfully defeated my mother's insult, complimented me, and forced my father to either support his wife and offend me, or support me and upset his wife.

I'm almost sorry for Dad, except, for the first time, I have my own champion. I love it. Rob always agreed with my parents. He never defended me as Levi did. I'm so grateful, I'm positive it shows all over my face.

My father avoids making eye contact with Mom when he responds. "Well, Levi, certainly Lindsey will be an asset to this organization. I think, however, what Helene means to say is she's capable of more." Dad's strategic answer angers me.

Levi's praise renewed my spirit. I'm stronger now than I've been all day. "More what, Dad? Making more money? Having a fancy office or title? Was writing for a magazine *better* than advocating for neglected and abused children? That job paid so little, it was practically an internship. We all have enough money. For the first time, I'll be making a difference in people's lives. Maybe I'll start my own foundation after I've learned from this experience, or write a book."

Mom's radar hones in on my newfound self-assurance and she torpedoes me. "Lindsey, these cases must take years to resolve. Won't you end up devastating a child or two when you inevitably return to New York? Have you even consulted with Rob about this decision? Obviously, Levi's got your ear. Why do you deny the rest of us our opinion?"

On the heels of her admonishment, Levi intercedes. "I never tell Lindsey what to do. I respect her and understand she alone lives with the consequences of her choices."

As soon as Levi finishes, I curtly respond to my mother's remarks. "*If* I return to New York, I can consult on cases and fly back to appear in court. As for Rob, I've no need to discuss my life with him now. He and I are not married. We're not even together."

"Considering the flowers he sent, he's not aware you've made a definitive decision about your relationship. Is he aware of your 'friendship' with Levi?"

I blanch from shame. I've never mentioned Levi precisely because of my conflicted emotions. I'm sinking, without a response. Fortunately, Levi pipes up.

"Excuse me, I think I'll excuse myself from the table. My back could use a stretch and I've no wish to cause Lindsey, or either of you, further discomfort. Please take your time to order dessert or coffee. Lindsey, I'll wait for you in the lounge area. Don't rush." He squeezes my knee under the table to emphasize his point before he stands. "Mr. Hilliard, it was a pleasure meeting you. Mrs. Hilliard, have a safe return to New York." Before any of us respond, Levi departs.

My face is aflame as I turn on my mother. "I can't believe your behavior tonight, Mom. You humiliated me. Why'd you question him about his mother and education, and provoke him with your insinuations about our relationship?"

Then, sick of my father's passivity, I turn on him, too. "Dad, you sat there, as always, letting her run roughshod over me. This, *this*"—I say, wildly waving my hand back and forth among the three of us—"is a big reason why I don't miss New York. Removing myself from your constant criticisms has been freeing. It's thrilling to make decisions for myself without considering your opinions. For God's sake, you act like my new interest is a drug habit or something."

"Sh, we're in public." Mom cuts me off. "Obviously you've been spending too much time on the beach to remember how polite society behaves." She leans toward me. "I'm not stupid, Lindsey. You think I can't appreciate what you see in Levi? You're letting your hormones dictate important choices. If you want to have a little romp with a handsome man, then do it. But don't mess up your entire life over him. He has nothing in common with you. He's not from a decent family, he's not formally educated, and he's not connected to anything more than himself. One of you will tire of the other when those differences become aggravating instead of romantic. Meanwhile, you'll lose Rob in the process and regret it later."

"Dad, do you share Mom's opinion?"

My father is ashen, caught between the two women in his life. "I don't know, honey. I don't recognize your defiant attitude tonight.

Levi's a decent young man, certainly self-made, which I can respect. However, if you're basing life-altering decisions on an infatuation, then I'd advise you to reconsider." That's my dad—always the diplomat, king of the evasive response.

Fortunately, he has no intention of prolonging the drama, so he asks the waiter for the check. We're all surprised to discover Levi's already taken care of the bill. I push back from the table and place my napkin in front of me. Struggling not to cry, I keep my eyes on my napkin while speaking.

"I wish you could be proud of me instead of undermining my confidence. I'd say thanks for dinner, but I guess I'll thank Levi. Have a safe flight home. I'll talk to you in a few days. Good night."

My insides feel wrung dry by the time Levi and I get into my car. We drive home in relative silence. I fight back the tears for most of the trip, but ultimately lose the battle.

CHAPTER FOURTEEN

Levi

A tear trails down Lindsey's cheek as we pull into her garage. I follow her inside without an invitation. I shouldn't have gone to dinner, knowing her mother had been baiting a trap. I'd only considered my own ability to tolerate it without stopping to think about the effect it might have on Lindsey. Now I must set this right before she goes to sleep.

Lindsey sniffles and wipes her eyes while blankly staring into space. She won't look at me. I suspect she's contemplating whatever her mother said about me once I left the table. It can't be flattering, so I need to draw her attention. My gift sits, unopened, on her dining table.

"I see you didn't open your present yet." I hand her the bright-pink box. "Go ahead. It's nearly your birthday now anyway."

She grins weakly.

"Nice wrapping." She takes the box from me and begins to untie the ribbons. "I should have known you'd do it well, considering your years of practice folding things neatly."

Hearing a little humor as her tears subside relieves me. She opens the box and removes the apron, laughing at the saying "I'm Not Bossy, My Way's Just Better" written across the chest. Then she finds the two knives in the box and smiles at me appreciatively.

"Levi, I love this gift. It'll always remind me of you and your patience with me in the kitchen." She places them on the table and stands to hug me. "It's perfect."

My lungs balloon in response to her embrace and my heart pounds against my ribs. She fits so perfectly in my arms. Against my better judgment and plans to slowly pursue her, I don't release her.

"I'm glad, though they're not as pretty as jewelry." I glance at the roses displayed on the coffee table. "Or flowers."

Her breathing slows. "Not as pretty, but more thoughtful and sentimental."

Her eyes reflect my own feverish desire, and when she trembles in my arms, it's my complete undoing.

Without warning, I lift her chin and kiss her. Unsure of how she'll react, I'm tentative at first. When she parts her lips and returns my affection, my heart races. A groan rumbles deep in my chest as my tongue seeks hers and tastes every sweet corner of her mouth.

Too quickly, I'm craving all of her. My hands grasp behind her head and waist to crush her against me. I've never, in all my life, wanted anyone more than her. A faint moan from her throat intensifies the longing rippling through me.

Her fingers weave through my hair. She matches each of my kisses with equal passion. My eyes search hers, and our breathing becomes more uneven and ragged.

I can't get close enough to her. Her skin smells like flowers and grapefruit; her mouth is warm and welcoming. When she whispers my name, everything in my body thrums so wildly, I feel a little dizzy.

Unwilling to break our kiss, I waltz her around in search of the sofa while keeping hold of her. She's removing my jacket, but I'm having trouble fumbling with the ties on her dress.

"My God, Lindsey," I hoarsely moan. "I want you so damn much."

Waves of lust crash over me as I lay her back against the sofa. Her frenzied hands reach under my shirt and up my sides. My heart pounds furiously, and I'm harder than I've ever been. I rub myself against her, anticipating what's to come, and let my body enjoy the tingling sensations temporarily blocking my back pain.

"I need you, Lindsey." I move to lift my leg from the floor and accidentally bump the coffee table, tipping the vase of flowers.

We catch it before it spills over, but seeing the roses again sets Lindsey on edge. When I try to resume our kiss, she pushes gently against my chest.

"Wait, Levi, wait. This is wrong. I'm not ready. I can't—I can't do this now. I'm sorry."

I can't release her. I kiss her again.

"Lindsey, please," I beg. I nibble her earlobe and make my way down her neck with my mouth. She arches toward me, but then she pushes away again.

"I'm not ready for this yet. For you. I'm confused about you and Rob. I owe you both better than this. Please. I'm a wreck tonight with everything that happened at dinner."

I brush my nose back and forth along hers. As the rush of excitement subsides, the throbbing in my back warns me of my limitations. Of course, that's not why she stopped me.

Christ Almighty. Rob. Rob? How's she not ready to dump him after his lies? Close to three years spent loving him and he repays her with deceit?

I want to scream, but I don't. I don't because I knew it already and it didn't prevent me from exposing my desire too soon. I couldn't stick to my plans, so now I'll suffer this excruciating refusal, as I predicted, just as Pop warned.

I kiss her forehead and pull back. She looks worried, fearful almost. Jesus, what's she think I'll do?

"I'm sorry," she says. "Are you annoyed?"

I know she's affected by what's happened—by me. I could push it and have her tonight, but it'll only make things worse for both of us. With every ounce of control I possess, I pull away.

"Frustrated. Not annoyed."

"I'm sorry." She's still clutching my forearms with her hands. "Obviously, I care for you. I'm attracted to you. But I've unfinished business with Rob. I don't know how to handle my feelings."

I lower myself back into a hug and stroke her hair.

"Hush. I know." I stay locked in a sad embrace for a while. "It's okay."

She ran from Rob and almost immediately began taking care of me. She's barely spent a single day alone. No wonder she's mixed up.

"Lindsey, I'm leaving." I start to sit up, but she keeps her arms around me.

"Will I see you tomorrow, or are you walking away?" She buries her face in my shoulder, anticipating my reply. I wrest her from my body and sit next to her, holding her hands in mine. I'm torn as hell but need to be strong for both our sakes.

"Our relationship's been unnatural from the start. Spending so much time together too quickly has thrown us off balance. Until you came along, I'd never let anyone get so close. But I know what you expect from people and, truth is, I probably can't deliver it. I should make myself scarce and give us each time to clear our heads." I kiss her hand because, while what I said is true, I still don't want to leave.

"Levi . . ." She drops my hands and folds her arms across herself in an act of self-comfort.

"What? What'd you want to say?"

She worries her lower lip and then lowers her head. "Nothing. There's nothing else to say. Neither of us can make any promises, so it's better to say nothing."

I can't argue, so I lean down and steal one final kiss. "I'll miss you. If you need anything, you let me know." I retrieve my jacket from her floor.

Her eyes spill over, but she doesn't deter me, so I leave through the front door. My chest is on fire from the rage swarming like angry bees under my skin. I loathe Rob and Helene, hate my parents for handicapping me, and despise myself for breaking my rules and setting myself up for this misery.

I'll be stuck living next door to Lindsey and watching her move ahead, maybe away and back to Rob. My gut had told me she'd be dangerous. I should've listened and stayed away instead of playing with fire.

When I get home, I check my PICC line and stretch out on my back. Hell, I probably couldn't even have made love to her in my current condition. I sure as hell wanted to, though.

I pour myself several shots of tequila to numb the pain. Better to pass out rather than dwell on the few minutes of ecstasy I've just enjoyed and may never experience again.

≈

Lindsey

The sunny day mocks my sorrow. My pillow's damp from the tears I cried throughout the night. I've no desire to get out of bed, although it's already nearly eleven o'clock. I can't concentrate. My parents' accusations overlay everything, causing me to doubt my motives.

Am I merely infatuated with Levi or, worse, using him to break away from the past? Is my interest in advocacy simply another fleeting whim that will fade once the real work begins and the bureaucracy bogs me down? Do I belong in California or New York? Am I really in love with Rob, or do I only miss the idea of us? Does being so drawn to Levi mean I don't love Rob?

Each time I close my eyes, I feel Levi all over me. Memories of his mouth, his voice, and his touch wrack my body with erotic, desperate shivers. Granted, my sexual experience is limited, but even fully clothed, Levi teased out aching needs with intensity I've never before experienced. Could I even survive being skin to skin, having his mouth on my breasts, my stomach, or my thighs?

Heat and dampness pool between my legs at the mere thought of making love with him, but is it purely lust? I can't play with Levi's heart to test my own, especially not with his history with his mother's rejection.

I'd be cruel to encourage him without being more certain of my own heart first. Of course, how much does he really care? *I know what you expect from people and I probably can't deliver it.* He walked away last night without a fight. Perhaps we're both equally confused.

My silent phone sits on the nightstand. I pick it up: no messages. Instinctively, I call Jill. She's much better at analyzing these matters than I've ever been. It's two o'clock in New York, so she'll be available. Shoot, voice mail.

"Jill, it's me. Desperately need your ear. Big blowup with Helene, Bill, and Levi. Help. Call me back!"

I turn on the ringer before rolling out of bed and hauling myself to the shower. After I dress, I check my phone. Jill still hasn't called. Neither has Levi.

My room's so balmy. I open the door to let the breeze inside. Lingering on the upper deck, I scan the beach and spot Levi talking to Elena near the water's edge. She's flirting, of course. Touching him. Surely he didn't confide anything in her, did he?

He's tossing shells into the waves while they talk, then she nods and holds up three fingers. He nods and squeezes her hand. She turns and ambles down the beach. I duck back inside to avoid being caught spying on him. What are he and Elena planning at three?

My phone rings. I dive on my bed and look at the screen. Jill. Thank God.

"Hey, thanks for calling back."

"How could I resist? You left me hanging with lots of questions. By the way, happy birthday! Did you get my gift yet? It ought to arrive today." Her rapid-fire comments distract me.

"Oh . . . thanks. No, not yet. Are you alone?"

"Sadly, yes. So what happened with your parents and Levi? Did they meet?"

"Mom insisted Levi come to dinner with us and then provoked him about personal issues. She wasn't subtle, but he handled her well. It upset me more than anyone else."

"So, what's the crisis? Helene's interference is nothing new."

I draw a deep breath, anticipating Jill's reaction to what I'm about to admit.

"When Levi and I came home, he kissed me and it heated up quickly. I panicked, thought about Rob, and stopped it from progressing. I told Levi I wasn't over Rob, so he left. Now I don't know what to do. I think I made a mistake."

"What do you want to do?" Her basic question has no easy answer.

"Jill, I told you. I don't know what to do."

"I didn't ask what's the *right* thing to do, I asked what you *want* to do. Did you want Levi last night?"

"God, yes. But what about Rob?"

"Why's Rob a factor? You're not even talking unless you're coming home, right?"

"Well, technically that's true. But it seems unfair to carry on with Levi without telling Rob."

"No, unfair is what he did with Ava. Your being with Levi is none of his business. You're broken up, for God's sake. You don't owe him any explanation."

"It's not that simple. And what about Levi? You know his history with abandonment. How can I lead him on and then maybe burn him by leaving? I need to be more sure of what I want."

"You're being irrational. Every relationship has the potential to end and hurt someone. Look at you and Rob. Despite the promises, he betrayed you and you left him. Even if Rob weren't in the picture, neither you nor Levi would have any certainty about each other, or the viability of your relationship. Levi's a big boy. He can handle the consequences."

"Maybe. I don't know. My parents hammered away at our incompatibilities last night. Maybe they're right and it's simply an infatuation that won't ever be anything more." I hear Jill chuckling on the other end of the line.

"Every woman on the planet, with the exception of your mother, is probably infatuated with him. So what if that's all it is? You need a little fling before you settle down and get married. You didn't exactly date around a lot, you know."

"You're not helping."

"Lindsey, time to grow up and make a decision. You can't please everyone, so do what you want to do."

"You and Levi, always turning everything back around on me."

"Well, I like Levi more and more with each new thing I learn about him. And, if you toss him aside, don't you dare complain to me when you see him with someone else, or if I visit and take a shot at him."

"You're horrible! You know that, right?"

"Just being honest. Trust me, there will be someone else waiting to take him off your hands."

"I know." The image of Shari's face flickers through my mind, inspiring intense jealousy. "Okay. Thanks for listening to me gripe on my birthday. I knew this day would suck."

"Happy birthday."

"Bye."

Downstairs, the fragrant roses remind me I've yet to thank Rob for remembering my birthday. I know he'll be wondering if they're freshly cut or dying. It's always been one of his pet peeves. He's sent back more than a few orders when they've arrived in poor condition.

These roses, however, are perfectly firm and beginning to open. By Monday, they'll be glorious.

I snap a photo of myself with the flowers and attach it to my thank-you note. It takes some thought to compose an appropriate, simple message.

> *Rob,*
>
> *Look at the gorgeous flowers you sent. You can see for yourself they're in perfect condition. ;-) Thank you for remembering my birthday. Getting older forces me to acknowledge the need to make some decisions. I know you are waiting for some answers from me. I hope to have them soon. Until then, be well. Again, thank you for the flowers. You surprised me. Thinking of you.*
>
> *Love,*
> *Lindsey*

I hit Send and sit back, realizing I'd been holding my breath. Okay, enough dwelling on thoughts of Levi and Rob. I should schedule the rest of my training sessions and do a little extra reading on guardian ad litems and the legal system.

≈

It's just past three when I return from the bookstore with a book about foster care and another about cultural diversity. Educating myself about the foster care system and related hardships has really made me realize what a bubble I've lived in for most of my life. The courage shown by the children, and volunteers in many instances, is uplifting. But other stories bring me to tears. I want to be admitted into this group so I, too, can stand up for a defenseless child or two.

I lift the book bag out of my car. Rather than enter the house through the garage, I walk outside to pick up the package—probably from Jill—the mailman left at the front door. On my way out of the garage, my heart skips a beat when I see Levi in the passenger seat of Elena's car as it pulls out of his driveway.

I'm glad they didn't notice me, but can't help wondering where they're going together. Did he have a follow-up appointment today? A therapy session?

Although he has no interest in Elena, envy gnaws at me. I should be with him today, not her. If my mother hadn't interfered, everything would be normal today. I'd be spending my birthday cooking something with him tonight and playing Scrabble or listening to him read more of *Unbroken*.

Instead, I'm sitting here alone, my heart torn between two dissimilar men, with no one to talk to about any of it, except for Jill, whose best advice is to abandon all caution and start something with Levi.

I open the box Jill sent. Inside are two smaller boxes and a card, which reads, *Hope you enjoy these little gifts. Feel free to use the spray on your mom, Rob, Levi, or anyone else (except me, of course, because I'm immune). Happy birthday!* Puzzled, I open the smallest box to discover a pretty pair of silver and turquoise earrings. Inside the second box is a gag gift: a can of "asshole repellant." In spite of everything, I can't help but laugh. This is why I still love Jill.

～

But at ten thirty, I find myself on my deck for the fourth time tonight. I can't believe Levi never even called to say happy birthday. I still don't see any lights on in his house, either. He's never returned since taking off with Elena. Curiosity and concern are killing me. I won't call him, not when I'm not even sure what I want to say.

He said we needed time apart, and he sure meant it.

I don't like it, not one bit.

CHAPTER FIFTEEN

August 18, 2013

Levi

I spent the past week at a local hotel near the Ranch at Live Oak retreat and participated in the Ranch to Farm Culinary Experience cooking classes with its executive chef. I escaped Lindsey while staying close enough to return quickly if she called. Of course, she never did.

At least I'm turning the corner in terms of healing. The PICC line came out yesterday and my back pain subsides a little each day. As for my time away, the cooking classes have been the best part of the week—the silver lining, so to speak.

It's been costly, but worth it. I couldn't have steered clear of Lindsey those first couple of days if I saw her on the beach or sitting on her deck. I can't handle the forceful pull of my novel affection.

In the mountains above Malibu, I was removed from temptation. But as I sit in the cab on my way home, I'm ready to face Lindsey without losing my nerve or my mind.

She's a wonderful person, but she's not mine. Truth is, she's not anyone's. None of us really are, but some vow to belong to others. If she belongs to anyone, it's Rob and her parents, not me.

I'm an interloper, the fortunate beneficiary of her empathy.

Whatever interest she has in me is probably linked to my face more than anything else. I know better than anyone how quickly physical attraction dies when it's not paired with more.

If I could trade this face for a normal one in exchange for a healthier emotional life, for a chance to be inwardly lovable enough to keep a parent or a woman in my life, I might do it. But wishing won't make it happen, so I'll live as I always did until recently.

The taxi pulls into my driveway at six o'clock. I drop my luggage inside, return to the cab, and ask the driver to take me to Duke's. I'm hungry and not quite ready to sit alone all night. Funny, being alone never bothered me before—I'd preferred it that way—but now it's the last thing I want.

I glance at Lindsey's house, wondering what she's done all week. Has she missed me? Has she made any decisions about her life? I know I'll bump into her soon, but right now I'm going out to be around other people.

After dinner, I sit at the bar and talk with Joe. The place closes early on Sundays, so business is slow. Joe's breaking down the bar for the night.

"You look better than last time I saw you, Levi." Joe pours me a tall, cold beer. "They ever find the driver?"

"No." I play with my beer glass by twisting it around on the counter. "No trace of him. I spoke with the cops again this week, but they doubt they'll find the driver without new evidence. Guess I'll never get reimbursed for my medical bills or pain and suffering."

"Probably some illegal alien—vanished into thin air." Joe wipes down the back bar while we talk.

I nod, having not considered that particular scenario. Seems as likely as any other at this point, which means they wouldn't even have any assets to pursue.

I can't imagine hitting someone and leaving them to die, but I've experienced a lot of things in my life I wouldn't have imagined.

At the end of her shift, Shari comes over and sits with me while Joe finishes cleaning the bar.

"Hey, Levi, honey. Where's the new lady friend you brought here the other week?" She winks at Joe and then looks back at me.

"At home, I suspect." I grab a final mouthful of peanuts and act blasé about Lindsey. "Not sure."

"Huh. She seemed different from your usual 'friends,' but maybe I was wrong." She raises her eyebrows to challenge me, but I just smile and tease her to shut her up.

"Shari, does Joe know you're still interested in my love life? How do you feel about that, Joe?"

Shari laughs and Joe smirks. He's cool with our past, mostly because he knows it never amounted to more than passing pleasure.

Shari slaps my shoulder. "Go ahead, change the subject. But you acted different with her. You admired her, too."

Jesus. Now I'm an open book? "She's a neighbor and a friend. She took care of me for most of my recovery when I needed a lot of help. I'm grateful to her." I hide behind a swig of beer because I don't want to talk about Lindsey. "Joe, can you call me a cab?"

"We'll give you a ride home, no worries." Joe looks at Shari to confirm and she nods in assent.

"Thanks. I'll take that offer."

When we arrive at my house, Joe asks to use the bathroom, so he and Shari come inside. Shari tours the first floor and deck while Joe's indisposed.

"Shoot, Levi. If I'd have known where you lived, maybe I'd have prolonged our little fling." She laughs as she opens the door and strides onto the deck.

"Oh yeah? If only I'd known," I tease.

"You're so lucky you can sit here listening to the ocean under the stars." She sits on a chaise. "Joe and I have nothing special planned tonight. Want company or do you need to rest your back?"

"No, I'm feeling fine. I'll grab some beer."

I bring my Bose speakers, iPod, and three Harp ales outside, with Joe in tow. The three of us reminisce about past shenanigans at the bar for a while, then they both head inside to use the bathroom and get another drink.

I'm reclined on a lounge chair, gazing at the stars, when Lindsey runs up my back steps calling out my name. She arrives in her pajamas and steps toward me, her eyes full of relief. Then her hands find her hips and her expression turns irate.

"I saw your lights when I was going to bed. I couldn't believe it. Where have you been?" She's speaking quickly; her voice is strained as she sits beside me. "I didn't call because you said you wanted some space, but after everything that's happened this summer, I can't believe you never once checked in with me. I almost didn't come over because I'm so angry with you, but I needed to know you're okay."

My will weakens the instant she nestles up against me. Memories of her kiss torment me, but I don't embrace her. I've worked hard all week to rebuild my wall. I need to be cautious and not fall prey to her whimsical emotions. I gently lift her from my chest until she's sitting alongside me.

Brushing her fallen hair back behind her ear, I drink her in with my eyes. I speak in quiet tones.

"I'm fine. I took a little vacation, that's all. Sorry you worried. It didn't occur to me you might be concerned."

She blinks in surprise, like I'm crazy for not realizing how she'd react.

At that moment, Shari steps onto the deck with more beer. Upon seeing Lindsey, she cheerfully greets her.

"Hiya, you want one, too? I can get another." Shari waits for Lindsey's answer while she hands me a cold beer.

Lindsey recognizes her immediately and jumps up from the chaise, retreat in her eyes and body language. I know she's misreading this situation and can see her mind adding two and two together and coming up with five.

Within three seconds, she's assumed Shari and I spent the past week together. I don't fret. Joe will appear any second. But then Lindsey's bitter, resentful eyes shoot me a death stare. She bolts off the deck faster than a lizard slipping under a rock.

Shari stares at me wide-eyed and mouths the word "sorry." I pry myself from my lounge chair to chase down Lindsey. Unfortunately, I can't move with any speed, partly because of my back, and partly because my heart's in a vise.

I call after her, but she won't slow down or turn around. By the time I reach her back door, it's locked and the lights are off. I bang on the frame and call her name again, but she doesn't answer.

Using my hands to shield the sides of my face, I press against the glass to peer inside. I don't see her anywhere. I bang once more before giving up and heading home. Joe and Shari are waiting on the deck, full of apologies.

"It's not your fault. She didn't even bother finding out the truth. Obviously, she mustn't think much of me if she believes what I think she does. Anyway, I'm not about to lose sleep over it." I lie because I won't admit the truth.

Shari pipes up. "You men are so damn stupid and stubborn."

Joe squeezes her shoulder and suggests she mind her own business, then bids me adieu. On her way out, Shari turns to me.

"Levi, I've known you a while. You didn't run off this porch because she *doesn't* matter to you. Lay your pride aside and tell her. If you can't be honest, then you deserve what you get." She leans up to kiss my cheek then gives me a fairly stinging pat on the cheek to emphasize her point.

Once they leave, I call Lindsey, but she still doesn't answer. I don't leave a message, but call twice more during the next hour. She must've turned her phone off by my third attempt, because it goes straight to voice mail.

Hell, I won't spend my night begging her to talk to me. She's the one who ran off before learning the facts.

I lie in bed wide-awake. When I saw Lindsey earlier, everything inside me lit up. For those precious seconds, I felt completely happy and wanted to wrap her up and run away with her.

I never understood brokenhearted love songs until now. Part of me wants to scale the walls of her house and force my way in—but it's no use. Without trust, and with Rob still in her heart, there's no chance for us.

Plus, for better or worse, I'm damaged goods and I know it. I've done all right for myself, by myself, but I've never learned how to love anyone. Never trusted anyone to care a whiff about me, either.

At the end of the day, I doubt I can make Lindsey happy. She'd leave me broken and embittered. Lindsey's like a rainbow, beautiful and vibrant. But I can't really hold on to a rainbow, can I?

~

Lindsey

I'm starting to hate men, especially Levi and Rob. I spent the better part of last week worrying about Levi's state of mind, and blaming myself for sending him running from his home. All the while, he was off having a grand time with his tart from the bar.

Pleasure—that's all men care about. Goddamned sex. And Shari, so cheerful, with her sensuous hair and victorious grin. I practically handed him to her on a platter.

I'd convinced myself I meant something more than his flings. But he replaced me with Shari without any hesitation. If he expects me to talk to him now, he's crazy. He can bang on the door and call me all night long for all I care. I have nothing to say to him.

Damn it. I can't sleep. Images of Levi and Shari intertwined keep coming quickly, one after another, driving me crazy.

Of all the reunion scenarios I'd dreamed up this week, I didn't foresee this one. Honestly, I don't know why I'm surprised. Rob risked everything during our engagement for one night with Ava. How'd I not anticipate Levi finding a willing substitute when we weren't even dating?

Relief filled me when I saw activity at his house tonight. I'd been so glad to see him on the deck, relaxing peacefully. Without a second thought, I threw myself at him—literally. My body naturally melted into his, but instead of embracing me, he practically pushed me away.

Guess he accomplished his goal of clearing his head. He's returned to his home and routine lifestyle without looking backward.

Maybe the most shocking thing is feeling as upset now as I felt over Rob. How's that possible? Rob and I had made a commitment to each other; we were in love. We'd spent almost three years dating, and lived together for one of them. His choice to bed Ava—whether only once, as he claims, or more often, as I suspect—tattered the ties that bound me to him.

I can't accuse Levi of doing the same. The only ties in place were the ones I created in my own fantasies. My rescue delusions, as Jill would claim. Yet my heart aches as much today as it did months ago in New York.

Levi never lied to me. He never uttered a romantic promise or offered more than friendship with benefits. In fact, even the friendship had been a difficult bridge to cross.

I infringed on his privacy, insisted on helping care for him, and invented a deep connection where none existed. At every turn, Levi warned me off, admitting to a disinterest in close friendships or exclusive romantic entanglements. To top it off, I refused his sexual advances, so how can I blame him for pursuing another woman who's free to meet him on his terms?

I'm angry with myself, and weary. I didn't travel across the country looking for love. I came to contemplate my life. But what, of lasting value, have I learned?

I've offended my parents, although truthfully, I've spent too long allowing their opinions to override my own. I've vexed Rob, although

I suspect he's still not been completely honest with me. I've quit my job, which isn't a proud professional moment and, after years of diligent work, probably not my smartest maneuver. The only positive recent development is the child advocacy program. At least that's genuine. Now that I've finished the training, I hope they'll admit me and assign me my first case soon.

But perhaps I should pursue it in New York. There's no reason I need to stay in California. I've not built any friendships other than my undefined relationship with Levi.

Granted, the distance from my family's allowed me to discover this passion and enabled me to question compatibility with Rob. *Rob.* Maybe Rob's learned from his mistake. If Ava wasn't his one and only past transgression, will she be his last? He continues to fight for me, unlike Levi, who so quickly retreated and moved on.

Levi. His face is the last thing I picture as I fall asleep.

∾

It's already breathtaking by six thirty. On my return from my run an hour later, I see Levi standing at his deck railing, surveying the waves.

I fear he'll push his luck too soon and hop on his surfboard, but I must absent myself from his recovery. Let Shari, or whomever, become the person he relies upon from now on. My immediate dilemma is getting inside without a confrontation. I'm unhappy, but in truth, he didn't break any promise. I need to grow up.

I wave without smiling. "Good morning, Levi."

His brows raise and a slight grin stretches across his face. He probably expected me to continue ignoring him, considering my behavior last night.

"Lindsey." He stiffly grips his deck railing. His mouth opens then closes, as if he wants to say something but can't.

I hesitate but then nod and progress toward my door.

"Hey, can we talk a minute?" He's moved closer to my house.

"I don't want to argue, Levi. I'm not in the mood."

"That's unusual." He smiles. "You love butting heads with me."

Normally his teasing lightens the tension. Unfortunately, I'm not up for banter. "Well, as you insisted upon the other week, we've both had time to clear our heads. I'm glad you're better, but I have my own recovery to address." I put my hand on the door to open it.

"Five minutes, please." His hopeful expression diffuses my resentment. "I have some things to say."

I almost refuse, but the truth is, I want to talk to him. I don't know why, since I'm sure to end up unhappy afterward. Perhaps I'm an emotional masochist.

"Let me shower, then I'll be over."

He nods and watches me until I disappear into my house.

Twenty minutes later, I leave home dressed in jean shorts and a pink T-shirt, my wet hair hanging freely around my shoulders. I intentionally dressed down so he wouldn't have the satisfaction of believing I care whether or not he's still attracted to me. Now I feel self-conscious. The realization I'm playing girlish games embarrasses me, but it's too late to turn around because he's opening his door to let me inside.

I sit with my hands under my butt and cross my legs to keep them from bouncing. "So, what's up?"

The scent of his house triggers flashbacks of time spent here with him. My foot starts to swing like a pendulum.

He's still standing near the door, arms folded in his typical defensive posture. The room's charged with his commanding energy.

"I want to clear up a misunderstanding." He shifts his weight to his other leg.

"About?"

"Shari."

I hold up my hand. "No need. You don't owe me explanations, Levi. We had no agreement. You're free to do what you want, with whomever you want. So, if that's all, I'll be on my way."

I stand, enormously proud of how well I handled myself—no tears, no judgments. However, I'm not tough and detached, so I need a quick escape before he uncovers the truth.

"You're right." He hesitates.

My heart drops. Although I know it's true, I'd still hoped he'd apologize or offer some explanation. I lower my head and continue toward the door. Instead of moving aside to let me pass, he grabs my hand.

"I don't *owe* you an explanation, but I still want to offer one." His grip is tight on my hand. "If you'd stuck around an extra minute last night, you'd have seen Shari's boyfriend, Joe, come back outside. Instead, you jumped to the worst conclusions about me, then refused to talk to me." One of his eyebrows arches accusatorially.

"Joe the bartender?" It's the first thing that pops into my head, along with a little ray of hope. He's holding my hand, and I'm holding my breath.

"Yes, Joe the bartender. He and Shari have been seeing each other for a few months. I went to Duke's for dinner last night. They drove me home and stayed for a drink." Both of his eyebrows rise in triumph over his redemption.

"So, she didn't go with you last week?"

"No."

"Who'd you take? Elena?" I know it can't be true, but I want confirmation.

"I went *alone* to a resort. Took some cooking classes." His answer catches me completely off guard. He went away alone, to cook?

"Oh." My voice is small. We stand in silence for a minute, my hand still held in his.

"'Oh'? That's all you're gonna say? No 'I'm sorry for doubting you, Levi'?"

It dawns on me he's affronted by my assumptions. "Wait, you're mad at me? That's pretty rich, Levi." I glare at him. My anger rushes back. "You kiss me, then cruelly take off for a week without telling me anything. I went crazy worrying only to find you drinking with your ex–sex partner, and you have the gall to be mad at me?"

Infuriated, I attempt to remove my hand from his grip so I can firmly plant it, along with my other fist, on my hips. Levi has other ideas. He yanks me up against him, looking at me with eyes full of heated resentment.

"I'm furious. I've never given you any reason not to trust me. I've always been honest." He's looking down at me and I'm not sure if he's ready to wring my neck or kiss me. Regardless, I'll not let him have the final word.

"Yes, you've been honest. Honest about the lack of interest in any kind of meaningful relationship, about your doubt in the foundation of whatever feelings may have developed between us, and about how you and Shari have some kind of ongoing, open-ended sexual relationship. You've also told me, repeatedly, that no one can be trusted. So I didn't think the worst of you—I thought exactly what you told me to think."

Levi's face abruptly transforms from smug to rueful. He stares at me, unable to offer a snappy or surly retort. In that moment, I want to bring him home. I touch his face. He shuts his eyes and lays his cheek against my palm. His grief-stricken appearance squeezes my heart.

My arms wrap around his neck and I rest my head against his chest. His arms hesitantly encircle me. I tighten my hold, hoping to ease his tension, wanting to break through his walls.

I tilt my head so my lips brush against the base of his neck. His breath catches and he pulls me closer. My pulse quickens and I kiss his neck, coaxing him to meet me. To my displeasure, he pushes me away again. He's shaken and conflicted, still setting himself apart.

"I meant what I said last week. I can't be what you want, what you deserve."

"Why'd you bother setting me straight if you just want to shut me out?"

"Because I'm selfish, Lindsey. Because I didn't want you to assume the worst, despite knowing, in the end, the truth doesn't make any difference."

"It does make a difference." I step closer to him, but he holds me apart.

"Stop it. Jesus, I can't think straight when you're so close. You throw me off balance. I can't do this with you."

His sad eyes take me in and then, despite his earlier protests, he unexpectedly drags me into a kiss.

His hands sink into my wet hair. Unlike our fiery kisses last week, this one is slow and sensual. This kiss has soul. It weakens my knees and my weight falls against him. I hear my own whimper before he pushes me away again. I'm dazed.

"Goddamn it." He savagely rubs his hand through his mop of hair. "I can't do this with you, Lindsey. Please go."

"Why? Because of Rob?"

Levi's face registers surprise, as if he'd totally forgotten Rob.

"No. Well, hell . . . partly, yeah. Lindsey, I don't know how to be different from how I am. And you, you keep pushing me into uncomfortable territory, taking control away from me. I don't like being powerless. I can't let go, not even for you."

"You can, but you *won't*. This is because of your mother. You won't try, because you're afraid." I'm treading on thin ice, but I must speak my mind.

"Leave my damn mama out of this. If it makes it easier to call me a coward, fine. The result's the same, no matter the reason."

"That's bull, Levi, and you know it. You're quite the hypocrite, telling me to cut the apron strings and stop basing my decisions on other people's opinions, yet you won't go to Atlanta to confront your mother and lay this thing to rest so you can move on with your own life!" I bark, realizing, too late, my slip about his mother's whereabouts.

He, however, didn't miss it. His eyes blaze.

"How'd you know about Atlanta?"

He's white-hot mad. I can't breathe or move. Time freezes.

"Lindsey, how do you know where my mama lives?"

My hand moves to my stomach and it seems like my knees are melting. Panic splits my voice when I speak. "I read the letter from your dad the day you were so sick."

Levi takes two steps back and plows both hands through his hair. He squeezes the sides of his skull like he can shut out what he heard me admit. Seconds that feel like hours pass before his booming voice cracks open the air.

"I can't trust you!" His eyes bulge in disbelief. "You came into my house, read a highly personal letter, and questioned—no, *tested*—me about my family when you already knew half the truth. You've lied to me every day since then."

He starts pacing around in a circle with a scowl on his face, then stops suddenly and turns on me. The expression of disgust in his eyes makes me want to throw up.

"I thought you were different, but you're not. Pop's right about not being able to trust *anyone*. Thanks for the reminder—it'll make saying good-bye a lot easier."

His eyes turn cold. His hands are fisted at his sides. This is the Levi from Florida—the callous, closed-off man I first met.

My entire body starts trembling, along with my voice.

"Levi, wait. Let me explain. I was looking for paper to write you a note. I happened to notice the photos of you and your dad in the desk drawer. When I picked it up to see what you looked like young, I saw the letter underneath it."

Shame swims through my veins and pours hot tears from my eyes. "I'm sorry. I know it was so wrong, but you'd never tell me anything and I just—I couldn't help myself. I didn't do it to hurt you; I did it to know you. I only wanted to know you better."

I wipe my cheeks then step toward him, reaching out to close the distance between us. He jumps back and points at the door.

"Get out, Lindsey. I don't want to see you or talk to you. I mean it. You need to leave. Right. Now."

"I'm sorry, Levi. Please, don't be mad." My lungs burn as I break into a heaving sob, but it doesn't budge him. He covers his ears with his hands and closes his eyes to block me out. Crushed, I turn and run out of the house.

Once at home, I fling myself onto the sofa and cry. A tapestry of little moments, not all of them pleasant, blend together in my mind and make me feel connected to him despite his attempts to loosen the binds. Ironically, my own behavior severed them, probably for good.

He may forgive me in time, but he will never trust me. Not really. I lied to him, and as I can't seem to get beyond Rob's lie, Levi won't get past mine. It's over and I'm to blame.

For the first time since May, I empathize with Rob.

CHAPTER SIXTEEN

Levi

When I return from my latest post-op checkup, I stop at my mailbox to grab my bills before entering my house. At least I received encouraging news about my recovery today. Doc says I'll be driving and starting therapy by the end of the week.

Thank God. I needed a little good news just about now.

Opening a beer, I sit on the sofa to flip through my mail. Amid the bills and junk mail, I find a letter from Lindsey. I stare at the envelope. Lifting it, I tap it against the table several times and then set it aside. I'm not ready.

Beautiful, generous, loving Lindsey lied through her teeth. I opened my heart, and she deceived me by sneaking through my private belongings. Pop warned me caring too much blinds a man. Looks like he was right.

I ignored everything he taught me and took her at face value. Somehow she tricked me into believing she was unique, that she honestly cared. I brushed aside my suspicions because she made me feel so damn good. All along, she played me.

I didn't do it to hurt you. I did it to know you. I only wanted to know you better.

Even if her motives weren't malicious, she still inserted herself into my personal affairs without an invitation. Not that it surprises me, considering her entitled behavior, but I won't be taken for a ride.

My whole life's been based on my ability to discern others' thoughts, plans, and secrets. If I can't depend on my instincts anymore, what the hell do I have left?

Worse, I'm having a hard time returning to the way I lived before she marched herself into my life. I just spent seven days and several thousand dollars last week forgetting about her. I failed miserably, it seems.

As soon as she entered my house—the instant she bared herself—I faltered.

Her kiss differs from any experience I've had with other women. Being near her blocks out the rest of the world. Everything appears more vivid with her by my side. Christ, my daydreams of making love with her exceed any actual sexual encounter I've had in years—maybe ever. Now she's doomed me to a hellish life of never being satisfied.

I don't want to read any lame apologies for her outrageous behavior. If I remain furious, it'll be easier to free myself from her clutches. I'll keep myself distracted with other things until the time comes when I don't even think about her.

I recovered from losing Mama; I'll get over Lindsey.

I lie back on the sofa. Have I really recovered from losing Mama? Looking at my life, there's a good argument against that declaration. I rub my temples, then jab one of the cushions with my elbow.

To hell with this. I just want to feel normal again.

I pick up a book, but the words swim before my eyes. I surf the TV channels, looking for an escape, but give up and go to bed early with a new book, tucking Lindsey's envelope inside its cover. After an hour of reading and rereading the first pages of a new chapter, I shut my eyes and pray for sleep.

~

I'm standing alone, beneath a gray sky, in the middle of an expansive field of tall grass. On the horizon, the sky explodes with bold purple and orange flashes. Suddenly, I'm carried along with a herd of people rushing into a makeshift emergency center.

All around me, people are crying, getting bandaged, and searching for others. My own face somehow ends up wrapped in gauze bandages. I touch them, confused, then go search for Pop.

I'm magically alone and outside, bracing against strong winds. The grass field has been replaced by a paved lot, and I see a forest in the distance. I reach the tree line, but then it morphs into a familiar, shallow riverbed, which I recognize as the riverbed behind my childhood home in Tifton.

I wade into the wide brook, trying to reach the road on the other side. The freezing water rushes over rocks and around my legs, and I lose my balance. I splash into the water, soaking my bandages. As I cross the raging brook, the wet bandages unravel.

The riverbank ahead of me begins to incline, like in a cartoon. I try to climb it, but the loose soil continually crumbles under my hands and knees.

"Levi, grab my hand."

I look up to see Lindsey leaning down with her arm extended.

"Hold on, Levi. Don't let go."

I grab on to her and she yanks me up onto the dirt road. Without another word, she begins walking ahead of me along a path leading away from the road, into the trees.

I stand at the fork, watching her meander through the shadows of the wooded path.

Now I'm floating above my body. I can see my face. There are no burns, only a small scar by my right eye.

I look for Lindsey to show her, but she's vanished.

I sit up, gasping. The bedroom's still dim, so I turn on a lamp and shake my head. I don't often remember my dreams, but this one's so graphic and unusual, I'm uneasy.

I glimpse the unopened letter on the nightstand. Hesitantly, I pick it up and slide my finger along the seal, ripping it open.

Dear Levi,

You trusted me in your home and as a friend. I abused that gift with my inexcusable invasion of privacy. There's no justification for what I did. I'm ashamed and more sorry than I can say. Please believe I never intended to hurt or betray you. My desperation to know more about you got the better of me.

Now I've proven your parents right, which is ironic because I wanted so much to be the person to prove them wrong.

I pray my mistake doesn't make you retreat from reaching out to others, or refrain from experiencing real friendships and love. Despite what you've been taught, and how you view yourself, you deserve love in your life and are strong enough to withstand the occasional disappointments and bumps along the road.

I hope, eventually, you'll forgive me. You're important to me. You've helped me discover things about myself I might not have otherwise learned, and I'll always be grateful.

If you shut me out, I'll miss you. Whether or not you believe me, I am your friend.

Love,
Lindsey

I read her letter twice more. *I'm important to her. She's my friend. I deserve love. She'll miss me. Love, Lindsey. Love.* I crush the letter against my chest and stare at the ceiling.

I've missed her so much since her damn birthday dinner. I don't want her to disappear from my world like she did in my dream, even if I can't trust her not to spy on me or take off to New York.

The truth is, I'm set up for pain whether I let go now or she walks away later. But with the second option, there's no pain now, and maybe, none later.

Mama really screwed me up worse than Pop. He tainted my thinking, but Mama killed part of my heart. Maybe I should confront her, if for no other reason than to finally look her in the eye and make her face me.

I'm curious to know how she started a new life—one without me—but I've been afraid of the answers. Damn, I liked it better when I didn't know where, or if, she lived. Now that Pop's thrown her whereabouts in my lap, it's harder to ignore my innermost fears.

All of these years, I'd convinced myself I controlled my destiny and feared nothing. In fact, I've allowed fear to dictate most of my decisions. My fear of loss, rejection, and failure has kept me apart from others.

Lindsey's parents may assert too much control over her life, but at least they didn't destroy her ability to believe in people. If I conquer the fear of hearing Mama's story, perhaps I can learn to embrace the way Lindsey's changing my outlook.

Would Lindsey come with me?

～

Lindsey

After a failed attempt at studying this morning, I decide to lounge on my couch and watch *Downton Abbey* on Netflix. I'm inhaling a pint of Ben & Jerry's Cherry Garcia like my life depends on it when I see Levi approaching my back door.

I hadn't expected him.

Anchored in place from shock, I wave him in without getting up. The remaining evidence of my pity party melts slowly in the container on the table in front of me.

"Hi." It's all I can say while my heart is in my throat.

"Got your note." He holds up the paper before tossing it on the table.

I sit forward. My hands grasp the edges of the seat cushion. I can't take my eyes off him, but I can't read his thoughts, either.

"Can you forgive me?" I hold my breath, wincing in anticipation of his reply.

He seats himself at the other end of the L-shaped sofa.

"For which, snooping or lying?" His face reveals no emotion. He's scrutinizing me, evaluating my behavior and responses.

"Both, Levi. Honestly, from the moment I read the note, I've been so sorry. I was too afraid to confess, so I questioned you in the hospital instead. Once you told me the truth, I figured the letter didn't matter anymore. I'm not justifying the lie, but I was worried about your recovery. You were so sick with that infection. I couldn't risk being pushed away, not when you needed me most."

Levi stands and begins pacing around the room. I assume he's debating my remarks, but his tension seems to be emanating from something more. If I didn't know better, I'd think he feared something. I wait without speaking. To press will only send him scampering. I take reconciliations with family and friends for granted, but this is new for him. *Be patient.*

"I'm going to Atlanta." He stops and stares at me, his eyes reflecting uncertainty with his decision.

Without flinching, I cross the room and embrace him. "That's very brave."

He doesn't respond to my hug, so I draw back. He catches my hands in his and caresses them with his thumbs. I love the sensation of him drawing these gentle circles on my skin.

His face wrinkles under the strain of anxiety. "Will you come with me?"

My mouth falls open at his request. His eyes narrow and brows arch.

I'm simultaneously overwhelmed and terrified. This confrontation may well be the biggest moment of his life. I'm not convinced my presence is a great idea. But, after what I've done, he's taking a huge leap of faith by extending the invitation.

I can't possibly refuse.

"If you want me to come, I'll be there."

His worried expression fades into a shy smile. "Thanks." He pulls me into a brief hug, releasing me too soon.

I hesitate, unsure whether he plans to say more about my snooping. When he doesn't, I decide to let it go.

"So, when are we taking this trip?" I ask, once he steps back from me.

"Before I change my mind. I'll purchase the tickets and pay for the hotel rooms. Leave Thursday, return Friday?"

"Oh, okay." Separate rooms—a good, if disappointing, idea. I smile awkwardly. "I don't have any plans, so that's fine."

He holds my gaze. "Thanks."

Questions tumble from my mouth when he starts to leave.

"Wait a sec, can't we talk?" I motion to the sofa and take a seat myself.

Levi hesitates before sitting. His typically calm, controlled demeanor is replaced with the air of a young, uncertain boy.

"I don't want to talk about what you did, Lindsey. I'm not happy about it, mostly because you hid it from me for weeks. It makes it difficult to trust you, but I'm trying to keep it in perspective."

The hard edge of his voice signifies the extreme difficulty he's having giving me a second chance. His steely hazel eyes remain aloof and detached, but don't scare me away from speaking my mind.

"I understand. That's not what I want to talk about, though." I'm leaning forward, resting my elbows on my knees. "I want to ask about the trip. What's your goal? Only yesterday you wouldn't even consider seeing her. What's changed?"

"I don't know exactly." He scratches the back of his neck. "I don't want to talk about it, though."

"How will you talk to her if you can't even discuss it with me? Maybe we should role-play or something?"

He smiles for the first time today, apparently amused by my suggestion.

"Role-play? Jesus, I haven't seen the woman in more than twenty years." He's closed himself up again. The air around him pulses with frenetic energy. "I have no idea what she'll say, or do, when I show up. This isn't the kind of discussion we can plan."

"Well, what do you remember about her?"

"Not much. I've blocked a lot of it out." The left side of his lip curls upward. "She's nothing like you."

"I hope not. I'd never leave my child." Fudge. I need a filter!

His brows leap upward. "Look, I thought I'd handle it better if you were close by, but I don't expect you to be involved."

"Well, do you hope for some kind of reconciliation? Do you want a relationship with her in the future?"

His features pinch in discomfort. "No! I don't know. It's complicated. I need answers, mostly." His gaze shifts. "I don't want to talk about it right now."

"Okay." Since he appears to be on the edge of an explosion, I concede.

"I'll let you know once I have our itinerary." He stands. "Thanks for coming with me."

"Thanks for asking." I smile broadly. Before I can ask him to stay for dinner, my phone rings. I view the screen and grimace.

"Hi, Mom."

Levi waves and silently exits through the screen door. Although I'm disappointed he made no effort to stay, I'm thrilled that he asked me to accompany him to Atlanta. It's a significant step, and even though he's still mistrustful, I now know I'm important to him.

My mom's voice interrupts my reverie. "Hi, honey. I'm calling to see if you plan to come home for your father's birthday next month."

I take the gooey ice cream carton to the garbage and toss the spoon in the sink. "Oh, that's right. Are you planning a big party?"

"Just something intimate here at the house. I'd like you to be here."

"Of course, Mom. I want to come. It'll be nice to see my friends, too. Maybe I'll stay for a week."

"Wonderful. Perhaps you can meet with Rob and make some decisions." A cool silence hangs between us.

"Perhaps." It's not a bad idea. By then we'll have spent four months apart. Despite my growing realization we couldn't share a happy marriage, I should discuss it with him face-to-face. Maybe seeing him again will settle the matter for good.

"Your father will be pleased. Shall I make reservations at Bliss Spa or the theater or whatnot? You must be missing some of your usual activities."

Actually, I haven't missed those things much, but I don't mention it to Mom. She's extending a peace offering, so I humor her to keep things pleasant. Old habits die hard.

"Sure, whatever you'd like to do is fine with me. Maybe Jill will join us."

"Maybe." She pauses before launching into less-pleasant territory. "So, what are you doing these days? I assume Levi's needing you less and less as his recovery progresses."

My insides bristle at the obnoxious tone she affects whenever mentioning Levi.

"Well, I'm traveling to Atlanta with him to confront his mother."
I can't help myself from adding, "Looks like he's taking your advice
after all. That should make you happy."

After a short pause, she launches into a lecture.

"Lindsey, where's your mind? Stay out of his family situation.
What's it got to do with your issues or reasons for running off in the
first place? You're getting too involved with him."

"I care about him, Mom. He's taking a huge emotional risk and
asked for my support."

"He's using you, Lindsey. Men like him don't settle down and
fall in love. Maybe you haven't ended up in his bed yet, but you're
letting your imagination run wild if you believe he'll become a man
who can commit and be a real partner, like Rob."

"God forbid Levi turns into Rob. Rob, a man so committed he
cheated on me. News flash, Mom: Rob isn't the only man on the
planet. He looks great on paper, but he's proven himself to be unre-
liable, untrustworthy, and unsafe." I'm surprised by my conviction
as the words fall from my mouth. Perhaps I'm more decided than I
realized. "I'm not discussing this with you. I'm traveling to Atlanta,
whether or not you agree."

"I don't recognize you at all, Lindsey."

"That's a shame because, for the first time in years, I'm finally
rediscovering myself." I smile at the truth of my statement.

Silence.

"Mom, I don't want to be at odds. You're taking matters personally that have little to do with you. I wish you'd chill out and let me
spread my wings."

"You say that as if I don't want to see you happy. Why is my
experience and advice suddenly so repugnant?"

"I respect your advice, Mom, but you need to respect my right
to reject it on occasion." I hear her sigh.

"I'll see you in a few weeks. Levi's not invited to stay here, Lindsey."

"What a surprise!" I spit out. "Bye."

I flop onto the sofa. Not even my mom can dampen my spirits today. Levi forgave me, basically, for my meddling. He's taking me with him to meet his mother. He needs me and I'm happy.

CHAPTER SEVENTEEN

Levi

My eyes open at four a.m., before the alarm rings. It's no surprise, considering I barely slept. We're booked on a seven o'clock flight to Atlanta, so I need to hustle. I should have taken a sleeping pill last night. Now my typically limited patience is sure to decrease due to the lack of rest.

Needless to say, I've been plagued with doubts for the past two days. The closer this trip got, the worse I felt. I seldom make uncalculated, impulsive decisions, and I'm still clueless about my goals.

I've no idea what to expect, or how I'll feel, when I see Mama's eyes. For the first time in my life, I'm walking to the table blind, deaf, and dumb. I swear, Lindsey's turned me into an idiot.

Of course, she's inexplicably happy about this trip. I'm still upset with her, but I've kept my mouth shut. She's under the impression all's been forgiven. I don't dispel the notion because my anger's subsiding anyway, and I need her to come with me.

She lacks the courage of her convictions in her own life, but she's very strong when it comes to everything else. I'm counting on her to back me up if I stumble. And ultimately, I'm confronting my past so I might have a different kind of future, one that involves her. She should be with me when I do.

The knock at my front door disturbs the quiet of my house. I roll my suitcase out to greet Lindsey. Despite the obscenely early hour, she's bright-eyed and brimming with nervous energy. The morning breeze blows her yellow dress around her knees. She's wearing makeup, earrings, and heels.

"Tell me you didn't get all dressed up to impress my mama, Lindsey." I shake my head.

"I wanted to look nice. So what?" Her hand skitters along her skirt. "It's the proper way to meet." She sighs when I roll my eyes. "Give me your bag, grumpy." She hoists my suitcase from my hand. "Would you rather I be in cutoff shorts and braless when I meet your mother?"

I suppress the sudden arousal that image evokes, then seat myself in the car.

"That'd probably be more appropriate, under the circumstances." I narrow my gaze to get her attention. "This isn't a date or something. I'm not bringing you home to meet my beloved mother. This is a skirmish with a virtual stranger."

My terse response is meant to remind her of the circumstances, not to hurt her. She winces nonetheless, at my tone or message, or both.

～

Several hours later, after a turbulent flight and a terrible lunch, we check into the hotel. I'd have preferred one room, but between her confusion about Rob and our recent fight, I doubted she'd have been comfortable.

"So, what time are we meeting with your mom?" she asks before I enter my room.

"The sooner the better." I insert the key card and open my door. Truthfully I could use some time to lie down and recover from the flight. My back's sore, but I'll pop a pain pill to numb it. Maybe it will numb my mind, too, which would be helpful. "Can you be ready in fifteen minutes?"

"Oh, sure. Is she expecting us already? It's midafternoon. Doesn't she work?"

"Hell if I know." I look at her as if she's from Mars. "I didn't call her. We're just going to show up."

Lindsey follows me into my room. Her huge eyes reflect utter shock as she drops her luggage by her feet.

"What? Tell me I didn't hear you right, Levi. Tell me we're not descending, unannounced, on your mother's doorstep!" There they go—her hands are planted on her hips again. I grin.

"No can do, darlin'. That's exactly what we're doing." I scratch my cheek defiantly, then wonder why I'm standing here ready to rumble with Lindsey. She's not the object of my anger, but she's the one who's here.

"What if she's at work, or away, or who knows where?"

"We'll wait a while, or leave and go back after five."

"Why did you come here this way? An ambush can only end badly. Did you really fly across the country to fight?" Her hands gesticulate all over the place, which is helpful, because it tickles me to see her all worked up. "And I get a front-row seat to the brawl. Oh, great. Thanks so much!"

I chuckle.

"Oh, of course this is funny to you." She frowns.

"No, this ain't funny." Damn, grammar. "You're funny, though."

Lindsey leans against the wall and sighs.

"Levi, please reconsider. It'll be a shame to have come all this way only to leave worse off than when you arrived. I thought you wanted to make peace. Not start a war. You're blindsiding her on purpose. That's not fair."

"Fair? *Fair?*" Thunder explodes in my head. "Why the hell should I be fair to her? She didn't give a lick about fair when she walked away from me." My booming voice surprises Lindsey. Scares her, even. I blow out a breath and quiet down. "If I'd have called her, do you honestly think she'd have agreed to see me?"

Lindsey scowls and purses her lips together. "Maybe not." Resignation dims her face. "I don't know. I guess we'll never know." She picks up her luggage. "It's your show, Levi. I'll go along. I can't imagine everything you feel, especially since you refuse to share it with me." She casts me a hopeful glance. When I offer no reply, she sighs. "I'll be back soon, then we can go."

My blood pressure's climbing. I toss my suitcase on the bed and wander to the bathroom to splash cold water on my face. Staring at myself in the mirror, I question whether Lindsey's right. Am I wasting this trip by planning a battle? What do I truly want from Mama?

The elusive answer is what's kept me awake these past few nights. All I know is I want to feel better. But what will make me feel better? Do I want to wreck her life, the way she destroyed mine? Will vengeance make me feel better?

I'd bet big bucks her new husband doesn't know about me. What man could fall in love with a woman who left her child? Yeah, I feel the ugly part of me that wants to rob her happiness since she stole much of mine. In the long run, however, that small victory won't improve my life, and it might even give me another thing to regret.

Obviously Lindsey's not pleased with my intention, either, which doesn't sit well with me. I don't need her approval, but I don't particularly like her disapproval, either. Hell, she's one big reason I came here in the first place. If I end up lowering her opinion of me, it sure will have been a waste of my time and money.

She knocks at the door but I'm not ready to face her just yet. I take a deep breath, staring into the mirror, searching for the answer.

Nothing.

Guess it's simply showtime.

~

Lindsey parks the car in front of Mama's house, which is located in a middle-class suburb of Atlanta. It's a decent street, safe and all, littered with small homes and smaller yards. The moss-green house has a large front porch with a swing, and is surrounded by flowerbeds. Angst stretches throughout my chest as I consider how different my childhood might have been here, with her.

My jaw hurts from too much clenching, and I'm perspiring. Granted, it's hot and humid today, but that's not the cause of my discomfort. I'm staring out the passenger window, gathering my thoughts, when Lindsey's hand pats my forearm. I haven't felt this much trepidation since my adolescence. It must be obvious, because Lindsey's eyes fill with concern.

"Levi, are you ready? We can sit here if you're not. Or I can drive around a little."

Lindsey's support, like cashmere-wrapped steel, saves me. I lift her hand to my lips to kiss it. A surge of uneasy emotions renders me unable to express my gratitude, so I deflect with a compliment.

"You look real pretty today, by the way." Smiling, I open the door. If I don't move forward right now, I'll retreat.

As we walk up the driveway, she takes hold of my hand.

"You know," Lindsey says, "if she's not here, we should get a strong drink before we come back. Maybe we should have done that first, actually." She smiles, trying to help me relax.

I appreciate her effort, but my heart's still slamming in my chest with each footstep toward Mama's front door. I can't turn back now.

I ring the doorbell and step back, holding my breath. Lindsey squeezes my hand with both of hers. "No matter what happens, Levi, I'm right here with you."

The door opens and, through the screen, I see Mama. She's older, but it's her. She's still a wisp of a thing, with the palest hair and eyes . . . a ghostly reminder of unbearable pain. Her former beauty's muted by age, despite her being only forty-nine. She mustn't recognize me at first, because she looks at Lindsey.

"Can I help you?" she asks, but then tilts her head and narrows her eyes when glancing back at me. I know I resemble my pop, so I wait an extra second before speaking, giving her an opportunity to realize who I am. I feel Lindsey fidget beside me.

"Hello, Mama." I stand still, peering through the screen door. Lindsey's got my arm in a death grip.

Mama steps back slightly and whispers, "Levi?"

She looks haunted, which pleases me. Seconds pass while the two of us stare at each other. When she doesn't open the door, I break the silence.

"Aren't you going to invite me in? It's been so long. There's much to talk about."

I hadn't intended to be sarcastic right off the bat, but the cork on my bottled-up rage has been blown off by more than twenty years of pressure. Now I wish Lindsey weren't here to witness my fury, but it's too late.

Mama struggles to regain her composure.

"Levi, I can't. You can't be here. I'll meet you tomorrow, anywhere but here." She's pleading, but I have no sympathy.

"Sorry, Mama. I flew across the country to see you. My return flight leaves tomorrow morning, so we'll be talking here and now." I reach for the screen door.

"No, Levi. Please, go." Her frightened eyes search mine for mercy but find none. "My husband will be home soon. He doesn't know about you. Please!"

Foolishly, even after all these years, some tiny part of me had hoped she'd welcome the chance to meet me. Embarrassed by my stupidity, my mood darkens.

"Well, then, the longer you delay me on the porch, the more likely I'll be meeting my stepdad, I suppose."

Lindsey tugs on my hand, but I shake her off and open the door to my mama's house. Adrenaline is pumping through me now, so I can barely feel my body.

"You're a selfish man." Mama's eyes narrow with contempt.

Fixing a smug smile on my face, I rest my chin in my hand and tap my finger against my lips, as if I'm considering her remark.

"I suppose I inherited that trait from you, then, didn't I?"

Without invitation, I brush past her, waltz into the tiny living room, and wait for her and Lindsey to join me.

❧

Lindsey

His mother's mouth falls open after his insult. I'm desperately seeking a way to smooth things over, then her brittle voice splinters my thoughts.

"I can see your daddy's manners rubbed off on you. You look like him. Tell me . . . are you a no-good hustler like him, too? Did he put you up to this, to shake me down or something?"

Her haughty tone and lack of remorse embitter me. Levi's camouflaging his emotions, but I'm sure he hurts. Of course, I had warned him an ambush wouldn't be pleasant.

Levi's icy stare, though directed at her, makes me shiver. I hold my breath, unsure what he'll say next.

"Don't speak ill of the dead, Mama. Pop may not have been the best man, but at least he didn't abandon his child. In the scheme of things, your sins are at least as bad."

I'm standing apart from them, rubbing the fabric of my skirt between my fingers, when Levi smiles at me.

"Where are my manners?" He reaches toward me. "Mama, this is my friend Miss Lindsey Hilliard. Lindsey, this is Mama."

"Hi." I extend my hand to her. "I'm sorry to meet you under these, um, circumstances."

She hesitates before shaking my hand, then returns her attention to Levi. "Okay, Levi. What do you want? Do you need money?"

Her obnoxious attitude and accusation piss me off. It's a struggle to keep quiet.

Levi sneers and nonchalantly promenades around her living room. He picks up a photograph of her and her husband and studies it before returning it to the table. I suspect he intends his leisurely pace to heighten her anxiety. It seems to be working. I also suspect it's helping him find his own footing. For all his threats, there's still a hurt little boy buried under all the hate on display.

"I don't need your money, Mama. I came here for answers. I know how my life turned out, but I'm curious about yours."

He takes a seat on the sofa and crosses one foot across the opposite knee as if we have all day. He grins at me and pats the cushion beside him, so I join him on the couch.

His mother glances at the clock on the mantel and then sits on a chair near the sofa. She observes me, probably wondering why I'm a party to this reunion.

"Lindsey? Perhaps you'd prefer to wait on the porch." She starts to rise from her chair. "I'm happy to get you a beverage."

"She's fine right here with me." Levi pins his mother with his eyes.

Much as I'd love to bolt from this powder keg, I can't desert him. Although he came with guns blazing, his mother hasn't done or said a kind or contrite thing since we've arrived. I'm convinced his behavior's largely a reaction to her chilly demeanor.

She sighs. Her only option is to satisfy his curiosity.

I don't know what I expected today, but I'd thought she'd have shown some sign of remorse or interest in Levi. Instead, she's merely interested in getting rid of him—again. My angry thoughts are interrupted by her next remark.

"Fine. What do you want to know? This is where I live, this is how my life turned out." She straightens her spine and sits back into her chair.

Levi pauses, staring through her. "Where'd you go when you left?"

Her cheek twitches. "At first I went to Houston for a few years. When my daddy got sick, I returned to Tifton." She looks to her lap and toys with her skirt. "After his death eighteen months later, I moved to Atlanta."

Donning an exaggerated, mocking frown, Levi leans forward. "Grandpappy's dead? Sorry I missed the funeral. The invitation must've been lost in the mail." He then tips his head sideways, like he often does when he's discerning something. "So, you've been here since then. When'd you remarry?"

"Thirteen years ago. John's a decent man. Honest."

"Huh." Levi grins. "Odd how you value his honesty but don't pay him the respect of giving him yours."

His mother smarts at his remark, briefly averting her eyes.

Levi leans toward her, his jaw firmly set. "Do I have any siblings?"

My eyes involuntarily pop open. Could Levi have siblings? I'd never considered the possibility. God, I hope not. If she's borne and kept other children, it'll only compound his pain.

For the first time this afternoon, her tone softens.

"No, Levi. I never had any other children."

I notice relief flicker across his face. In a flash, he dons his stony mask once more.

Levi and his mother sit in silence for what seems like forever. He's waiting for her to say more, but she refuses. In my mind, I imagine grabbing his mother by her shoulders and physically shaking her, as if my aggression will force her to apologize to her son and beg for his forgiveness.

Finally, Levi speaks again, in quiet, anguished tones.

"Why, Mama? Why'd you leave me?"

Her gaze fixes upon her hands, which remain folded in her lap, white knuckles visible to all.

"I was pregnant at seventeen. By eighteen, I was a mother and married to a handsome charmer who turned out to be a cheat and a low-life liar. I did the best I could, for as long as I could, but I didn't want to live that way—in shame, with regret. It was no life for me. Your daddy wouldn't change. So, after too many squabbles, I left."

"You escaped a bad life." Levi's dead-calm voice alarms me.

"Yes, I did."

"So, either I was part of what made that life bad, or you left me to grow up in a bad life. Which is it, and why?"

There it is—the crux of the matter, the root of Levi's insecurities and intimacy issues. I wish I could throw myself around him like a shield.

Surprisingly, his mother's emotions finally inundate her and unshed tears dampen her eyes. Her voice breaks apart a bit when she answers.

"I doubt there's any answer to satisfy you. It wasn't an easy choice, despite how it may have appeared to you. At the time, it seemed the best option. If I took you, I'd have always been tied to Jim. But more importantly, I knew in my heart I wasn't meant to be a mother. Other mothers bonded with their babies. But I never did. I never did, Levi. Maybe I was too young or too unhappy with Jim, or maybe I'm simply not meant to be anyone's mother."

"That's it? You weren't meant to be a mother?" He locks his eyes on hers so she can't evade him. "But you *are* a mother."

Her penitent comportment swiftly reverts to antipathy. "Don't make me out to be a monster. I didn't abort you, which, at seventeen, surely crossed my mind." Her venomous retort knocks Levi back a minute, and his retreat emboldens her. "I tried to be your mother, but I couldn't. Do you condemn women who give their babies up for adoption? I left you with your father. I didn't leave you in the streets or foster care."

Levi squeezes my hand so tightly I bite back a yelp. I notice his lower lip quiver, but can't tell if he's furious or despondent, until he speaks. His palpable raw pain lashes my heart. I'm in over my head and don't know how to help.

"You think you're a saint because you didn't kill me? Jesus, that's fucked up." Levi's features change shape as his rage deepens. "You didn't make some grand sacrifice by giving up your infant to some lovin' family for a better life. I wasn't a baby, Mama. I was nine. You *knew* me. You knew I loved you. You never even said good-bye or wrote me a damned letter." He draws a deep breath. "You left me with a man you hated, not respected. A man you knew couldn't give me a stable home. You did that to me, after nearly a decade as my mother."

A tear slips from his eye, but he wipes it away in disgusted anger. He's trembling. If I could scoop him up and run, I would. But he's not making any move to leave.

His mother's remorse has long subsided. I shudder in anticipation of her next response.

"What else do you want me to say? I've told you, I'm not mother material. It's why I never had more kids. It was too much." She leans closer to him. "You needed too much attention. Always 'Mama this' and 'Mama that.' You'd cling to me constantly. When I was cooking, you'd be hooked around my ankles like a monkey. When I was napping, you'd crawl beside me and squirm around. When I was watching TV, you'd interrupt me with your laughing and playing. You suffocated me."

Levi's astonished face collapses under the weight of his mother's blame. Outraged by her insensitivity, I abruptly stand and stomp my foot.

"Shut up!" I stare at her and, God forgive me, embrace my lack of filter. "How dare you? How *dare* you make Levi responsible, in any way, for your pathetically weak choice? You've just described a loving, adoring son. The kind of child any mother would be blessed to have." I shake my head. "But the worst of it isn't even that you left. It's that you never looked back, never apologized, and never asked for forgiveness."

Avoiding Levi's eyes, I continue my rant. "Your son's a beautiful man. But you damaged his soul, leaving scars so deep he's afraid to trust anyone. Yet still you show no remorse. You've spent this afternoon defending and protecting yourself. Now that I've met you, I agree with your self-assessment—you aren't mother material!" Disgust courses through my body.

I reach out my hand to Levi. "Levi, we're leaving. You shouldn't be here anymore."

His mother doesn't let my insults pass without comment. "Missy, I, too, got drawn in by a handsome face. If Levi's closed off, that comes from him, not from what I did. You'd better watch out or you'll end up running, like me."

Her self-satisfied insult pushes me too far. Without thinking, I whirl around and slap her cheek. "I'm nothing like you."

Levi's shock snaps me back to reality. I rub my own hand, surprised by my outburst. I've never, in my life, hit anyone. His mother stands, with her hand on her cheek, staring at me with her eyebrows raised.

On our way out the door, Levi pauses to face his mother one final time.

"In case you're curious, I stayed with Pop until I turned eighteen, then I left and built a good life for myself. Pop died in May and left me your address." He turns to go, then faces her once more. "I've imagined this meeting many times over the years. Can't say it went as I might have hoped, but I'm glad I learned the truth. At least now I know I'd have been worse off if you'd stayed with me. I finally have peace, not that you care. I won't be disturbing you again, ma'am."

He inclines his head and we walk out the door.

His last-ditch effort to share something about his life with that awful woman, to make her know him in any way, rips my heart apart. She doesn't deserve to know him.

Levi falls deadly quiet during the entire ride back to the hotel.

CHAPTER EIGHTEEN

Levi

I keep my eyes closed in the car. I refuse to break down in front of Lindsey, but am having a hell of a time assimilating all my feelings. Mama's remarks replay, over and again, in my mind. Christ, she's hateful. A frigid bitch of a woman. Thank God she didn't have any more kids.

Lindsey's right, I was better off without Mama in my life. That woman resents me, as if I chose to be born just to ruin her life. Comparing herself to selfless women who give up babies for adoption. She's crazy.

Yet I can't shut out the little voice that wonders whether she'd have stuck it out with me if I'd been less clingy.

Lindsey's long sigh breaks my concentration. Boy, she sure got fired up. I still can't believe she smacked my mama. I couldn't even react at the time. Just watched it unfold like a movie.

I shouldn't have dragged her into this mess. No doubt she'll consider all she's learned about my genetics and run from me as soon as we get back to California.

Damaged soul. That's how Lindsey sees me. A beautiful man with a damaged soul. She thinks I was made, not born, this way.

But maybe it doesn't even matter how I became distant. I am distant. Lindsey deserves someone who isn't detached and fucked up. God forbid she ends up with the wrong person and becomes unhappy like my mama.

"Levi, will you talk to me?" Lindsey asks as she pulls into the parking garage. "Please say something."

I don't know what I expected from the day, but now I just want to escape her and her questions before she sees my weakness. "I can't talk now. Sorry."

"Are you mad at me for how I spoke to your mother—for slapping her?" A tiny whimper escapes her throat. "I'm sorry. I couldn't help myself. Exploding is so unlike me. Please don't be mad."

She chases me through the hotel's parking garage, reaching for my hand. I yank it away, still averting eye contact.

"I'm not mad at you." I shift my gaze to the buttons inside the elevator. "But I need to be alone for a while."

"No." She grabs for me again. "Levi, look at me. I came all this way for you. The least you can do is look at me. Don't push me away."

I take her by her arms and shove her away.

"Lindsey, leave me be. Please." Thankfully, the elevator doors open, providing an escape. I stalk into the hall and dash toward my room, but she's on my heels. "Darlin', I appreciate everything you've done, but I don't want you to see me this way." I'm losing the battle against the swelling tide of self-pity. "Please, let it lie."

Unfortunately, as usual, Lindsey's undeterred by the word *no*. She slips into my room behind me, refusing to respect my wishes. Ignoring her, I head straight to the minibar, find some vodka, and then sit on the edge of my bed.

She kneels in front of me. She gently clasps her hand around the bottle, trying to pry it away from me.

Her other hand rests on my thigh, and I suddenly ache with a startling need.

"Please don't run away, not when I feel closer to you than ever.

There's no shame in feeling vulnerable after such a painful experience. I won't think less of you. I'll still be here."

I let go because right now I'm too weak to fight my way out of a wet paper bag. Her compassion undermines my determination, and my tears flow. Damn it, I've never cried in front of any woman.

She whisks the bottle from me, then lowers her head onto my lap and encircles her arms around my back.

Suddenly I'm no longer thinking about Mama. The weight and warmth of Lindsey's body affect mine. I want to bury myself in her and make everything else disappear. She's what I need, like air and water. But I can't have her; she made that clear the other week.

"Lindsey, please go. I can't have you here and not *have* you. I know you're trying to help, but you're asking too much from me. Don't stir up something you can't finish."

Instead of pulling away, she looks at me and strokes my thighs. "I want to stay here with you."

My eyes scan her face. "You're sure?"

She nods.

The heat in her eyes dissolves my restraint. Before she can rethink her decision, I yank her up against me and claim her mouth with a growl. I'm completely overwhelmed by the softness of her lips, the scent of her skin, and the taste of her.

My breath comes fast and hard. Hers speeds up as well. I lie back onto the bed, bringing her with me. When I loosen the knot of her hair, it falls around her face and I bury my hands into it while eagerly crushing her lips to mine. My hands run along her neck, down her back, and around the curve of her hips and thighs.

Her breath catches, sending shock waves of pleasure through me. *Lindsey.* My greedy hands and mouth seek every part of her, desperate to make her mine. I'm ravenous for her.

All that matters now is us.

She wants me, too. Every mew, gasp, and moan she utters pushes me closer to the brink. I roll over and she squirms beneath me, her arms hugging me tightly. Desire courses hot and heavy through my body.

I open my eyes. Her hair's tangled, her lips are swollen from our kisses, and she's panting and groping for me. The sight of her arousal sends shivers across my skin.

"Lindsey." Her name rumbles from deep within my chest.

I force myself to slow down, to savor the feel of her and the affection in her eyes while I kiss her—slowly, deeply.

Her hands tremble as she unbuttons my shirt. I can barely breathe when I realize she's undressing me. Fascinated, I watch her fingers undo each button, her chest rising and falling in anticipation.

She's surrendering to me, and the realization that I'm about to make love to her nearly knocks me out. I moan and kiss her harder when I feel her touch against my bare skin. I'm torn between the need to take her now and the desire to make this last a lifetime.

Slowly, I unzip the side of her dress. Within a minute, she's lying beside me, wearing only her frilly underwear. I feast on the sight of her. My hands roam the planes of her waist, her thigh, her breast, and up her neck to her jaw. She's the most beautiful woman I know, and she's about to be mine.

Finally.

Raising myself above her, I kiss her neck and then trail my tongue down between her breasts and onto her stomach. She arches her back and threads her hands in my hair. Oh, God, she's perfect. The slow rise of her spine and each muffled response hurl me closer to heaven.

Her hands fumble with my pants, but soon enough they fall to the floor. When her hand reaches under the elastic of my boxers, I shudder and then notice her smile in response to her own power.

Her playful grin teases me, so I remove her bra and take her breast in my mouth to regain control, to make her submit. My hands are free to fondle the rest of her, after removing her last stitch of clothing. She fists the sheets.

Her restless legs kick as she arches and thrusts her hips forward, seeking more of my fingers and mouth.

"Oh, Levi. Yes . . . yes."

Jesus, she's so responsive. I'm shaky from yearning, and afraid I won't last one minute once I'm inside her. Just the sound of her voice makes me want to explode.

I stroke her skin, memorizing each hollow and slope of her body. Lust rages through me and I press kisses along her thigh. She sucks in her breath and it muddles my brain.

With each caress and nip and tickle, her tension builds. She shifts her hips and rakes her fingers through my hair until I bring her to a shattering orgasm with my mouth.

"God, Levi. Oh, yes!"

The experience breaks open a wholly unfamiliar emotion in my chest. A swelling need to cradle her in my arms overpowers me. I kiss her mouth and fit myself between her legs. When I enter her fully, I can't breathe for a moment.

With slow, easy thrusts, I move inside the amazingly hot tightness of her body. It's different from any other sex I've had. I don't only want her body; I want her soul.

I murmur, "Look at me."

Her topaz eyes dreamily open. Locking my gaze with hers, I relish every movement of my body and hers, joined as one. When I see a tear slip from her eye, I panic.

Does she regret this already?

I freeze. "What's wrong?"

She smiles. "Nothing." Her hands curl around my neck and she pulls me into a kiss, but I'm not convinced.

"Why are you crying?" I'm stilled, inside her, brushing her hair from her face.

"Because I'm happy."

I stare at her for a long moment while a heady pressure builds in my chest. I'm thrilled and terrified at once, possessed by a fierce need to make her mine.

Her legs wrap around my hips, edging me deeper inside. She's magnificent and intoxicating, and suddenly I'm moving at a frantic pace. Her fingers dig into my back. She releases a guttural moan. I reach my own climax and collapse against her, smothering her neck and face with gentle kisses.

My eyes close. I'm completely and utterly satisfied. I could stay here, holding her, forever.

Sadly, I know reality will come. We'll leave the sanctity of this room and return to our real lives.

For now, she's mine. And it's enough.

∾

Lindsey

I awaken, spooned by Levi's warm body. It's five in the morning, but I've hardly slept. He's insatiable. While I've never before had sex so frequently in such a short span of time, I won't complain.

His fingers graze along my breasts and thighs. The damp heat of his breath whispers against my ear until he clamps his mouth against my neck. His erection presses against my hip, then he enters me from behind. The low groan deep within his chest pleasures me. I'm drowsy, yet aroused. He tenderly rocks me into another dizzying orgasm. Each time he exclaims my name in passionate, rasped whispers, shivers trickle up and down my spine.

Sex with Levi's nothing like I imagined. Knowing his past, I expected an impersonal, purely physical repartee. Surprisingly, he's been affectionate, emotional, and has kept me wrapped in an embrace throughout the night. Again, I'm not complaining. It's been an awakening.

I can't help wondering if he's like this with other women, or only me. Did the confrontation with his mother affect what's happened here, or not? Neither of my prior lovers has sent me spinning into ecstasy quite this way.

Whatever comes next, I know my situation with Rob's forever changed. Even if Levi and I leave everything between us here, in this hotel room, I could never resume my relationship with Rob like this never happened.

Passion, however, isn't the same as love. Rob claims to love me and to want to spend his life with me. I'd like to be a wife someday, but Rob's wife? If I return to him, so much would need to change. He might not even be willing, once he learns what I've done with Levi.

Frankly, I'm shocked by my own behavior. Yet I've never felt more alive and roused. Something's changed deep within me. I can't dismiss it and return home to being the dutiful daughter and fiancée, living my old life.

If I return to New York, it will be on new terms. But what about Levi?

Has seeing his mother put ghosts to rest, or will it cause him to bolster his fortress? And what of our intimacy? Considering his penchant for casual sex, I suspect he'll start to put distance between us when we reach LA. I can't blame him. He begged me to leave him alone, but I ignored him.

My concerns abate when I roll toward him and he hugs me against his chest. I'm too tired and content to raise my head to see whether his eyes are open.

"Levi?" I whisper.

"Hmm." He peppers tiny kisses across the top of my head.

"Are you okay about everything that happened . . . with your mother?" I trace my fingers along his ribs. "Did you get what you came for?"

He captures my hand and kisses it. "I got everything I want from this trip. More than I expected." Curling his fingers around my hand, he brings both to rest against his chest.

The groundwater of hope feeding my heart bubbles up. Unfortunately, shame revisits me in the form of the memory of my violent reaction to Levi's mother. No matter what he contends, some small part of him wanted a reconciliation or, at least, a minor show of affection from her. Instead, she laid blame on him for driving her away. My heart aches recalling it. Reflexively, I tighten my hold on Levi.

"I'm glad," I say, although I don't believe him.

～

At six o'clock, we land safely in LA. I recovered a few hours of sleep by napping during the long flight. Now, I'm starving. We've hardly eaten anything during the past twenty-four hours. Levi kept me quite preoccupied until we had to catch our flight home.

He's continued to keep me close all afternoon, rarely releasing my hand. I'm not sure what to expect going forward, and I'm afraid to ask. Jill would advise me to keep my mouth shut and roll with it. For once, I think I'll follow her lead.

We stop for dinner on our way home from LAX. By the time we return home for the night and I unload the luggage from the car, I'm exhausted. Levi takes hold of my hand and starts walking out of my garage toward his home.

"Levi?" I stop. "What are you doing?"

"Going to bed. I'm beat." He tugs me into another wonderful kiss. "Come on."

He tastes yummy, like the red wine and chocolate he enjoyed at dinner. But I'm not staying in his bachelor pad. I push away from him.

"To your house?" I arch one brow. "Uh-uh."

"Why not?" He frowns. "What's wrong with my house?"

"Your house is lovely, but I'm not sleeping with you in the bed where you've made love to countless women."

My cheeks color, but I don't care. I'm not comfortable and I won't pretend I am.

He casts a seductive smile in my direction.

"I've had sex with other women, but I've never made love with any woman in that bed . . . yet."

His words cause my heart rate to climb, but I hold my ground.

"Smoothly played, Levi. But I'm still not sleeping there tonight." I hug my arms around his neck. "You can stay with me at my house if you'd like."

"Still bossy." He searches my eyes, then smiles. "All right, you win."

Within minutes, we've tumbled into my bed, naked. The glass door's open, allowing the sound of the waves to float through the air. Levi's husky voice rouses me. His fingers sweep across my skin, drawing ribbons of goose bumps and shivers over my body. His day-old beard lightly abrades my breast before he takes it in his mouth, sending another wave of shudders through me.

My own hands explore the hard muscles of his chest and arms, the silky locks of his hair, and his bare chest. He's so gorgeous. When we're together this way, he looks at me almost reverently, reducing me to a quivering mass of Jell-O.

I like being on top, controlling the pace and having a perfect view of him. It makes me feel powerful.

Afterward, I collapse on top of him. We end up entwined with his leg thrown over my hip. I snuggle deeper inside his embrace. Exhaustion lays over me like a heavy blanket.

While drifting to sleep, I realize Levi hasn't asked about Rob or spoken of the future. He may assume I've agreed to his no-strings policy by sleeping with him before clarifying the point. That I won't share him may send him running. I need to talk to him before I talk to Rob, and I need to talk to Rob soon.

But my head throbs from the lack of sleep and the roller coaster of emotions. I think I'll put off dealing with it all until tomorrow.

CHAPTER NINETEEN

Levi

I can't keep Lindsey close enough to satisfy me—she's infused all my senses. To win the pot, I ought to be shrewd, to withhold and wait for her to reveal her hand. But I can't stop smiling or keep my hands—or any other part of my body—to myself.

Am I falling in love? It's a disastrous place to be, but my heart won't give it up. Not yet, anyway.

She yawns and shifts away from me to stretch. Holding her waist, I tuck her back inside my arms, pressing a kiss against the top of her head.

"Go back to sleep, darlin'." Resting my cheek against her hair, I inhale that captivating grapefruit smell.

She unlocks my arms to escape me, but I grasp her wrist.

"Where're you going?"

"To run." She smiles and kisses my nose. "Got to keep the blood pumping."

I yank her back into bed. "I'll keep your blood pumping." Grasping her behind her neck, I steal another kiss.

She grins. "I know, that's why I need my morning run—for sanity."

Reluctantly, I release her.

"I'll be back in forty-five minutes." She kisses me quickly and then dashes away.

Rolling onto my stomach, I notice two framed photos on her

bedside table. In a glass frame, she keeps a photo of herself with her parents. They're dressed up at some formal social event. Lindsey's wearing a low-cut, emerald-green gown, her shiny hair framing her face. I imagine escorting her to an affair like that, dancing close, having her on my arm all night. She makes me wish for something I never wanted before, yet now need like air and water.

Pulling my head from the clouds, I return the photo to the table. When I pick up the silver frame, my blood runs cold. Lindsey's toothy grin and twinkling eyes bestow a loving look, not at me, but at the man beside her in the photo.

It must be Rob. A large diamond ring resides on the hand she's draped around his shoulder. She beams at him, but he's looking at the camera—at me. His perfectly shorn black hair and cool-blue eyes warn me that she's his, not mine.

I set the photo down. The image of his smug face hovers above me, like a heavy weight pinning me to her bed. Why is his photo beside her bed? Damn it to hell. Didn't she end things with him yet? Jealousy lashes through me, causing my muscles to burn, then go rigid.

Calm down, Levi. Closing my eyes, I draw long, deep breaths. She didn't attempt to hide it from me, so maybe it's not important. Maybe she forgot it's even here. A few minutes later, the suffocating haze lifts. Whatever is or isn't in her heart, I can't know unless I ask.

But I won't ask.

She'll tell me when she's ready. Until then, I'll wage a campaign to make her mine. I'll make her forget he ever existed.

Heavy footsteps climbing the stairwell startle me. I pop open one eye when she enters the room. On a mission to make love to her, to erase him from her memory and my own, I sit up.

"Come here," I say gruffly.

"I'm all sweaty," she protests.

Lunging forward, I catch her hand and pull her into bed. "I like you sweaty."

I capture her mouth with my own and restrain her arms above her head. She parts her lips and immediately surrenders with a purr in her throat. Despite my impulse to take her quickly, I reel in my desire and commit to long, lazy kisses and caresses. I'll torment her and tease her until she can't breathe, can't think, can't do anything but beg to be mine. I didn't count on my plan to drive her wild to also send me over the edge.

"Levi. Please." Her breathless command is what I've been waiting to hear. "Don't stop."

I need to know it's me, not him, she wants. I can only know it if I see her eyes.

"Look at me."

When our eyes lock, I enter her and swallow her in a kiss.

"Jesus, Lindsey. What you do to me . . ." I've lost control. Consumed with passion, my thrusts rapidly become uneven, convulsive.

"Levi, I lo . . ." she trails off.

Tell me. Tell me you love me. But she doesn't finish, so I'm unsure of what she'd intended to say.

I lie on top of her, spent and motionless, while her legs stay clamped around my hips and her hands gently sweep up and down my back and along the scar on my spine. If not for that accident, I wouldn't be here with her now. Funny how something awful can turn around and become wonderful. Could Lindsey be right about destiny?

I drag her with me as I roll on my side and kiss her again. She smiles while touching my face. Real happiness eluded me for most of my life until recently. I wish I could enjoy it without apprehension.

Abruptly, Lindsey props herself up on her elbow. "I need to shower."

I draw one side of my mouth upward. "Me too."

"Levi, if we keep up at this pace I won't be able to walk, much less run."

"Hm. Well, I can think of a lot of entertaining things we can do that won't impede your ability to walk."

"Is that right?" she teases.

I quickly follow her into the shower. "Yep, let me show you."

~

I leave Lindsey in the shower and go downstairs to prepare breakfast. While I'm rooting through her refrigerator and cabinets, someone rings the doorbell. Who's here so early in the morning?

"Lindsey, someone's at your door," I call up to her.

"Can you get it? I'm not finished dressing."

The doorbell rings again just before I unlock and open the door. The ground beneath me shifts when I come face-to-face with the man in the photo by Lindsey's bed. He stands on her doorstep, with red roses in hand, staring at me with cool-blue eyes.

Rob steps back to match the address on the door with the one on the piece of paper in his hand.

Did she invite him? My defensive instincts take over and I hide my change of thoughts.

"Can I help you?"

"I'm sorry. Perhaps I have the wrong address." Rob's face colors, but he remains calm. "I'm looking for Lindsey Hilliard."

His clipped New England accent serves as a reminder that I'm not from their world. I want him to leave, and selfishly, I don't care what I have to do to make that happen.

"She's here. Just getting out of the shower." I smile, pretending I have no idea who he is. "May I tell her who's callin'?"

Rob's eyes focus on my wet hair and bare chest. I'm supremely pleased to make my relationship with Lindsey obvious.

"Rob Whitmore." He waits for me to recognize his name.

"Huh. The ex from New York?" I tip my chin up. "She didn't mention expecting you." I'm still blocking his entrance.

Through gritted teeth, he utters, "It's a surprise visit."

"Indeed it is." I step back and wave him into her house. "Come on in. I'll get her for you." Now I know she didn't ask him to come, which improves my mood considerably. "Take a seat." I motion toward the sofa before trotting upstairs.

Lindsey is putting her hair in a ponytail. "Was it a delivery or something?"

"Or something." I stare at her, waiting for her full attention so I can read her facial expression when I tell her about Rob. "Rob's here . . . with more damned flowers." I cross my arms in front of my chest.

Lindsey's hands whip up and cover her mouth. Her jaw drops, and her feral eyes dart around the room. Not the response I wanted. Her eyes glisten as she holds her stomach and bends over.

"You answered the door . . . like that?" She gapes at my lack of clothing.

"Yes." I scowl. Her guilt and remorse shred my heart. "What's the problem, Lindsey?"

"This is not good." She's shaking and talking to herself. "This isn't the way . . . This is messed up. . . ."

"Messed up?" The edge in my voice catches her attention.

"Levi, I'm sorry. I—I should talk to him. Alone."

"You're asking *me* to leave?" I glower. "Why's he even here, Lindsey? I thought you and he had ended things." I choke back my anger, because I suspect he's listening to us.

"It's not that easy, Levi. Yes, technically, we're not together. But there are a lot of things still unsaid. I haven't seen him in months and this is not the way I'd have preferred he learn about you."

"What're you gonna tell him?" I grab my shirt. I need to leave before I do or say something I can't take back.

"I'm not sure." Lindsey stops fidgeting and looks at me expectantly. "What do you want me to do?"

Jesus. Really? She's asking me to tell her what to do? Now I'm furious.

"Christ, Lindsey, it's your damn life. I don't want you to do anything because of me, that's for sure." I grab my shoes, but stomp down her steps in my bare feet.

Rob waits near the bottom of the stairs with a grin on his face. He's gloating. I compose myself, unwilling to cede more of the upper hand to him.

"She'll be down in a minute. If you'll excuse me, I'll leave you two alone to talk." I start toward the door, then he speaks.

"How was Atlanta?" His arrogant tone slices through me.

Caught off guard by his remark, I can't summon a snappy retort.

"None of your business." My icy tone doesn't deter him.

"Helene mentioned your circumstances to me. She expressed concerns about what might develop between you and Lindsey. I hope you didn't get too attached. I'm not slinking away without a fight, and I don't usually lose."

I'm ready to pop the cocky son of a bitch in the face, but Lindsey appears.

"Hi, Rob." She's pale and upset. "I'm surprised to see you."

He turns his attention to her and then glances back at me. I stare at Lindsey, but she makes no overture to me, so I back away and go home.

~

Lindsey

I can't think. I'm torn in two. I didn't want to hurt Levi or Rob yet managed to level both of them. As Levi left, his walls came slamming down around him, like heavy metal doors. What have I done?

Before I collect my thoughts, Rob hands me a bouquet of roses. The look in his eyes indicates he's here on a mission.

"When I brought these for you, I didn't expect to find you in a compromising position with another man." He's too calm. "Lindsey, did you sleep with him to strike back at me because of Ava?"

Oh, he's made it all about him. Is it so inconceivable I might simply prefer someone else? Perhaps I have moved on. I deposit the flowers on the table without care.

Time to seize control of the conversation. "Rob, why are you here? Without invitation or warning, I might add."

He places his hands on my shoulders. "I received your thank-you note. Seeing the picture of you with the flowers I sent made me miss you more. Then I ran into your mother, who told me about your growing infatuation with your neighbor. I assume he's the guy who just ducked out of here. Anyway, desperate measures were required to bring you back where you belong."

"Where I belong? Or where you and my mother think I belong?"

"Let's talk, Lindsey." Rob sighs. "We're on even footing now. I slept with Ava; you've dallied with your surfer. I admit it hurts like hell to see you with another man. You've got my attention."

He doesn't look nearly as ruffled as he proclaims. The strain of the situation weakens my knees, so I pull out a dining chair and sit.

"Contrary to your assumptions, what's happened with Levi has nothing to do with revenge. In fact, it has nothing to do with you at all."

"Lindsey, don't kid yourself." Rob sits beside me and jerks my chair around to face him. "You wouldn't even be here if it weren't for my stupidity. Maybe you didn't intentionally hook up with him to hurt me, but you turned to him because he's my opposite."

His sympathetic expression seems phony to me, but he continues. "I hurt you, then you removed yourself from everything, and everyone, that reminded you of me, of us, of our life. Even you must admit you don't really expect a happily ever after on the beach with a drifter. You sought to investigate the road not taken, and now you have. But eventually you've got to consider the future you really want."

"Rob, I don't want to hurt you, but you're mistaken if you think this is all about you." My eyes search his. "It's about me. I tried telling you weeks ago, but you mocked me for 'finding myself.'" Do I want affirmation, denial, hate, or love from him? I'm ambivalent.

"You're right, I did mock you." Slouching back into the chair, he sighs. "I've been unhappy since you left. Every time I felt you pull further away, it upset me. I haven't handled this well. I should have chased you down as soon as you left, but I believed you'd be back. Not because I deserved it, but because we have an amazing future waiting for us. How can you turn your back on it?"

I wish I shared his confidence about the future, or us. "You don't believe me, but I've changed. I'm not the same girl anymore. I want to forge my own path. Maybe the new me no longer fits with the old us."

"I've never stood in your way before, so why do you think I'd do so now? I don't care what you want to do, as long as you're with me when you do it." He takes my hands in his and stares at me. "You'll never not fit in my life."

His grip tightens. "You think you'd have a better life here, with him? Has he made you any promises, or is he just enjoying the moment? I'm here, despite it all, fighting for you. Doesn't that count for anything?"

I don't want you to do anything because of me, that's for sure. Rob's right—Levi hasn't told me how he feels about me. But the past intensely passionate thirty-six hours could not be an illusion. It means something, even if Levi left here without any promises. Knowing him, he did it to force me to draw my own conclusions.

"It counts for something, Rob." I blink back shameful, nervous tears. "But doesn't it matter to you that I've started a relationship with another man?"

Rob's hands break away from mine to ball into tight fists.

"You know it matters," he barks. "I hate it. I can't stomach it, in fact. But I'll put it behind us if you'll come back with me, now. I won't share you. You need to decide where you want to be."

Despite his loving words and affirmations, I feel bullied. Rob's played this well, and treated me with respect, yet it feels hollow and showy. Deep in my soul, I'm unable to shake my distrust.

"I'm not sure you really love me." I avoid looking in his eyes, all the while knowing somewhere inside I don't really love him anymore, at least not enough to commit my life to him.

"You keep saying things like that, but I'm here begging for another chance. Why would I be here if I didn't love you?"

"To win." As soon as I say the words, it makes perfect sense.

"Win?"

"Win me back, away from Levi or LA. You thrive on challenge. Winning me back, after your betrayal and my move, well that's a seductive victory. But how long until another secret fling comes along?"

"You don't get to pull the guilt card again, Lindsey. Now I can say the same thing to you. You jumped into someone else's bed, so don't play high-and-mighty."

"I didn't cheat while we were engaged. We broke up months ago. And unlike you, I didn't go to bed with someone I don't care about."

"Him? You care about him? Come on. You enjoy pushing your mother's buttons." His tempestuous eyes betray his contained rage. "Helene saw it, but I'd have never believed you'd be so gullible. You can't care about him."

"I'm not gullible. I do care about Levi. A lot. I won't pretend my feelings aren't real simply because you and my mother don't like or understand them. Maybe I don't completely understand them yet, either, but it doesn't diminish their significance. Please don't force me to hurt you by pushing me to say more."

"You don't love me anymore?" He looks humbled.

My throat aches. "I suspect I'll always love you in some ways, Rob, in spite of everything. I'll always want good things for you." I gulp. "But I don't see the same future for myself that I once did. I'm sorry, Rob. Marrying you now isn't what I want, and it may never be. I don't expect you to wait for me."

I'm shocked to hear the words leave my mouth, but the instant they do, a weight lifts. "I think we should say good-bye."

Rob's face clouds over. He turns to me, repulsed. "You're a piece of work, Lindsey—a cold, punishing piece of work. So, this is for the best, then, because God forbid I be tied to an unforgiving bitch for the rest of my life."

He's lashing out because he's in pain, but it stings.

"I'm sorry you see me that way." A tear falls down my cheek. "I never set out to hurt you."

"*I'm* sorry I ended things with Ava when you left. That's my second-biggest mistake, the first being chasing after you."

His words leave me cold. I'd always suspected more went on between him and her. His comment confirms my suspicion. Now I'm equally revolted.

"Then you'd better hurry and catch the next flight back to New York." I grab the roses on the table—his predictable gesture—and hand him the bouquet. "Under the circumstances, perhaps you should take these to Ava."

He snatches them from me and stalks toward the door. Just before leaving, he turns and snarls. "When things fall apart with your neighbor, don't come crawling back to me. If I never see you again, it will be too soon."

A picture in the hallway rattles against the wall when he slams the door closed behind him. A loud screech tears apart the air as Rob's car peels out of my driveway.

Sinking to the floor, I cry over all of the pain we've caused each other. I was naive to believe we could end things as friends. Despite his abominable behavior, I don't hate him. I loved him. A tidal wave of nostalgia causes me to erupt into sobs over lost years and lost love.

CHAPTER TWENTY

Levi

I'm going to lose her. Goddamn it, she's going to forgive that dishonest ass. When she discovered he'd arrived, her shame over being with me thrust a dagger in my chest. I'm disgusted by my own foolishness.

I march over to the closet, take the box of ashes off the shelf, and then set it on the kitchen counter. I place my hands on either side of the box and just stare. Somewhere in the great beyond Pop's shaking his head. I can almost hear his big ol' "I told you, son" echo through the house.

My fingers grip the box more tightly. What have I been thinking these past months? How'd I convince myself I could handle this? I've never acted like such a moron as I have this summer. Lindsey enticed me with her "friendship" and promises of the benefits of baring your soul. Jesus, she sure played me.

It ends now.

I refuse to sulk around my house or run off and hide for another week. I'm gonna treat today as I would have treated any fine Saturday afternoon in August before I met her.

Before Lindsey. Is this how I'll think of my life now, in terms of before and after Lindsey, like she's the second coming or something? Good Lord.

I should be riding my bike up the coast. The doc gave me the green light to drive, but we never discussed my bike.

On my way to my garage, I put Pop back in the closet, then I admire the new Ducati I had delivered last week. The shiny red-and-black beauty beckons me to touch her. I sit on her for the first time, to get a feel for the equipment. Feels pretty good.

Subconsciously, my hands rub my lower back. I consider whether or not I can endure the ride. Probably not advisable, but I'm sick of listening to everyone's advice. I'm done being a patient—a victim.

I'm about to strap on my helmet, then I pause. Despite the mixed emotions raging within me, I never want to end up in the hospital again. Doc's warnings about the danger of pushing before the fusion takes whisper in my ear. He said it'd be a minimum of four months . . . possibly a year. In either case, it's too soon to ride the bike. Goddamn it! Everywhere I turn, I'm facing a wall.

I return the helmet to the shelf and get into my Jeep. The roof's already removed, so it's ready to roll without any effort on my part. I'll still enjoy a drive up the coast, even if not on my new bike. When I pull out of the garage, I notice the rental car still in Lindsey's driveway. Are they talking or doing something else? Just the thought of her with him makes me see red. Without looking back, I pull onto the highway.

An hour later, I arrive in Santa Barbara and stop for lunch at Brophy Brothers to enjoy the clam chowder. The gorgeous day acts as a Band-Aid on my wounds, but the cut underneath's still sore as hell. Normally the activity of the marina stimulates me. Today I notice couples and families—normal folks who have someone in their life who gives a damn. I'd always considered them suckers. Now I just feel jealous.

After lunch, I detour to Santa Ynez to stop in at Kalyra Winery. It's a fun, casual place to sample wines and talk to strangers. It enjoyed a boost in popularity after being featured in the movie

Sideways. Fortunately, today it's hosting a blues and BBQ event, so it's my lucky day. Promising to limit myself to the equivalent of two glasses of wine, I take a seat and enjoy the music.

Within ten minutes, I notice two young women vying for my attention. On the heels of Lindsey's rejection this morning, my ego appreciates the flattery. Hell, I need it. I smile openly, signaling a willingness to receive their company. Ronnie, the redhead, is a stunning woman, while her brunette friend Callie is simply cute. Within a few minutes, Ronnie's vanity becomes tiresome, though I find Callie's shy flirtation to be sweet.

Turns out they're from Vegas, so we discuss our experiences in that delinquent magnet. I haven't been there since my pop died in May. I can hardly believe all that's happened to me since.

Before Lindsey mattered to me, this day would have satisfied all my pleasure-seeking needs. Basking outdoors, enjoying good food and drink, romantic intrigue.

Sadly, now it's leaving me empty. My thoughts slip once more to Lindsey, and how her company would've enhanced the entire day.

"Where'd you go?" Ronnie asks.

Her voice yanks me back to the winery. She's leaning against me, brushing her breast against my arm. I'm so disinterested that the closeness of her body merely inspires annoyance. I turn to Callie. She has gentle eyes, like Lindsey's. I surprise myself with the question that tumbles from my mouth.

"Have you ever fallen in love?" I sip the wine in my hand.

Her face registers humor and shock. When I stare, awaiting her response, she smiles pensively. "Once, but it didn't end well," she admits.

"What happened?" I'm curious now about a subject I've never discussed with anyone.

She looks embarrassed, but then shrugs.

"Basically, he dumped me." She laughs it off, but I read the enduring pang of sorrow behind her eyes.

"Why, if you don't mind my asking?"

She hesitates before launching into her story.

"He'd come in and out of my life, telling me he loved me, then stating he wasn't 'in' love with me. He'd date someone else, then run back to me, claiming I was the only one who understood him, the only one he could talk with and be himself. Weeks later, he'd take off again. It would have hurt less if the breakup had been clean."

She sighs and her eyes drift, her mind somewhere far away, before her attention resumes and she flashes a weak smile.

"Did he know how you felt about him?" I ask.

"Oh yeah, he knew." She smiles. "I've always worn my heart on my sleeve."

"Like a fool," interrupts Ronnie.

Callie rolls her eyes. "At least I don't suffer from the 'what ifs.'"

"'What ifs'?" I ask.

"What if I had told him I loved him, what if I had tried harder, what if . . ."

What if I had told Lindsey I'm falling in love with her.

"Do you regret loving him?" I press, seeking insight from a stranger. Jesus, I've lost my mind.

"No." She draws a slow breath. "We shared as many good moments as bad ones. My only real regret is that I took him back time after time. I wish I'd been stronger . . . respected myself more."

She smiles at me even as Ronnie huffs at my diverted attention. "Is this why you're sitting here, alone, drinking? Trying to get over someone?" Callie asks.

I raise one eyebrow, slightly embarrassed at being busted. "Maybe."

"Maybe?"

"Let's just say I'm having a major case of the 'what ifs.'" I smile at her and drain my wineglass.

"Oh!" Her brows rise. "You'd better hurry up and fix it before it's too late. You can risk your pride and gain the girl or keep your pride but lose the girl."

Ronnie cuts in again. "Now you're dishing out relationship advice?"

I really dislike Ronnie. Why has Callie saddled herself with this pseudo-friend?

"Thank you, darlin', for listening and for sharing your story. I hope you find your Prince Charming some day. In the meantime, don't be anyone's doormat. You deserve better."

She blushes. I stand and nod good-bye to Ronnie.

Sitting in my car, I replay my conversation and think about Lindsey. I've never told her how much she means to me. Of course, taking her to Atlanta should have proven something to the woman. Don't actions speak louder than words? Regardless, my stomach burns when considering her moving away.

I'd gone to Atlanta hoping to close the lid on my past by facing Mama. Perhaps all I accomplished was substituting one extreme brush-off with another.

I certainly didn't help my case by yelling at Lindsey after Rob showed up on her doorstep. Instead of pouring my heart out, I walked out.

Not Rob; he kept his cool. He's outplayed me all summer with the flowers and presents. Well, if I'm going down, I'm going down fighting.

On my way out of town, I stop at a jewelry store. I've never bought jewelry for a woman. Desperate times call for desperate measures. I skim over the light-filled glass cases loaded with formal-looking pieces. None of that stuff looks like Lindsey to me. Plus, considering her upbringing, she probably owns all the platinum and diamonds she can wear.

In the corner of the store, I spy a collection of casual, bohemian necklaces by an outfit selling under the name Love Heals. That's so corny, but apt to our situation. Plus, Lindsey strikes me as the corny, sentimental type.

One necklace, made of pearls spaced loosely along a thin, brown leather strap with a silver floret clasp, catches my eye. It can be worn as one long strand, or wrapped two or three times along the collar-bone. It looks like Lindsey to me, sporty yet feminine.

I picture Lindsey, naked in my bed, wearing it coiled around her neck. I want the image to be real. Even if she takes off, I'd like her to take this little remembrance of me with her. Whatever happens, I know she didn't fall into bed with me easily. I doubt I could feel so much if she felt too little. I probably have just one last shot at convincing her to stay. I'd better make it count.

~

Almost two hours later, I arrive safely home. My back's screaming at me for being so boneheaded today. I spent too much time in the car. That, plus I strained it over the past two days in bed with Lindsey.

Rob's rental car isn't in Lindsey's driveway. Her house looks dark. Are they out to dinner? Surely she didn't pack up and leave without saying good-bye. Then again, Rob might have pressured her to leave immediately. I frown at the possibility.

My back hurts when I exit my car, so I decide to run inside and grab a painkiller before I go over to her house. I try to hurry because time is no longer on my side.

Once inside, I head straight to the kitchen. I set the gift on the counter and look for aspirin, but then I feel an electric awareness. I turn the corner and stop. Lindsey's curled up asleep on my sofa. She's here, in my house, and Rob's car is nowhere nearby.

She senses me watching her, stirs, and sits up, blinking in confusion. The pain in my back dissipates instantly, but my lungs feel compressed.

~

Lindsey

Levi's standing across the room, guarded, saying nothing. All my planned speeches and sentiments vaporize. I'm rooted to the cushion, unable to manage a fully formed thought.

"You're home." My paper-thin voice drifts through the air.

"You're here." His face remains contemplative.

I'm going to have to take the first step. I knew it would be the case. Levi's not comfortable with emotional declarations. Even if he were hopelessly in love with me, he'd never admit it first. Love's never brought him anything but heartache, so he doesn't trust it.

Dating Levi will require a lot of patience, but I can't walk away. I hope he'll give us a chance.

"Where have you been all day?" I hold my breath.

"Santa Barbara. How long have you been here?"

"A few hours." I bite my lip. Will he be sarcastic and accuse me of snooping again?

"Where's Rob?" Levi steps a little closer, but his arms remain folded in front of his chest. His anxious eyes pin me in place while he waits for my answer.

Shrugging, I check my watch. "Cooling his heels at LAX, I hope."

Levi hesitates. Did I see a smile? He takes another step in my direction.

"Will you be joining him?" The silence is broken only by the rasping sounds of Levi's shallow breath.

I shake my head. "No."

I expect him to smile, but he narrows his eyes.

"Why not?"

His need for reassurance runs so deep. He truly is a wounded soldier in need of rescue, if ever I met one. Lucky for him, I'm the perfect woman for the job. I'll love every minute of it.

"I'd rather stay here . . . with you." Now it's my turn to hold my breath. What if he doesn't want more than a casual fling?

I scan his face, praying for a grin, but he turns and walks back toward the kitchen without saying a word. I can't breathe. He walked away?

Thankfully, he returns quickly, carrying a small bag in his hand. When he sits on the coffee table, I resist the impulse to touch him. He faces me and drops the bag in my lap.

"I bought you a gift." He straightens his back, grimacing from what I presume is back pain.

"Wow. I'm stunned." My eyes shift between him and the bag. "What did I do to deserve a present?"

He evades the question by asking his own. "Don't you want to open it?" One brow quirks up while a grin forms. I love those wonderful dimples.

I gingerly open the bag and pull out a flat, square box. It's a jewelry case. Involuntarily, I gulp. My mind scatters in several directions. When he left my house this morning, he'd been dour. Why, between then and now, did he decide to purchase jewelry . . . for me? I open the box and lift a funky pearl and leather necklace from the case.

My mouth falls open in surprise. I lace it through my fingers and hold it up for inspection. Blinking back tears, I look at Levi, who's nervously observing my reaction.

"It's beautiful. I love it." I twist it around my neck twice and continue touching it. "I don't understand. Why'd you buy this for me, Levi?"

He's battling to find the words. My heart grows larger just watching him work so hard for me.

"I'm not good at talking about feelings. Hell, until recently, I hadn't experienced so many of them." He smiles to himself and then looks at me. "Earlier you asked me to tell you what to do. I wouldn't, but not because I didn't care about the outcome. When I left your house this morning, I'd convinced myself you'd be leaving. I vowed not to let it affect me. So I took off for the day, the way I used to before you came along. It didn't take long to realize nothing's the same without you. I came back hoping to talk you into staying here. I figured the necklace might help advance my cause."

"Turns out you didn't need the necklace after all." I lean forward to kiss him. Within two seconds, he's pinned me back against the sofa with a hungry kiss.

He drags his lips from mine, wincing. "Sorry, it feels like someone's using my back as a dartboard. Scoot over. I need to lie down. I think I've pushed too hard these past few days with all the travel and other activity."

Once he's on his back, I burrow against him and lay my head against his chest to listen to his slow, heavy heartbeat. His fingers comb through my hair, and he kisses the top of my head.

"Lindsey, are you sure about me? It's nearly impossible for me to trust anything good to last. And I've never been in a relationship. I can't make many promises, but I swear I'll never lie to you or take you for granted."

Exhausted from the emotional fallout with Rob, I'm not particularly in the mood for a serious discussion at this moment. But this is important. I touch his face.

"Would you consider a suggestion?"

"Sure."

I take a deep breath. "Well, you've mentioned your inability to trust, your disinterest in emotional intimacy, your feelings of unworthiness—"

"Can we skip to the point, rather than reciting all of my faults?" He cuts me off, but his fingers continue to lightly skim up and down the length of my arm.

"I wouldn't call them faults. Learned habits, perhaps." My fingers brush along his collarbone. "Anyway, the point is, maybe you should consider talking to someone, professionally, who can help you. Especially now, since you've seen your mother and everything's been dragged to the forefront."

He's silent for a minute. "Is this a condition of your decision to stay?"

"No." I caress his chest. "But I think it would help us if you heal some of the damage your parents caused and learn to have faith in love."

I feel his lips on my scalp. "I'll consider it."

I smile and prop myself up to kiss him.

"'Have faith in love.'" He toys with my necklace. "Does that mean you love me?"

I bury my hands in his hair, kiss his neck, and whisper into his ear, "Yes, I believe I do."

His eyes glow in response. "That's good." He kisses me with possessive need. "Then we're both all in."

All in. His fingertips trace along my jaw, down my neck, and over my breast. "You were opposed to staying here last night. Are you still boycotting my bedroom, or can we move this reunion upstairs later?"

Embarrassed by the memory of my silly declaration, I blush. "The boycott's over."

EPILOGUE

August 2014

Levi

Everywhere I look, Lindsey's presence is evident. She moved in with me several months ago, after her lease expired. Since then, she's started a slow campaign to modify the decor.

My monochromatic color scheme's been punctuated with splashes of turquoise and silver. Gleaming silver picture frames now adorn the tables and shelves. Fresh-cut flowers are often in the living room and bedroom. Half my old books are boxed up and have been replaced with vases, statuettes, and other such nonsense. My bathroom now smells like grapefruit and perfume.

I have to count to ten every time I open a closet or cabinet. The girl simply can't keep anything orderly, despite her efforts to try. At least she's trying not to leave her things piled up on counters anymore. All in all, the small sacrifices on my part are worth it, since having her here full time is pretty close to heaven.

This past fall she got admitted as a volunteer and assigned two cases. She spends about fifteen hours each week working on them, takes on some freelance writing assignments, and has been outlining a book about foster care. Other than that, we've been attached at the hip. She's even become a decent cook, with a lot of help from me. Her new confidence has spurred her to start entertaining friends at our house—another first for me. While I wouldn't claim to look forward to chatting all night with the boyfriends or husbands of her few new pals, I love seeing her animated and cheerful.

Every morning I wake up awed by the impact she's had on my life and my own happiness. It's hard to remember I once preferred being alone. I've feared love for so long. While I won't lie and pretend I don't get anxious, I'll never regret the leap of faith I took with Lindsey.

My head doc's helping me address my trust issues, but all in all, things have proceeded smoothly for Lindsey and me. Waking up next to her, hanging around the house or walking on the beach, or even just sitting together, working independently—it's all better with her than without her.

As for her family, Bill's become pleasant, but I may never win Helene's approval. In her mind, I'm not good enough for her baby. I probably can't argue the point. So, I've laid low around Helene, hoping not to provoke her. The few times Lindsey returned to Connecticut to visit her parents, I stayed behind. I wouldn't care about Helene, except I know it's important to Lindsey. Eventually, she and I will have to come to an understanding, preferably sooner than later.

I've met Jill twice now. She took Lindsey's decision to stay in California pretty hard and, during her first visit, grilled me to make sure I was good enough for her friend. I can't understand how two women different as night and day are so close, but perhaps old bonds can't be broken. I sure wouldn't know anything about that. In any case, she's not trying to break us apart, so I keep my mouth shut. I only have to tolerate her antagonistic sense of humor in small doses, which I can handle. And ultimately, despite her odd way of showing it, she cares for Lindsey.

Lindsey's birthday is next week. I'm planning on surprising her with an engagement ring. I've debated whether it's too soon, but we're happy and settled, and I don't see any good reason to put it off. I want to make things official. Doc thinks it's my way of needing to feel in control. That may be partly true, but mostly I just want to make her my wife. I want to know she's obligated to stick it out with me, for better or worse.

She's been down this road before, though. Planned a life and a big wedding, only to see it all fall apart. I'm going to do whatever I can to distinguish our relationship from her former one. To start, I picked a feminine, contemporary ring that I'm confident doesn't resemble what Rob gave her. It's unique, just like her. So, if I can pull off my surprise proposal, and she says yes, I'll be living with turquoise and decorative pillows for the rest of my life.

~

Lindsey

Levi chartered a private jet for my birthday and refused to tell me where we'd be going. We've come so far since last year's birthday debacle. The closeness we share is the only gift worth having this year, in my opinion. Despite our vast differences, at heart we share the same needs and goals. He's not out to prove anything to anyone other than himself. He's physically and emotionally available to me almost any time. He's not embarrassed by demonstrative shows of affection. Having finally created my own happiness, I've no regrets about Rob, New York, or my parents.

Levi's been working hard with his physical therapy and his shrink. He's back on his surfboard, which I now know is one of his favorite activities. One of our only real arguments is over that awful motorcycle. I hate and fear it. But it's one of the very few areas he's unwilling to compromise. When he goes for a ride, I hold my breath until he returns. He's made a lot of accommodations for me, so I try to bite my tongue these days when he takes off on that contraption.

As for his emotional therapy, it's been tough. Levi's gradually coming to terms with the fact that his father died before they reconciled.

Despite their unconventional life and relationship, Levi loved him. My heart breaks to think about it, and yet I'm awed at what a good, honest man Levi became, notwithstanding his father's influence.

We haven't heard from Levi's mother. I doubt he'll ever fully resolve that anger, but at least he's working hard to overcome the issues her actions created. She probably destroyed his ability to completely trust in my, or anyone's, love, but each day he wakes up beside me with a smile and allows himself to be vulnerable more often.

Sometimes I'm amazed at how willing he's been to make changes. Mostly, I love the way he's so genuinely happy to please me and to support my needs and dreams. I can only hope he's getting as much from me as he's giving. If only my mother could be more accepting. I know, however, that day is years away, if ever.

~

When we landed in Fort Myers, I could barely speak. I knew, then, where he planned to take me. My smile grew broader with each mile nearer we came to the Sugar Sands Beach Resort. For a tough guy, he can be wildly romantic and sentimental when he sets his mind to it. It's been interesting to revisit the place we first met. During this trip we sat at the very bar where he refused to serve me. When I look at him now, I still get the same flutters I experienced so many years ago. We've kept busy for three days, but now we're sharing our final evening here, where it all began.

I'm sitting at the dinner table, finishing my dessert, when he presents a gift—neatly wrapped, of course.

"Can I open this now?" I ask, eyeing the pink-and-yellow box.

"Not here. Come on." He reaches for my hand and then leads me out of the hotel and toward the beach. "One more stop."

Pink and yellow ribbons of cloud and sky light up the beach. Distracted by the scenery, I don't notice Levi's brought me to rest at a chaise lounge in the sand near the cabana where we fought eight years ago. My pulse begins to race, wondering what he's got up his sleeve.

He sits beside me and hands me the gift. When I unwrap it, I find a copy of *The Celestine Prophecy*, which he's inscribed.

To the beautiful woman who knew, before I did, that destiny brought us together. Thank you for loving me and making my life better than I'd ever dreamed possible. Happy birthday.

Love,
Levi

Tears slip from my eyes while I smile and turn the book over in my hands. When I look up for Levi, he's kneeling in the sand holding another, smaller box.

My body trembles. My hand shakes as I take the box from him. Inside, a fiery white diamond, set in a simple yet interesting platinum setting, sparkles against the deep-red velvet cushion. I look at Levi, afraid to speak. His eyes are glistening and his voice is still sexy as hell.

"Years ago I made a huge mistake by dismissing you right here in this spot. Someone took pity on me and gave me a second chance, and I'm so grateful. I know I'm not the easiest person, nor the most polished, but I love you, Lindsey. Be my wife, and I'll do everything I can to keep you happy, safe, and free to be whatever you want to be."

A little sob escapes my throat when he slides the ring on my finger. "I love you, Levi. Yes. Yes, I'll be your wife!"

He beams, his beautiful dimples gracing his cheeks, before he swoops me into his arms and kisses me.

I've taken a most circuitous route, but my heart has finally found a real home.

ACKNOWLEDGMENTS

I would like to thank my husband, children, parents, brother, and friends for their love, encouragement, and support.

I am grateful to my agent, Jill Marsal, and to Helen Cattaneo and the entire Montlake family, for believing in me and for working so hard on this story.

I owe so much to Kathryn Johnson, for her enthusiasm and mentoring, and to my earliest readers, Christie Tinio, Siri Kloud, Katherine Ong, Tami Carstenson, Shelley Eccleston, and Suzanne Harrison, for their input on various drafts of this manuscript.

I am also indebted to the wonderful members of my CTRWA chapter for their support, feedback, and guidance throughout the years.

Finally, I want to thank my readers for making my work worthwhile. With so many available options, I'm honored by your choice to spend your time with me.

ABOUT THE AUTHOR

Lorah Haskins, 2013

Jamie Beck is a former attorney with a passion for inventing stories about love and redemption. In addition to writing novels, she also pens articles on behalf of a local nonprofit organization dedicated to empowering youth and strengthening families. Fortunately, when she isn't tapping away at the keyboard, she is a grateful wife and mother to a very patient, supportive family.

For more information about Jamie and her upcoming books, follow her on Facebook (www.facebook.com/JamieBeckBooks) or on her blog (www.jamiebeck.com/everyday-romance).